The Town Speaks to You

Rebecca Mathis

Contents

1. Prologue   1

2. Chapter 1   9

3. Chapter 2   16

4. Chapter 3   22

5. Chapter 4   30

6. Chapter 5   38

7. Chapter 6   45

8. Chapter 7   52

9. Chapter 8   60

10. Chapter 9   69

11. Chapter 10   80

12. Chapter 11   89

13. Chapter 12   97

14. Chapter 13   103

15. Chapter 14   111

16. Chapter 15   119

17. Chapter 16   125

18. Chapter 17   133

19. Chapter 18   139

20.	Chapter 19	147
21.	Chapter 20	154
22.	Chapter 21	161
23.	Chapter 22	167
24.	Chapter 23	173
25.	Chapter 24	179
26.	Chapter 25	187
27.	Chapter 26	193
28.	Chapter 27	201
29.	Chapter 28	209
30.	Chapter 29	218
31.	Chapter 30	225
32.	Chapter 31	235
33.	Chapter 32	243
34.	Chapter 33	251
35.	Chapter 34	258
36.	Chapter 35	266
37.	Chapter 36	274
38.	Chapter 37	281
39.	Chapter 38	290
40.	Epilogue	299

Prologue

♥

Although the Chief Editor's son cut the ribbon and officially launched MIRROR's new office in Chennai three weeks ago (the Chief Editor was unable to attend due to food poisoning), the workplace still does not have a coffee maker. Miraya is unwilling to comprehend the factors contributing to the delay in establishing one. Even though she went to great lengths to arrange benches and create a welcome area for the machine, no attempt has been made to obtain one. What is an office without a smart coffee machine luring gullible human minds to take a break every half-hour to sip free wonderful coffee? Sure, the office is stylish and minimalistic, overlooking the nasty Chennai traffic (luckily noise-cancelled), but what is an office without a smart coffee machine?

Fiya looks at the huge takeaway cup of coffee that Miraya has placed on her desk and lets out an audible sigh.

Miraya seats herself with disdain, "Watch this lose all its warmth before I finish half of it," she remarks. Don't misunderstand her. She adores her job, her workplace, and the coworkers there, but without caffeine in her system, she simply cannot function well enough to appreciate them.

"The pain," Fiya replies.

"Well done, alien non-coffee drinker. Have you have your Alpha juice?

"Hey! Respect my ABC juice, please. It sustains my life. Fiya is dressed in a white shirt tucked into an ankle-length, lilac pleated skirt. Her eyes are heavily kohled, and she has French braided hair. Miraya becomes aware that she would be going out tonight with Ashraf. He's doing well, she thinks.

Miraya turns on her computer and reclines in her chair. The chief editor's room and the art director's office are both empty, she finds after taking a look around. The question "Is there a meeting going on?"

"Oh, absolutely. At the same time, all of the department heads barged into the cabin room. Using her computer, Fiya types, "must be a last-minute narrative that the Delhi unit has conveniently pushed to us.

When do you believe we will complete our South Indian cover story? We were only given the Life Essence section and the Rising Music Trends article. The music one is fun, but I can't wait to talk to famous people who I know from my youth and write a fancy essay about it. I have a lot of creative ideas to make it humorous and catchy.

"What if this meeting is to talk about a cover story?"

"No way. You are aware that we had previously secured celebrities for the cover? They would have told us about it if they were from the South, for sure.

Fiya cries. "This is terrible. When will we be able to do the fun things? Who, in any case, is on the cover of the issue due out in a month? If it's Deepika Padukone again, I swear —"

Miraya screams with laughter. "I'm positive it isn't. What exactly is your issue with Deepika?

"Really, I do adore her. But these days, she appears on the cover of every magazine. I want a fresh face. Do you not believe so?

It is real. People must read about newcomers and unseen voices. The undiscovered are more deserving of attention.

"It's not really up to us. Has your writing for the website been completed? I've been getting nags from Sam about it. On Thursday, he needs to upload it.

Fiya mutters and resumes typing, her face betraying her lack of interest. By today, I'll send it to you.

Miraya grinned and continued where she left off the previous evening. However, she starts to daydream about writing a cover story after all. Miraya is certain that she would be the ideal candidate to complete the piece if they were given the chance because she has the most expertise in the area. She spent two years working at a well-known fashion publication in Germany and one year in MIRROR's headquarters. Additionally, she recently received a promotion to editor. The staff writers lack the expertise to manage such a huge section.

Miraya chuckles to herself as she takes a drink of coffee.

The department heads emerge one by one from the cabin room, each holding a binder, notebook, or coffee cup in their hand. As Miraya and Fiya twist their heads to see what all the fuss is about, they become perplexed by Mrs. Nandhini's tense smile. She serves as both their head and main editor.

"Miraya. Please use my office," she adds as she passes by her. Miraya fumbles to get up from her chair and nearly drops her coffee. She rushes to Mrs. Nandhini's door but turns around and gets a notebook and pen before knocking on the door to request entry.

Mrs. Nandhini exclaims, "Miraya," as she arranges the enormous black binders on her table. Please sit down. There is huge news.

Her gut is filled with an ethereal ball of undefined feelings. She detests tension. She is someone who, as horrible as it may sound, will look up a movie's finale and spoilers during the interval if the anticipation is really intense. She finds it uncomfortable to eat.

"I'll be open and honest with you and let you know what is happening in the office right now. We can only accomplish this feat because it is so large then.

She is only made worse off by Mrs. Nandhini's foundational disclaimers.

So Aayush Sharma was meant to be the cover model for this month. He was scheduled a month ago, however it appears that he cancelled. Therefore, the main quarters smartly assigned us the task of finding a substitute.

Miraya's mouth gaped open. The woman sobs. "But it's not simple, though. How are we going to accomplish that so quickly?

Mrs. Nandhini sighs as she reclines in her chair. "I know. However, there is no point in grumbling about it. This is the first cover story for which we are responsible. No matter how unjust it seems, we can't complain. Do you know what people in the central areas say about us?

Looking down, Miraya. This bothers her. This is not possible.

"Don't appear so dejected. We've already secured a famous person. Additionally, we believe he can help us generate good or above average sales. Fortunately, we have access to sufficient funds and resources. That Grace spends her time creating fictitious mood boards for cover photos is a good thing. Good concepts have been proposed by the art team. Eliza has been requested to be the photographer. You don't need to stress over the photo shoot, that's the thing. It will be handled. I wanted to know whether you would be willing to provide the cover narrative.

She flinches. Holy divine shit, did her daydream just come true. It's a big deal.

"Really? Are you kidding me? Just in case she was hearing her own thoughts, Miraya inquires.

"Miraya, it was evident who to choose. You were asked to do it by everyone. We know how talented you are since we have seen your work, Mrs. Nandhini says with a smile.Are you prepared to carry it out?

"Sure, that. Of course.

Her heart is racing. She makes a lot of effort to contain her excitement.

But that's not the only piece of news.

Miraya looks upward.

The first week of October marks the release of the latest film from director Shankar. Next week, he's having a big party to celebrate, and several well-known south Indian celebrities are scheduled to show up. Everyone is aware of how expensive his gatherings are. The celebrities will arrive dressed similarly. Here's where we step in.

Her eyes enlarge. Saying "Don't tell me..."

"Yes. We have press passes for the occasion. Many stars and musicians that we haven't seen in a while will show up for the party, which will provide for excellent magazine content. Do you not believe so?

Compared to the feature, the party is a much more alluring option. In contrast to the quiet, couch-to-couch task she was assigned, this one is loud, wild, and nerve-wracking. Miraya enjoys lavish events primarily because she hasn't attended many of them. However, she is aware that it is her kind of place based on the tales she has heard.

All of Mrs. Nandhini's compliments for her suddenly become invalid, and she requests a change of assignments.

She starts off, "So," but she is at a loss for words.

Varun and Shreya are the reporters on this subject. Do they not work well together? Their joint work on Shah Rukh Khan's house was beautiful.

Miraya receives another stinging smack to the face when she hears the names. She's always desired to collaborate with Varun. His photographic abilities are amazing. If she had been given this task instead, it would have been so much better. Even though Miraya knows it is selfish of her to expect more than what she has been given, she can't help but feel let down. It resembles earning first place but getting the second-place trophy.

Hoping Mrs. Nandhini won't notice the enthusiasm slowly leaving her body, she reclines in her chair. She dislikes the sensation. Miraya looks for further justifications to rekindle her early enthusiasm. She mentally creates a list.

One, the cover story is one of an issue's most crucial sections. It may lead to a lot of exposure.

Second, Eliza took the photos for the cover. She is a young, thin photographer who began as an intern before quickly joining the Delhi office. She has a passion for jewellery fashioned from seashells and marine stones and is quite talented. They've already collaborated, and Miraya and her get along great. That's reassuring, then.

Three, she will have the chance to put her thoughts into practise.

Four, it's not that horrible to have a pleasant, in-depth conversation with a famous person. You know how things often go wrong at parties? Perhaps it's for the best that she was given this item to work on instead.

"Okay. When should I start, she wonders after realising the benefits outweigh the drawbacks.

"Once he has figured out the schedule, I'll ask Giri to give you the specifics. I anticipate it to happen sometime in the upcoming week. The party will also keep us busy. Also pending is the artwork for the Monsoon necessities section. This month is going to be incredibly difficult. After this, we'll wish the Delhi unit had completed the task entirely on their own.

Mrs. Nandhini makes an effort to laugh the stress away that is lurking in the background, ready to attack.

Miraya complies and beams. She gets up and walks out. Saying "Thank you, Ma'am."

When she realises she has overlooked a crucial detail, she is standing next to the door. "Who is the famous person we hired? Certainly not one of the best actors. Who am I collaborating with?

When Mrs. Nandhini finds she's failed to provide her the assignment's essential information, her laughter reverberates throughout the entire room. "My thoughts are jumbled up. As she begins to feel better, she apologises to Miraya. I'm shocked that I neglected to say that.

The emerging young star of the south will be featured on this month's cover story, says Mrs. Nandhini. Miraya only thinks of one person when she hears such words.

She hopes for anyone but him. This assignment would no longer be the one she had been looking forward to if it were him. Instead, it would turn into the task she has spent her entire life trying to avoid. There will never be enough benefits to outweigh the drawback of his existence. Please. No, he. No, he. Never him—

The name "Shray Nivas."

Miraya senses the departure of her spirit.

Such a good-looking face, no? I'm curious about where. She is completely deaf to anything else.

Hearing the one term she hates the most spoken directly to her face hurts like someone stuck a million needles in her lungs. The term, the two-word horror, echoes in your head.

Nivas Shray. Nivas Shray. Nivas Shray.

It permanently imprints his utterly flawless face in her thoughts. She is unable to get rid of the image or the knowledge that, of all the people in the world, he will be the subject of her interview.

It was inescapably him.

The evil scumbag who destroyed her life.

The only person she vowed to stay away from.

Chapter 1

♥

"I believed that you were the one calling for undiscovered and up-and-coming stars to receive greater attention. Why then do you recommend hiring a model instead? says Mrs. Nandhini.

With a false smile on her face, Miraya squeezes her eyes shut before opening them once more. "Yes, but don't we typically book models in the event that a celebrity cancels? Maybe with better organising and planning in the following issue, Shray Nivas? In this little amount of time, we can't do him justice. She wants to spit her tongue out when she hears his name because it makes it feel so strange. Leave her alone.

She won't be permitted to serve as the issue's cover story twice in a row. Everything would return to normal if she were able to move him up the assignment ladder rather than abandoning it altogether. It was a smart thought.

"No."

"Ma'am —"

"Miraya, I don't get what you're trying to express. Do you mean to say that we might not have the necessary tools to succeed in this? You should be aware that we carefully thought over our choices before making a decision. Shray's fan base is expanding, especially among women. If my niece has the opportunity, she will purchase all of the copies herself, hang his images in her room (if there is still room), and memorise his interview. Numerous girls resemble her. Right now, Shray is extremely pertinent. He has a hectic schedule, so we should be pleased that he still consented to do it. We are unable to make a decision. Miraya: "Beggars can't be kings.

Her lip is bitched. "Ma'am, would you mind—"

"Nah, Miraya. You lack comprehension. His team has already been contacted about it, and they share our interest in it, especially given the potential marketing it could provide for his upcoming movie. Despite the fact that they indicated certain venue and time changes due to his busy schedule for the month, we believe we can make accommodations, Mrs. Nandhini continues, every syllable shattering her heart.

She keeps on attacking. "Unfortunately, Miraya, your ideas and suggestions are futile at the moment. It only depends on whether you'll accept it or not. I can ask Shree to perform the task if you don't want to. She will be able to — with a little help.

"NO." Miraya screams. If the assignment belonged to someone else, she would be able to tolerate it, but not if Shree received it.

Shree is like a bothersome fruit fly that refuses to go away even when you swat it away.

Shree will make up a tale that she will tell 10,000 times a day if given the chance to do so rather than Miraya. The story will feature a woman (played by Shree) who is given an opportunity and is surprised when she accepts it. However, she won't accept it like a "greedy" woman and will insist that it be given to the "deserving" person (Miraya). Eventually, after extensive convincing, the 'greedy' woman decides to seize the chance.

Important point: She accepts it under coercion rather than out of greed, and she will quickly give it all away.

As if.

Miraya is consistently astounded by the story's level of non-sense. When she imagines listening to Shree turn her want to brag into phoney guilt and an apology, she cringes.

No.

She would not allow the fruit fly to overshadow her. Before it had a chance to take flight, she would swat it away.

"I'll accept the task. With a toothless smile, Miraya says, "It would be a pleasure. With a glimmer of relief in her eyes, Mrs. Nandhini brightens. Why are there so many individuals in my life that I despise? Don't they just have to be a pain, she muses.

The question "Is there anything else, Ma'am?"

If you require assistance, you may bring Fiya with you. She could learn something from it. Tell me how things are going. You may now leave, says Mrs. Nandhini. Miraya looks around, wanting to rip her hair out for getting into this predicament. How does she manage to keep making trouble? Where does all the misfortune come from?Miraya, too?

At the door, she halts.

Good fortune.

Oh, she'll require a lot of it.

Along with having the heavenly ability to endure the approaching painful days with the composure of a saint.

"I heard that the cover story is being written. You understood, didn't you? As soon as she exits, Fiya stays just outside the door and yells and whispers at her. Miraya gives her a phoney smile while hugging her while exerting all of her might. "I warned you. I guaranteed you would receive it. So, will I be joining you?" she queries.

Was that not obvious?

Fiya throws her arm around Miraya and exclaims with excitement that this will be her first time meeting a celebrity and that she plans to post about it on social media to show off the benefits of her profession. She is unaware that Miraya is strangely still in her arms or that she is struggling to contain her dismay.

"Shray Nivas is this month's cover model, according to the social media team. Is it real?

Miraya squirms. That name, drat.

Shray remarked, his fingers on his socks as he removed them but his eyes on her. "You said you'd be there," he said. The PE teachers asked Shray to heal his wounds in the nurse's room because the nurse had departed early that day. Miraya had been dragged along by him.

"I know. The choices for my throwball match, however, were scheduled for the same time as your game. Miraya murmured, kneeling in front of him and grimacing at the swelling on his ankle, "I attempted to come but since I am the team captain I couldn't. "It really looks bad."

"If you had been there, I would have won."

Eyes rolling, Miraya said. You wouldn't have, I'm sure. Instead of working on your skills, you spent all your time aggravating me. It is entirely your fault.

Shray extended his leg towards her and stated, "I knew I was going to lose from the moment I learned you weren't going to make it.

Miraya remarked, wiping rubbing alcohol on the bloodied scrape on his knee. "Stop being stupid," he added.

Just consider it. Every game you've came to, I've won. The two that you didn't lose, I have. Miranda, you're my lucky charm. No matter how you feel about it. Shray had dumped water on his head after the game, and it was dripping from his hair. She felt her breath catch when he uttered things like that while staring directly at her.

Blowing on his wound, Miraya. I'll think about attending your game the day you address me by my real name.

Shray supported his weight on his palms while leaning back. Miranda: "I'd rather lose my game than do that."

She shook her head and hurled the cotton swab at him. You are intolerable, I say.

Contrary to what she claimed, Miraya never skipped a game of Shray's after that since, as promised, he continued to call her Miranda, the name of an orange-flavored soft drink.

In the end, he obtained his goals. She was fine with losing to him.

"Miraya?"

"Huh?"

Fiya scowled at her but asked the same question again. "Is it true, I inquired? Do we need to meet Sh—?

"Yes."

You are aware of my intense crush on him, right? This is the finest news ever, my god. What if we instantly click when we first meet? When Fiya inquires, the first thing that comes to mind is that Fiya is not Shray's type. Never would he pursue her. Although Fiya is attractive and witty, there is little chance that they would click romantically. What if we became friends instead? But who knows? Anyway, today I'm going shopping.

"I believed you and Ashraf had a date?"

Her hand shoots up to her forehead. "Shit. I completely forgot about him.

As she moves by her to take a seat, Miraya rolls her eyes. She imagines what it could be like to run into Shray once more. Can she still look into his eyes with the same assurance she did in the past? Her greatest worry right now is running into him and having to relive the horrific history she left with him when she let him go.

She cannot afford to cry in his presence. He cannot be aware of how much she is still affected by his memory.

Should she go back and cancel the task so Shree can take it? The worst that can happen to her is some minor ego damage and a phoney apology from Shree. Right?

Saying, "You know what?" Fiya spins around in her seat and slouches. "Mr. Hari added that if this month's issue is successful, they will definitely get a coffee maker. This time, we are covering the majority of it, so if it sells better than expected, we might even buy a refrigerator.

"Really?"

It is verified news. So, Miraya, it's our responsibility to make Shray appear to be the lovely and charming man that he apparently is in order for this problem to cause a stir. If we take that action, the coffee maker is ours. That won't be an issue, in Miraya's opinion. Even if he wasn't trying, that jerk is endearing.

She gives her coffee a quick glance while wrapping her fingers around the cup. It no longer has any warmth. It is sitting on her table cold.

Miraya sighs, rubbing her forehead with her index fingers as she closes her eyes. She should be relishing this task and adoring the procedure. She is currently hesitant to even start it.

She is asking herself if the coffee maker and the assignment are worth all the pain that she will cause herself. Will she be able to endure him?

"Miraya, what are you contemplating? You're terribly disoriented. Is there a problem? Fiya questions.

Miraya instantly gathers her composure. "No. Never at all. Like cough syrup, she drinks the barely warm but not cold coffee, scarcely letting it rest on her tongue. She finishes by crushing the cup and discarding it.

The task will be completed by Miraya. She has his back. She is capable of enduring everything.

She must.

She definitely will.

Are you certain? pressing Fiya.

Her smile almost looks genuine. Indeed, everything is flawless.

Chapter 2

T he thing about Chennai is that no matter which time of the day, you will hear the buzz and rush of a crowd, the annoying horns from the impatient vehicles in the traffic, and see the swirling dust and familiar pollution. But this pertains only to the centre of the city.

Miraya loves to take a walk along Elliot's beach in the evening, drinking in the beautiful sunset and the soothing ebb and flow of the waves. And now, she walks barefoot in the sand, her skin relishing the delicious grind of sand against her feet. Past her, an old man with his granddaughter walks by, throwing his head back as he laughs at how the little girl skips with her red balloon. Just across them a couple sit together, their bodies propped on their elbows, half-sunk into the sand, as they talk and laugh. Once in a while, the woman turns and watches the man talk, smiling to herself.

Miraya lowers her head, watching her feet dip in and out of the sand. However many times she denies it, the truth is that she aches for love. A love like the couple on the beach. Genuine, simple and meaningful. Nothing extravagant or impossible. Just a walk on the beach with the man she loves, their hands intertwined as their faces reflect the pinkish glow of the sunset. A shoulder to lean on.

An arm to catch her when she stumbles. An ear to listen to her worries and excitements.

She drops her sandals on the sand like an anchor and sits next to it, her feet stretched and crossed at the ankles. Miraya sighs. Maybe she will never get to feel that kind of love. Maybe her chances of finding something like that had reduced to zero after what happened in school.

Just as she plugs in her earphones in her ears and listens to the first twenty seconds of a song, *Amma* calls. Her fingers hover over the red side because she simply doesn't have the energy to deal with her. But, if she declines this call, she knows ten more will follow. She will only be giving an opportunity to *Amma* to make her day even difficult to get through.

Swiping the green side, she says, "Hello."

"Were you busy? What took you so long to answer?"

"I was searching for my phone in my bag. It took a while. What are you doing, *Ma*?"

Lying was natural when it came to conversations with *Amma*.

"Your *Appa* wanted *Chapati* and cauliflower gravy for dinner. So before I start making them, I thought I'll call you and ask if you wanted to join us. It's been awhile since you came home."

Miraya presses her eyes close. "I know. But work has been really tight and I'll only become busier because of next month's issue. I'll see if I can find time and let you know. How is *Appa*?"

"He is the usual. Comes home at seven and he is so tired he falls asleep right after he's had his dinner," *Amma* says, the clinking sound of cutlery echoing in the background. "So, where are you?"

"In the balcony." Another lie again. See how flawless it is? It took Miraya years to perfect the art.

Amma thinks the balcony of her and Dakshina's apartment is her favourite place in the world. The balcony is so full of Dakshina's plants that there is barely any place to stand. Her mother doesn't know that.

"How is Dakshina? She is not bringing men to your apartment anymore, right?"

Miraya rolls her eyes. "*Ma*, she can bring whoever she wants. It's her apartment too. I can't control that."

"I hate that girl. She'll spoil you also."

"I can't have this conversation right now, *Ma*. Bye." With that, she hangs up and lies back down on the sand, closing her eyes.

Dakshina has a boyfriend and sometimes he stays over. Ranav knew the 101 about comforting a person when they are in a bad place. Dakshina says that's one of the reasons she keeps him around and that he's precious.

And that is why she can never ask Dakshina not to bring him to their apartment anymore. Miraya has grown fond of his presence too. She would never ever do that to him. And she wouldn't be the person to ruin someone's love for some crooked reason. Being a victim of it is enough trauma in itself.

Miraya rubs her forehead with her index fingers. This is exactly why she hates talking to *Amma*, especially on a bad day. She makes things worse. If Miraya had continued the conversation, she would've asked her to move back to their house, which would've led to a bigger argument.

The main reason Miraya was firm on moving out was to gain her freedom back. Choosing journalism as her major had been one way. She used her education to explore places and cultures.

Later when she secured a job, she didn't want to lose the freedom she experienced. Going to work from her house would be going back to square one so she chose to move out altogether. Even though it took a lot of arguments, second opinions and mini-hunger strikes to make her parents agree, Miraya deems that decision as one of the best decisions she's ever made.

Miraya's phone rings again. She quietly groans, expecting it to be *Amma*, attempting to make peace. But she sits up straight when she sees the caller ID.

"Hey. Kishore?"

She can hear the announcements from the airport before she can hear him. "Mira. Guess where I am?"

Miraya's lips curve into a smile and she balances her phone properly next to her ear. "The airport."

"That's kinda obvious, isn't it?" he says from the other side. She can bet that he is scratching the back of his neck. "Guess which airport?"

Her eyes go wide. She looks back at her phone screen and realises belatedly that he hasn't called her on Whatsapp like he always does. It is a normal call from an Indian number. "Don't tell me..."

"Yup. I am in Chennai!"

"Oh my god, are you on leave from work? Your presence is very much appreciated in this city, but why the sudden visit? How come you didn't tell me?"

"My school is hosting an alumni reunion. I really didn't want to miss it. I had to come," he says. "And I didn't tell you because I had difficulty getting leave. This trip was not happening until yesterday."

Alumni Reunion. Sometimes Miraya wondered what her school-mates were doing right now; if they were still the same person they were then.

At that moment, her brain painfully reminds her that she is, indeed, going to have a little reunion with an important person from her school life soon. And when she meets him, he would know that she isn't the same stupid school girl anymore and that she understands the cunning ways of the world now. After all, he had been the first one to teach her that lesson.

She also realises that, despite her curiosity, if Miraya is ever invited for a reunion in her school, she would rather die than attend.

But that doesn't stop her from feeling excited for Kishore.

"That's really great. Are you going to your hometown?"

"Yes. But before that, I want to see you. I've missed you, roomie."

She laughs.

Miraya met Kishore in her German class. He was from a small town in the south of Tamilnadu. He was so smart and sweet that Miraya clung to him from the moment she realised it. If it weren't for his help, she would've failed the exam. They kept in touch after the exams and even when they were working in the same German city in different areas. Miraya had roomed with an Indian girl who worked in an export company. Not even a few months into the job, she decided to go back to India and get married. Miraya couldn't pay for the rent on her own so she tried searching for a roommate and when that was a flop, she asked Kishore for help. He had suggested rooming with him, if she didn't mind.

She didn't.

Miraya had lied to her parents that she got a new roommate, creating a new woman named Mizra to keep them unsuspecting. She moved to Kishore's apartment for the rest of the year.

Their friendship only became stronger, since they got to learn each other's habits, likes and dislikes and accepted them as who they were.

They became inseparable best friends. In fact, he is the only male friend she has. And she thinks it's only possible because her parents don't know.

"Where are you staying tonight?" she asks.

"At my sister's. I wanted to see my niece."

"Dhriti? Aww. Give her a hug for me, no? I miss her early morning video calls," Miraya says.

"Sure."

"So, when do you want to meet?"

"Tomorrow for breakfast? Or do you want to meet me for lunch?"

"Maybe breakfast? A lot of things happened today. I want to tell you everything." Miraya *needs* to vent.

"I'll be all ears tomorrow. Oh — my baggage is here. I'll see you in the morning. Text me the details. Okay?"

"Yeah, yeah. Get home safe. Text me when you do."

"I know the drill, Ma'am."

She smiles. "Good. Now, go. Bye."

Sometimes she misses the days in Germany where it was just her work, the peers at her office and Kishore. No nosy relatives, no parents who had fallen prey to the norms of Indian society and no judgemental community. It was just everyone minding their own business. *Those were good days,* she thinks with a sigh.

When she stands up and dusts the sand off her dress, the sun has exited the scene completely. Mild grey clouds loom over, suggesting a possibility of rain. When she walks to her car, she notices the same old man she had seen moments ago. This time he is pacifying his granddaughter, handing her a different balloon. But the little girl's hands are pointing at the sky, at the bright red dot floating in the air. She cries and shakes her head.

Because she knows.

The little girl knows the first balloon can never be replaced.

She knows that because she loved it too much.

She knows that because it hurt when she let go.

Chapter 3

Miraya's sling bag slaps against her thighs as she runs towards the cafe. Heads turn and watch her whiz past by, some shaking in disapproval and some turning back without a care; she appreciates the latter.

The cafe is posh, serving both Western and Indian breakfast in the same place. It isn't very popular among the Middle-class crowd because of the cost of the food. Miraya suggested it because she needed to talk to Kishore without the possibility of running into her relatives and because it has a nice homey feel.

Miraya enters the cafe and scans the room for her friend.

"You dyed your hair black? Burgundy was so cool on you," Miraya says, dumping her bag in the empty seat next to her. Kishore's eyes light up at the sight of her.

"Ma specifically told me to do it before I came home. She doesn't want my hair to become the talk of the town," Kishore says, dipping the piece of crispy *Dosa* into a red chutney and then white chutney, followed by the green chutney. "God, I missed this. I think I could eat four more *Dosas*."

She throws a disgusting look at him as he gobbles food like a starved man. From what she's seen, every Indian who returns from a foreign country after a long stay appreciates Indian food like it's the last molecule of oxygen in the world. They'd go on and on about how much they missed the rich Indian spices, the flavour, the aroma and all the fancy culinary terms. Miraya had been one of these people. "Help yourself. The food is unlimited at the buffet."

"Aren't you going to eat?"

"I am," Miraya says, eyeing the well-crafted croissants and shimmery doughnuts on the buffet table. It has been so long since Miraya had a scrumptious breakfast. She usually chooses coffee over it.

"Bring me the *Dosas*, no?" he asks. Miraya rolls her eyes but her lips curve when she remembers how bossy he is. They used to have arguments about it back in their apartment in Germany.

"Fine. Don't eat the plate too," she snips and walks away from him. Miraya piles toast, scrambled eggs and every single dessert she can find on one plate. The next one has her favourite combo — *Vada*, *Idli* and *Sambar*.

"Don't touch," she warns Kishore as she places the plates on their table. Then, she takes his plate and returns back with what he wanted and a glass of watermelon juice for her.

Miraya starts with her toast. "So, how was your flight? And how is Drithi?"

"My flight got delayed an hour but otherwise it was fine. And Drithi... That little devil is the same bubbly giggling mess. Someone taught her to demand chocolates in return for a kiss so I got an earful from my sister when I gave her a big tub of M&Ms. I had to leave when Drithi was asleep because otherwise she wouldn't let me go."

"That's cute. You're living up to the title of the cool uncle who loves to spoil her. Every child needs one," Miraya says, sipping her juice. "So, what did you get for me?"

"I was supposed to?"

Miraya's jaw drops.

"I was kidding. It's in my bag. I'll give it to you later." Kishore shakes his head when Miraya's shoulders relax with relief.

"So, you slept through your alarm again?" he asks. Miraya was hoping he wouldn't bring up her tardiness because if there is one thing that Kishore hates, it's the lack of punctuality. Which, unfortunately, characterised Miraya.

"Actually, I forgot to set one," she sheepishly admits. "Before you say anything, I am sorry, okay? I took a quick shower and drove here as fast as I could. The traffic was another problem."

"Since you're paying for this, I am not going to say anything. Besides, I kinda expected it. And yet a tiny part of me wanted you to prove me wrong."

"Tough."

He shakes his head again but there is an affectionate smile tugging on his lips. Miraya notes at that moment that though he has been very unhappy with her tardiness, he had never once stayed angry with her. Meanwhile, Miraya had gone for days without talking to him for not refilling the ink in the printer and making her panic over unprinted schedules she had to take to work.

Kishore would give her a half-hour advice on why punctuality was important in life and he would go back to smiling and helping her out with whatever she needed. That has always been who Kishore is.

Miraya has a long-term relationship with grudgery. She knows it's not healthy but she can't help it.

"So, what did you want to talk to me about? Something at work? Or the usual with your family?"

"Um, both?"

Kishore is the only one who knew of the chaos that ensued during Miraya's 12th grade. He knew about Siddh and Shray and how her carefree school days ended with a horrible experience.

Reliving the memory was a burden but to Miraya, Kishore was her safety. She had felt compelled to open up to him for some reason and she had spilled it all one night.

So, Miraya tells him about having to interview Shray and not having a choice in the matter. She complains and rants and curses the man who had destroyed her life and settled nicely in the arms of the film industry without the least bit of guilt of what he had done.

"Did you talk to him? Over the phone, I mean?"

"No. I've been asked to be in touch with his team. I don't think he even knows I'll be the one talking to him."

"God, I wanna see his face when he realises it's you," Kishore says, breaking a piece of *Dosa* and offering Miraya a bite. She shakes her head. "I hope he wants to dig a hole for himself and hide the minute he sees you. He probably hurt you knowing he wouldn't have to face the consequences or you again. This would be a nice surprise. Like his mistakes visiting him. Like a *nightmare.*"

Miraya pauses her chewing and nods with consideration. "I didn't think of it this way. Kish, I was scared to meet him. But I wasn't the one who burned our friendship down, was I? So, why should I be scared? He should be the one ashamed. Yeah, you are right. Gosh, why didn't I look at it this way?"

"Miraya, you show him how you've grown over the years. Let it speak that he can't do anything to you now or twist your mind to his liking. When you are nervous, you always force yourself to appear confident. Do exactly that. Show him he doesn't affect you. Show it in your eyes."

"You should give me more pep talks. I am literally feeling the positivity radiating from you," Miraya says, using her left hand to demonstrate absorbing all the good energy.

Kishore chuckles. "God, I missed you. It's so lonely out there in the apartment."

"I thought you found a roommate."

"Yeah. Tyler. He is a good roommate. He was born deaf, but god, he has quite the humor. He even writes hilarious notes and uses a lot of puns. And I am learning sign language to communicate better with him. But you know... when you were there, the apartment was so loud and lively. It was as if you carried the life of the apartment in the palm of your hand. And since I am also a quiet person, the apartment feels soulless now."

Miraya's eyebrow rises. "You hated it when I made noise or spoke too loudly."

"Well, Karma is a bitch."

"True that. From what you say about Tyler, I think you will get along just fine. You love a person with humour," Miraya says and then adds, smirking, "Maybe because you lack it."

"Shut up. Don't start with the teasing," Kishore says, wiping the plate with the last piece of *Dosa* and managing to pick up every last drop of chutney. He puts it in his mouth and chews, leaning back against his seat.

"So, what's up with your family?"

"Same old. They're trying to get me to move back home. *Amma* is trying to use Dakshina as an excuse. She is bringing it up in every conversation. My life is going to get real hectic. I just hope I can survive it all," she says, spearing the egg.

"God save the Queen."

"Shut up."

"Hey, I am rooting for you," he says, sipping Miraya's watermelon juice. "I always will. You know that, right?"

Her chest feels warm at his words. "I know now," she says, smiling. "When are you boarding your bus?"

"At 6:30 pm. I bought chocolates and gifts for my friends around here so I have to drop by and visit them before I go home."

"Ah, the duties of an Indian who lives abroad. It was partly the reason I moved back to India."

"Some sacrifices have to be made," Kishore agrees dramatically and they laugh together. Looking at his black rough hair that refused to turn soft, his thick eyebrows, his pale brown eyes behind his oddly-shaped glasses and the tiny black mole just under his jaw reminds her of how much she had missed seeing him.

Being together from the moment she woke up to the moment she went to bed had gotten her so used to him that she had felt extremely lonely when she had returned back to her house in India. She had taken a lot of time getting used to it. And when she moved to an apartment, she felt it again. Rooming with Dakshina had faded the feeling over time.

"Why are you staring at me like that? Suddenly realised you are in love with me?"

Miraya snaps back from her thoughts and rolls her eyes. "You wish."

Kishore chuckles. It was amazing how their relationship, even after living together, had remained platonic. Sometimes, she would accompany him to company parties and he would tag along for hers. People would automatically assume that they were dating which had led to some awkward conversations that they had to awkwardly excuse themselves from. Sometimes they would just go along with it for fun.

Even Dakshina had once asked if one of us ever made a move on the other. The answer was No. *Is Kishore gay?* she asked next. A No again.

It is actively instilled in society that a man and a woman cannot remain best friends and *only* best friends. Even broad-minded

people, who claim that a man and a woman can have a platonic relationship, tend to find it hard to believe when it actually happens.
The worst part is that they don't even realise it. The belief is so
deeply buried in their mind because of what they grew up hearing
in their home, at their school and at their workplaces that their
mind refuses to adapt to something contrary. *It is so sad.*

"So, when do you have to be there at your office?"

"At nine-thirty. I told them I'd be late."

"But it's already nine."

Miraya's eyes go round. "What?"

Kishore shows her the time on his phone.

"Shit."

"Yeah, what did I expect?" he chuckles to himself. Miraya slyly
wraps the croissant, the sweet coconut balls and the choco-
late-bar-like dessert she doesn't know the name of in tissue paper
and slips them into her bag. She quickly chews on the *Idli* and
the *Vada.*

"Ask for the bill," she barks at him, before washing down the food
with a long sip of juice.

Miraya hands him her phone and instructs Kishore to pay from
her account, ignoring his attempts to pay instead. When the bill is
paid, Miraya starts to get up from her seat to wash her hands.

"Wait, come closer," he says and wipes her mouth with a tissue.
"You just love to embarrass yourself, don't you?"

Miraya grins and thanks him before running to the washroom. At
nine-ten, they are out of the cafe. She hugs him quickly and waves
goodbye to him. Just when she is close to her car, she comes back
running.

"*Aei,* where's my gift?"

The left corner of Kishore's lips tug upwards. "I thought you were
in a hurry."

"Well, *priorities*. Come on. Give it to me."

He fishes out a gift bag and hands it over to her. She throws a thank you at him as she climbs into her car and drives to her office.

Only when she is inside the four walls of the building, she breathes a sigh and opens the bag.

There is a used scented candle, a razor kit and a pen with a half-chewed lid.

A gasp leaves her lips.

He had given her the things she had left in his apartment. *Her* things. There is not even one chocolate inside the bag that he bought for her.

The *audacity* to prank her.

The absolute *nerve* of this idiot.

And when she calls him and greets him with a string of profanities, Kishore only replies with chest-heaving laughter.

Chapter 4

♥

MIRROR is buzzing like it has never before. Furious slaps of paper against paper, orders being yelled, people in crisp clothes zig-zagging through the narrow paths between cubicles to get work done and a chaotic rhythm of noisy keyboards. Miraya smiles. *Oh, I have missed this,* she realises.

"Mira! Oh, thank God. Mrs Nandhini has been asking for you. Mohan Sir from the communications team was in her office a moment ago. I think it's regarding the cover story," Fiya says. Her hair is a mess, a bad job at bundling it into a bun. And yet, she manages to look pretty. *God clearly has favourites,* she thinks, before nodding and heading to Mrs Nandhini's office.

The first thing she notices when she walks into the office is the sudden shift in room temperature. Mrs Nandhini hasn't even bothered to switch on the AC. Instead, her head is buried into a black binder, her round, metal-rimmed glasses inching down her nose.

"Ah, Miraya. Sit. We have some things to discuss."

Miraya obeys.

Mrs Nandhini removes her glasses and keeps them aside. "I had asked Vijay to get in touch with Shray's team to enquire about the schedule adjustments. He just got back to me about it. It seems there is a problem."

Hope sparks in her chest. *Please tell me he cancelled. Please,* she prays.

"Apparently, Shray's schedule is packed tight this month. He is shooting for his upcoming film. If it was around Chennai, it wouldn't have been a problem. We could have squeezed in the interview and the photoshoot somehow."

"But?"

Miraya's heart hammers in her chest. She would be the happiest woman in the world if this gets cancelled.

"The shooting for the film is happening in a hill resort in Ooty. His team has asked if we could send in our team and do an one-to-one talk and a photoshoot there. The expenses of the stay will be covered by them but the travel and other expenses should be covered by us."

"Wow," Miraya says. Honestly, she can't believe that asshole is so busy that he can't spare an hour or two of his time for them. Was he that popular already?

"I know. It's an odd request. I've spoken with the Heads and they say it should be doable. We have no other choice anyway."

Miraya frowns. It isn't too late to replace him with someone —

"I know what you are thinking. No, we can't bring in a model. It will make our quarters appear irresponsible and careless. You know what I am talking about, right?"

She knows. Opening an office in Chennai hasn't been looked upon as a promising investment at all. Most people in Delhi quarters have since scorned it. They deem the new quarters unnecessary so it was all the more reason to give them zero reasons to confirm their attitudes.

"We don't want a single thing going wrong with this issue. Somehow, we make this thing work. Understand?"

"Yes, Ma'am." Miraya forces a look of determination on her face.

Mrs Nandhini pushes a brochure towards her. "The details of the resort are given here. Look through it. You will be going there next week, I believe. Sort out everything before you go and please report to me about the progress."

"Yes, Ma'am."

"Eliza will be joining tomorrow. She is already briefed about the situation and the revised ideas for the shoot. Only once she and her crew go to the resort they can look into the lighting and technicalities involved. Besides that, Grace has been in touch with Shray's team. He wants to work with his personal stylist and makeup artist. The clothing and accessories should be acquired from the designers. I put Joyce in charge of that. I am telling you all this so that if something goes wrong, you know what to do. I will not be there because I have my son's wedding during that time. You should take responsibility."

This is huge, she thinks. She has never been trusted with such a big responsibility before. It makes her excited and nervous at the same time.

"Yes, Ma'am. I will."

"I know it's sudden but I trust you to handle it well. Please call me only in cases of extreme emergencies. Okay?" Mrs Nandhini asks, putting her glasses back on. She looks tired, the lines of grey in her hair looking more prominent than before.

Miraya smiles. "Got it. I am sorry I can't make it to your son's wedding. Please give him my wishes."

Mrs Nandhini's tired eyes light up briefly at the mention of her son. Everyone knew in the office that to Mrs Nandhini, her son was everything. Every chance she got, she spoke about her son's accomplishments, what he does and how he acts in response to something. She speaks about him so much that everyone feels like they know him personally. Anyone could feel her adoration for her son seeping through her words. It was apparent how much joy and sadness his wedding gave her at the same time. When that was added to the wedding-planning stress and the sudden workload in the office, Mrs Nandhini was undergoing a lot at one time.

Miraya tells herself that she shouldn't bring her any more trouble from her side. Afterall, that is the only thing she can do for her.

"I will. Thank you. You can leave, Miraya."

Miraya drags herself out of the room and slumps in her seat. Her head aches and her tongue craves for some coffee to soothe her nerves.

Miraya's life has been stagnant like a lazy lake that wouldn't care for a tiny ripple. For a year or so, she has been writing articles throughout the day, relaxing on the beach in the evening, having an awkward conversation with her parents, going home to eat and then sleep. Sometimes she watches a movie or two, or spends the night talking about nothing with Dakshina.

But in the past two days, her life has picked up tempo, attracting all sorts of mishaps and bad luck and opportunities to be thrown in her face. Her head spins when she tries to comprehend it.

She reviews the instructions Mrs Nandhini had given her a while ago and the enormity of the task overwhelms her. What if she messes things up? What if she manages to miss something important? Or what if she breaks down after seeing him?

Questions, doubts and insecurities drown her optimism. She needs to talk to someone. Miraya fishes for her phone from her bag and walks out, shaking her head at Fiya's questioning glance.

There were times in Miraya's life that brought her a storm of tears. It would be so powerful that she'd give in and get messy and real and cry her heart out. She would not be able to stop the tears so she'd ring someone close to her and ask them to distract her, talk something, *anything*.

That someone was Shray. It had been Shray for eight years.

"I told you I didn't do well. I expected only 400. I got 415. That's a good thing," Miraya said, forcing her lips to curve. Appa clapped her shoulders and told her that she did well and that he was proud of her no matter her marks. Amma was clearly disappointed but she smiled and nodded as well.

Miraya excused herself and took her phone to the terrace. She ignored the messages flooding in, asking her about her 10th grade board exam result.

Miraya squeezed her eyes close. She thought she did well in her exam. Yes, she was an average student; some teachers even called her below average. But, she had worked her ass off for the exams, had endless study sessions with Shray, sacrificed her sports practices and stayed late in school. She had done her best and expected a score around 450. Miraya was disappointed in herself. She had advised so many people that marks didn't matter but she was readily letting the numbers take a toll on her. She hated how worthless and useless it made her feel. Tears slipped silently over her cheeks.

Her fingers trembled as she called Shray and pressed the phone to her ear. The line was busy but before she could end it, Shray picked up.

"Miranda! How much? I bet you got —"

"Shray."

That one word spoke a thousand things.

"Oh, no," he said, his voice folding itself to the cosiness of a blanket. She sobbed. "Hey, I got you. I got you, okay?"

Her tears poured out of her eyes like a never-ending stream, slowly turning her loud sobs into sniffles and the sniffles into long gasps. Shray let her cry. She knew he was on the line, waiting for her to give her a sign. Waiting for her permission to talk.

"Shray?" she said, wiping her tears furiously on her skirt. Her chest was heavy. She hiccuped.

"I'm here. I'm here, Miranda. Let's talk about something else, okay?"

"Please."

"Okay. Hmm, I asked you to watch a Russian movie with me, right?"

"Yeah." Miraya's eyes felt hot and red. She pressed her palms on them and blew through her mouth.

"Well, since you refused to watch it with me I watched it alone. Miranda, you missed it. It was so good. You would've loved the hero. Totally your type."

"My type? How would you know my type?"

"Oh, please. Your type is guys who are goody-two-shoes, teacher's pet and use hair gels to set their hair everyday to school. Or in a word, Siddh."

"Shut up, idiot!"

"What? It's true. You are in love with him."

Miraya's face warmed up. She looked around her to see if anyone was there and then hissed, "No! It's just a tiny crush. It will go away."

"Uh uh."

"Shray?"

"Miranda?"

"Wipe that smirk off your face and shut up."

"How did you know I was smirking?"

Miraya swiped the last of her tears from her cheeks. "I can feel it."

"Then, can you feel my hug as well?"

Miraya found his words so endearing that she felt like crying all over again. Instead, she smiled and wrapped her arms around herself. "I can. I can always feel your hug even if you're a thousand miles away."

"You're my Miranda. I got you. You know that, right? I always got your back."

"I know."

Even after their fallout, even after she had hated him with all her heart and even if she had stopped speaking to him, the first person she wanted to call was him. Even now, when she feels like crying *because* of him, she still wants to call him and beg him to distract her. And give her one of his famous hugs.

Miraya bites her teeth, telling herself to get a grip. She calls Dakshina.

"Hello? Mira, I was just about to call you. Did you see my white socks? I remember seeing it under the tea table last night —"

"Daksh." Miraya's lips trembled.

"Hey, what happened?"

"Talk about something. Anything else," Miraya forces out, trying to mask the shiver in her voice. She sits on the stairs and buries her head in her lap, her phone glued to her ear.

"Oh, um, what should I talk about— oh god, I can't think of anything. Mira, why do you always put me in the most difficult positions?" Pause. "Suddenly my mind is blank, what the hell? You know I could talk for hours right? Shit. Okay, okay." Pause again. "Um, did you have your breakfast?"

"Yeah, I had it with Kishore," Miraya says, laughing weakly. Dakshina not having anything to talk about was a rare occurrence.

"Oh yeah, you told me. So, did he confess his deep, years-long love and pining for you this morning?"

"How many times have I told you? We are best friends."

"So were Ranav and I. Look at us now. We are thinking of marriage."

Miraya's eyes shoot open. "What?"

"Oh, didn't I tell you? I thought I did."

"Dakshina Gopinath!"

Her roommate's rich laughter puts a smile on Miraya's face.

"I'm letting you go now. I need the details tonight," Miraya says finally.

"Yes, Ma'am. And I think you have something to tell me as well."

Miraya hums into the phone and stares at the pattern on the marble stairs.

"Okay, I gotta go. I'll see you tonight. Italian for dinner okay?"

"Yes, please," Miraya says. "Thanks, Daksh."

"Shut up, bitch. Don't humiliate me by using the golden words."

"Okay, okay." Miraya notices Fiya waving at her to come back. She nods at her. "Daksh?"

"Yeah?"

"I wore your socks today."

"I knew it. Do you know how long I've been searching for —"

"Bye, I gotta go. Muah," Miraya says and hangs up. She flicks away the rogue tear that had slipped out of her eye. Then, she plasters a smile and joins Fiya at their table like nothing ever happened.

Chapter 5

♥

The following week disappears under a pile of planners, ideas, moodboards and several cups of coffee. Miraya is on the floor in a t-shirt that doesn't go with her printed shorts and with a pencil in her hand, editing the recent article that Fiya had written. Her eyes had given up on screen time so she had to do it on paper.

The door of her room is ajar. Dakshina is inside, packing Miraya's clothes into the tiny suitcase she has. "This one okay?" she asks.

Miraya looks up to see her holding up a pair of skimpy shorts that she wears to pools. "Let me remind you that I am going on a work trip and not to seduce someone into my bed. And I am going to Ooty. If I wear that, my legs would become popsicles."

"I bet Kishore would dig that popsicle," her roommate smirks and Miraya throws her eraser at her. It falls on the door frame.

Dakshina guffaws, kneeling on the bed over the suitcase in her black pyjamas. She is wearing glasses instead of her contacts and her latest tattoo of a crescent moon gleams on her collarbone under the faint streaks of sunlight. Her dark straight hair sweeps over her shoulders.

When Miraya had met Dakshina in college, she had perfect straight hair that every girl was envious of. Only after they had gotten close, she came to know that Dakshina used to have wild curly hair when she was young. Tired of having to tame the curls down each time she combed her hair, she gave up and straightened the damn thing.

Now, Miraya cannot imagine Dakshina with curly hair. It was too strange.

"Okay, this one?" This time it's a lacy black bra that Dakshina had forced her to buy on her previous birthday.

"I haven't worn that yet and I don't think I will *ever* wear that," Miraya says.

"Oh shush. Don't worry. Kishore will love that," Dakshina replies, smug.

Having enough of her nonsense, Miraya slams her pencil on the floor and chases Dakshina in her room. Her roommate cackles and runs around the bed. Miraya follows her. In the end, they both end up on the floor, their chest heaving from laughter and the accidental physical exercise.

"It's my fault for asking you to pack my clothes for the trip," Miraya says.

"Yeah, yeah. You say that after I am done."

"You finished?" Miraya asks, jumping up to inspect her suitcase. She opens it up to find her clothes folded and arranged so neatly that it looks like a DIY tutorial from Pinterest.

"Damn. I take back what I said. Asking you to pack my clothes is the best thing I did this week."

"Right. Now, in return, I have a favour to ask."

Miraya snorts. "Of course. I should have known."

Dakshina grins and props her chin on the bed. "Can I get a voice note from Shray? He can just say," - she clears her throat and adjusts her voice - "hey Dakshina. I heard from Miraya that you were a big fan. Lots of love and hugs. I wish you the best of the best."

Miraya's heart squeezes at his name.

"Or if that's too much you can just get a note signed for me. Please, *please*, Miraya."

Miraya forces a smile. "First of all, he doesn't speak like that. Sorry to say this but you suck at mimicry -"

"I know. No need to rub it in. When I was young, my dream was to become a mimicry artist. I changed my mind."

"- thank God you did. And secondly, yes, I will try my best to get it from him. Only because you're my best friend."

Dakshina makes a high pitched sound and throws her arm around her, shaking her shoulders in some kind of dance. Miraya smiles and wraps her arms around her. Dakshina always smelled like strawberries. The familiarity of the smell comforted her.

"Miraya?"

"Yeah?"

"Have you ever thought Kishore is hot? At least once?"

Miraya groans and falls back on the bed. "Will you ever drop the subject?"

"I will once you get a boyfriend."

"I guess I should just put up with all your teasing then."

Dakshina shakes her head and stands up. "Hopeless. You, woman, are a hopeless establishment of nature."

Miraya laughs. "I know."

□□□□□□□□□□□□□□

"Want some gum?" Miraya asks Fiya, trying not to laugh at the poor girl's condition. Fiya is strapped to her seat with her seat belt and has her hands on either side of her thighs, tightly gripping the cushion. The car winds its way up the hills of Nilgiris in circles, which makes Fiya extremely nauseous. She has already stopped the car once to puke on the roadside, tearing up while doing so. But, it seems her stomach hasn't settled yet. "It helps with nausea."

"I don't want to move. If I move, I think I'll puke again," Fiya mumbles. Her face is pale and tired.

"I'll pop this in your mouth then. Chew on it," Miraya says before doing so.

"Thanks."

Miraya plugs her earphones back in her ear and leans against the window. On her left side, there is a never-ending assembly of trees over brown rocky soil. Monkeys sit on the roots of the trees, watching cars zoom past them, wishing someone would stop to toss them food. On her right, is the open road, dotted with sign boards for hair-pin bends and accident prone areas. When she looks past that, she can see the gentle folds of the hills expand into a blanket of lush green. The sky, which feels closer and bigger than before, is like a painting - bright blobs of white over an evenly painted blue. It looks real and unreal at the same time.

Her eyes drink in the calming power of the picture before her and hopes that capturing the essence in memory could keep her going for the next few days.

"How many more bends?" Fiya croaks.

"Five more," the driver says.

She makes a pained sound and bites on her gum.

For some, the ride up the hill to reach Ooty is a torturous trip. Even thinking of the swirling road makes them feel sick. But the city and the view from up there is worth it in the end.

Miraya has plenty of good memories in Ooty. She used to come here often for the summer holidays and stay with *Athai* and *Mama*. She remembers the first time she went boating, her first horse ride and her first camping trip. It was all during her time in Ooty. She loves this place.

But now, to think it was going to be tainted with a permanent mark by this assignment made her sad. Miraya can only hope it is not as worse as she expects it to be.

The song ends and the next one plays. She has listened to it many times after her school days but maybe because of the fact that she has been thinking about school and Shray and Siddh lately, her mind takes her back to the memory linked with it.

It was a good memory when it happened.

It still is despite everything that went down.

"Okay, since we have a block period today, why don't we take a ten-minute break and have an ice breaking activity?" Miss Priya said.

The class groaned.

"Why can't we have a ten-minute break without any activity, Ma'am?" someone asked.

Miss Priya shook her head. "I know what will happen if I give you a break. I don't want the principal to walk in here and ask why the class is so noisy with the teacher present in class."

Shray, who was seated right before Miraya, leaned back. "I bet a hundred bucks that the ice-breaking activity is going to be you singing for us," he said.

"Aiyoo. I'm not doing it. Tell her I'm not feeling well." Miraya said before folding her head into her hands on her desk and closing her eyes.

"Since this class is too lazy to stand or engage in any activity, Miraya, why don't you come sing for us?" Miss Priya asked. She expected Shray to help her out but there was only silence that followed. Miraya looked up to see Shray's shoulders vibrating with silent laughter as he shrunk in his seat. Asshole.

She looked at others in the class looking expectantly at her, some boys even hooting in encouragement. She also caught Siddh's eyes on her, nudging her to do it. Miraya didn't want to let him down. She stood up.

"Go Miranda. Go entertain the class," Shray said as she passed by. She kicked him and gave him a glare that clearly told him he was going to pay for it.

"Hey, Mira, I can sing if you don't feel up to it," Sona offered. She was a part of the gang along with Shray, Siddh, Roshan, Pavithra and Suriya.

"It's okay."

Miraya stood in front of the class. She sang.

It was the song that Shray had introduced to her. He had asked her to sing that song so many times that she had memorised the lyrics and grown to love it equally. As soon as she finished the first line, Shray clapped and hooted. Miraya bit back her laugh and continued, her eyes landing on Siddh. He sat there, watching her with adoration, his arms crossed across his chest. Miraya's heart fluttered whenever he looked at her like that.

In his neatly ironed pale blue shirt and black uniform pants, Siddh was a dreamboat. It was true that Miraya wasn't a big fan of men with perfectly styled hair, with no room for a mess. But Siddh was an exception. The predictable hairstyle complimented his face and his button nose. She liked everything about him. Especially how his sleeves hugged his arms like a second skin.

She sang, staring into his eyes. He smiled the whole time, making her cheeks warm. She hoped it wasn't too noticeable.

When she was done and the applause poured in, she walked back to her seat. Miraya expected a comment from Shray but he looked out the window like a foreigner in a city. She kicked his chair.

"What?" he snapped.

"What is your problem now?"

"That was our song," Shray said through his teeth.

"So? Am I not allowed to sing it in front of the class?"

He mumbled something that she didn't quite catch and turned back to the window. Miraya rolled her eyes and kicked his chair again. He didn't respond. She blew a breath of frustration.

At that moment, Suriya passed her a note from Siddh, wiggling his eyebrows. Miraya blushed, snatching the piece of paper from him and opening it between the folds of her notebook.

I just fell for you a bit more.

She leaned back and glanced at Siddh. Making sure the teacher was facing the board, he put his hands on his chest and shook his head as if to say his heart can't take it anymore.

She scribbled a note. Not my fault.

When Siddh got it, he narrowed his eyes. She grinned, shrugging her shoulders and feigning innocence. But in truth, she fell for him a bit more in that moment too.

Chapter 6

♥

"You know something?" Fiya asks, her smile restored in her face after freshening up in their assigned rooms in the resort. "This resort had very slow business, it seems. The owner is the director's best friend so the director decided to help him out. Most of the film is being shot in this resort so it is rented now. After the film is released, this resort will be a shooting spot which will attract more customers. So clever, no?"

"Yeah. How did you sniff this out?" Miraya asks, clicking a picture of the tall wooden swing before sitting on it.

"I have sharp ears," she shrugs, capturing Miraya in her phone. "Oh, this one is so good. You look like you could get a role in this movie."

"Shut up," Miraya says, closing her eyes and tilting her head back. The resort was aesthetic and their rooms were cosy and luxurious at the same time. This might have been a nice getaway if not for the heavy burden that sat on her shoulders, posing as a constant reminder that she has work to do and she has to hustle. Soon, when Shray's schedule clears out, she will have to face him (which requires a lot of energy in itself), help supervise the dress fitting and discuss his timings for the photoshoot and the interview.

Miraya is nervous and scared and feels like sprinting into the woods and cursing out his name. She is anxious that she is going to mess things up in some way. She imagines everyone getting to know her sob story through Shray and feeling bad for her. There are so many things running in her mind that it makes her sick to the stomach.

Now, *she* is the one feeling nauseous.

"Eliza and her crew done?" Fiya asks, snapping her out of her thoughts.

"Yes. They've surveyed the resort and picked out the spots they could do a photoshoot in. The aesthetics of the resort helped them a lot. She said she'll show them to us and Grace later on once we've had our rest."

"How many days do you think we will get to stay here?"

"I don't know. The quicker we get the work done, the better."

"Why? It's nice here. I have already planned a trip here with Ashraf."

"So, are you guys serious?"

Fiya tugs her sweater closer. "Very. You know, only with a few people, you can picture yourself getting married to without shuddering and cringing badly. With Ashraf, after a few dates, I saw it. And marrying him feels like the most natural thing. Like, if you ask me to marry him right here right now, I will. You just know these things. It's difficult to explain but it is what it is."

Miraya smiles. "I'm genuinely happy for you, Fiya."

"I know you were secretly rooting for us."

"I hoped it wasn't obvious," Miraya says, chuckling along with her. But deep inside, she realises that most people around her are getting married soon. They are with the love of their lives, happy and eager to start a new life. She feels happy for them but something aches deep inside her. Will she ever get someone like that? Will she ever get back from work, knowing there would be someone waiting for her?

Her phone rings.

"Hello, Grace."

"Where are you?"

"Um, I came outside with Fiya. We are by the swing. What's up?" Miraya says. Fiya comes next to her at the sound of her name.

"Shray's team told us he is free for dress fitting in thirty minutes. Would you like to join?" She doesn't want to join. A polite no is almost out of her lips when Grace adds, "You have to report to Nandhini Ma'am, right? I think it's best if you are there with us."

"Okay. Yeah, you're right," she mumbles, clearly having no option. "I'll be there."

With that, she hangs up and fists her fingers around the swing's rope. This is it. The moment she had been dreading is here. She only has to walk right into it with a smile on her face.

Fun.

Miraya had to be there but no one said anything about being on time.

Despite Fiya's interrogation about her behaviour, she lounges in the fluffy white bed in her room, flicking channels on the TV without any interest to while away the time. To Fiya, Miraya might come off as a too-cool-for-being-punctual, uncaring and nonchalant employee but internally every single cell in her body is freaking out, filling her lungs with bubbles of anxiety and fear.

She wasn't ready to meet Shray.

It was the first time she would be meeting him personally after school. She wasn't aware of how her body and mind would react.

To be honest, Miraya found it hard to hate Shray. When you look at some people, hatred bubbles in your chest for no reason at all. Or for reasons you've forgotten. The heart does its work without the mind's help. But with Shray, every time she looked at a picture of him, or watched his movie, the first feeling she felt was happiness. He had made it after all. Then, Miraya would force herself to think about what happened in school, how he had stabbed her in the back when she had trusted him with the knife. She would have to muster up her disgust and hate for him each time she saw his face and it wasn't different this time, apart from the fact that she has to muster up the courage to talk to him like nothing ever happened at all as well.

"Don't you want to see him? I can't wait to see him. Let's go, Mira!" Fiya whines. Miraya checks the time on the phone and takes a deep breath. *I can do this. I can do this.* She chants the words in her head as she straightens her dress and takes a last look at the mirror before heading to the venue.

The room has familiar faces, a good change from the filming crew she has been seeing all day. There is Grace whispering into Eliza's ear while she nods to whatever she hears. Joyce has a notepad in her hand as she scurries into what Miraya assumes to be the dressing room. In hindsight, she realises she has nothing to report at all. It's not her department. And even if Mrs Nandhini expects the details, she can simply ask Joyce to feed her information.

She contemplates announcing her presence to Grace and walking out after a chat. Or ask Fiya to stay here and let her know about anything worth reporting. Before that, Joyce walks out of the dressing room and beelines for Grace. She leaves the door open.

Miraya's heart races.

She can recognise that laugh anywhere — loud, piercing and heartful. It was like a particular drum beat in your favourite rock song that always put the pep back inside you. Most of the time in school, Miraya would laugh along with him, not because of the joke but because of how contagious his laughter was. She can almost picture his face, the way his right cheek rose higher than the left, causing his right eye to crinkle more. Shray always laughed with his mouth open, without a care in this world. It was one of her favourite things in the world.

Was.

But he's so close. Just a few steps from her.

So so dangerously close.

Miraya marches towards Grace and Joyce and barges into their conversation. "Hey. How was the fitting?"

"Yeah, there is a mild alteration in the shirt but otherwise everything is perfect."

"Oh, great. I'll be off then," Miraya says.

"Wait. Miraya," Grace stops her. "We were about to schedule the photoshoot and the interview with his team. Can you stay for a bit?"

The lie slips from her lips effortlessly. "I'm sorry. I'm not feeling very great. I think the travel and the food has unsettled my stomach. Um... I can work with whatever you decide. Is that okay?"

Joyce, thankfully, believes her lie and takes it one step further by adding onto it. "Yeah, you look pale, Mira. Should I have someone bring you something to drink?"

"No, I'll go to sleep for a while. It might make me feel better."

"Okay then. I'll check in on you later. I'll ask Fiya to let you know about what we discuss," Grace says, giving her a smile. Miraya wastes no time in telling Fiya a hasty goodbye and walking out of the room.

She walks until she can't see the room anymore and leans on the pillar, breathing out. Miraya realises it wouldn't have been this difficult if she had to meet Siddh instead of Shray, even though he was her ex. They hadn't mutually broken up but it was clear as crystal that their relationship was done and dusted after what happened. Even then, if she can, she would gladly switch Shray for Siddh at the moment.

But she can't.

She has to face him eventually. She can't escape forever.

Miraya has to insert a big black boulder between her personal feelings and her work to stop it from mingling together and messing with her mind. She can't afford to make a mistake. She has to compartmentalise her thoughts into boxes so that they don't —

"Care for a round of carrom?" A voice comes from somewhere close that she wonders if the question is directed at her. It's a feminine voice, minute traces of a foreign accent sticking to her words.

"Now? I thought you were supposed to have dinner with Vinay," Shray's unmistakable voice floats in the air. Miraya presses herself to the wall. There is no other place to hide. If she runs, she'll only be attracting attention. Her only option was to hope they'd ignore her and walk by.

"He cancelled. Last minute meeting with the producers," the woman said.

"I'm sorry, Ria. You were so excited," Shray says. Ever the empathetic one. *Then how did he have the heart to betray her?*

And Ria, as in his co-star? She didn't know they were close.

"It's fine. I understand him," she says and it's clear, even to Miraya, that it is to convince herself more than Shray. "So, what do you think?"

The voices are so close. If they turn right, Miraya would be there, slotted in the space next to the door frame. She pulls out her phone and leans against the wall so that if they catch her, she can appear to be casually hanging out with her phone and not hiding.

A gust of expensive perfume hits her nose before she could see them. Miraya hides her face with her hair.

"I wanted to take a nap. I'm so tired. But okay, I'll play a game with you. Just one, though," Shray replies.

"Thanks. I'll buy you a drink later."

Miraya holds her breath as she stares at her phone. Shray and Ria walk past her but before she could exhale out her relief, her phone rings. Her mind gives up on her and her fingers fumble to decline the call or mute the damn ringtone.

But it was too late.

Without thinking straight, she glances up and meets Shray's curious black eyes that instantly round with surprise and recognition.

His lips part, beginning to shape out a word.

Miraya freezes.

Don't say it. Don't say it. No, don't you dare say —

"Miranda?"

And her world comes crashing down.

Chapter 7

♥

Every time Miraya watched a horror movie, she dreamt of being stranded in a haunted island alone, wishing she could kill herself instead of walking through the trees that moaned eerily every time the wind blew and whispered absurd things in her ear. She feels the same way as she stands frozen under Shray's shocked gaze.

And as soon as the cursed word slips out of his lips, her heart thumps. It brings back a thousand memories but instead of slipping into a happy reminiscing trip down memory lane, she schools her anger together. He still had the nerve to call her using that stupid nickname?

She snaps out of the trance and clears her mind. Like a slate wiped clean except that burning red anger she has harboured for him all these years.

He called her Miranda. That's not her name, is it?

She wills her legs to take a step forward and then another. She doesn't look at him again and struts forward like the last few seconds didn't happen.

What seemed like a badass move in her head turns out to be her asking for trouble. Because the next thing Shray does is grab her wrist and spin her around.

Ria steps forward, asking if he knew her. He gruffly says he will have to take a rain check on their game and drags Miraya to another room.

"Shray, let me go," Miraya hisses through her teeth. She is so used to him moving her like a sack of potato that it takes time for her to realise he was crossing a boundary. A boundary that he had clearly drawn with a bold red pen. His grip isn't very tight so she uses her other hand to peel them off her wrist.

But it was too late. They were in an empty room.

"Miranda, oh my god!" He grins. "Why— How are you here? Why did you pretend to not hear me?"

"Because Miranda isn't my name, Shray," she spits out.

He visibly coils back. *Good.*

"I know but that's what I call you all the time," he reasons. His voice isn't squeaky with happiness anymore.

"Not anymore. Don't ever call me that."

"Miran— *Miraya*, what's wrong? This is the first time I see you in seven years and I always thought it would be all tears and laughter and hugs."

How does he have the heart to say such a lie? Did stabbing her in the back turn his heart black and cold? Or was it always like that? Or was it her fault that she failed to see past the flimsy golden cover over his heart of stone?

Anger bubbles in her chest. He had ruined her life and had the audacity to ask what's wrong? Did she, by any chance, step into a multiverse? Did he have amnesia?

"Look Shray, I'll be candid with you. I didn't want to meet you."

His face crumbles. She feels the stab of pain inside her but she bites her jaw to steel herself. No, she will not act on the instincts she had grown up with. She will not give in to the urge to empathise with him.

He deserves to be hurt.

He ruined her life.

This was Miraya's mantra from now.

"I tried every possible option to avoid this meeting but bad luck is a clingy friend of mine. You might be wondering why I am here. I work at MIRROR —"

"I know."

She's totally going to ignore the way the question HOW? is itching in her mind. Never scratch an itch however tempting it gets. She's going to take that advice for once.

" — and I'm here to interview you for the cover story. I am here for work and work only. So, please, save yourself the trouble, and don't talk to me about anything that's not work. I don't want to be associated with you in any way other than this one conversation we are going to have. Don't try and change my mind and ask me stupid questions like why*You know why.*"

Shray opens his mouth but Miraya cuts him off. "If you try, I'll write shitty things about you in the article and trust me, any news of you, good or bad, is juicy enough to blow up. I don't care about you."

He closes his mouth. The look on his face reads *Processing Delay.* She hates herself for knowing him so well that she can read him by his eyes only.

Miraya takes advantage of his shock and the lag. It is the best way to put it all out there without any interruption, giving no room for him to change her mind.

"I don't know you, Shray. And don't pretend like you know me. After what happened, I don't think we even knew each other in the first place. Unbelievable and quite the cruel joke, considering we were friends for twelve years."

With that, Miraya walks out the door.

She doesn't stop until she is inside her room, safely locked between the pristine white walls of the bathroom.

Shray.

That goddamn asshole.

The pictures she had seen and the movies he had starred in did him dirty. He looked way better in person, so much better.

He had grown some more muscles over the years, the way his shirt tightened around his arms when he raised it being enough proof. In school, he used a perfume that she forgot the name of. But now he smelled like expensive mandarin and musk. His jawline was sharper than before and his skin was fairer, shinier. On second thought, she recalls that she didn't see the prominent scar on his left cheek, just next to his lips, and realises he had makeup on.

But other than the differences here and there, he hasn't changed much over the years. Shray grew out of his awkward boyish phase at the end of tenth grade. The last time she had seen him he was a very attractive and manly man. He had a stubble growing that he oh so religiously maintained, tried to keep his hair the longest the school would allow and took care of his skin like it was his goddamn wealth. Miraya always fussed over how unwantedly long his lashes were and how thick his eyebrows were. The muscles and the toned fit body that the girls crushed on him for were a perk from his sports practices and work out.

As she pictures that guy from twelfth grade, snippets of memories play in her head. When Shray had started to grow a moustache and she had ordered him not to sit next to her because he looked weird as hell, when Siddh and Shray arm-wrestled to claim the last piece of *Kaju* sweet in her snack box, when Shray wouldn't let her move out of her seat until she tied her shoelaces because she had scraped her face a week before. She remembers during Sports Day, how Siddh sipped water from her bottle suggesting an indirect kiss and before she could revel in that flirty move and contain her blush, Shray had barged between them, panting, and slurped on her bottle like it was his own. She chased him around and threw that bottle on his face in the end.

Miraya's heart aches.

She has desperately wished many times over the years to reverse time and go back to when Shray had been her best friend and not a traitor. More than the sharp pain of the stab wound on her back, losing him forever scarred her the most. She knows she could never go back to the way they were. Miraya and Shray's story died when Shray decided to tattle away her one secret to everyone.

What happened that day is still fresh in her mind.

It was February 16th, the Monday after Valentine's day. It was their last week before their study holidays began. Valentine's day was on a Saturday and usually all the young lovers in school avoided bringing any gifts to school because of the bag-checking that happens to catch victims of love and destroy their lives. That's just how Indian schools worked.

But the school was smarter. After two years of absolutely no confiscation of gifts on Valentine's day, they decided to switch up their tactic and check the bags during the next few days.

That day the bag-checking had started in the junior block and word reached Miraya's class. 12B. She panicked. Not because she brought along a gift for Siddh or he for her but because she had collected all the love notes they had exchanged over the years and kept them in a pouch.

"What are you going to do?" Sona asked.

Siddh suggested the dustbin and she disagreed immediately (in hindsight, she shouldn't have). She thought hiding them in her file was too obvious. She can't stuff them in her sock as well. Then, it clicked.

"Shray?"

"Yeah?"

"Your secret zip inside your bag," Miraya said. He looked confused. She whispered in his ear, *"The one where you hide your cigarettes."*

Shray coughed and looked almost guilty. *"You knew?"*

Miraya looked at him like he was stupid to ask something so obvious.

"Of course you knew."

"Miraya, I'm sorry. I know you don't like it when I smoke but I tried —"

She stopped him and batted her eyelashes. *"I'll forgive you if you let these notes share that space with your cigarettes. Please."*

"You weren't even angry, were you?" he asked. Miraya only smiled. He regarded her repulsively. *"Look at you using the golden words and smiling like a creep. Give it to me."*

He took the stack of papers and went outside to hide them in his bag. The zip was hidden to mankind unless they searched the bag knowing it was there. Miraya blew a breath of relief and squeezed Siddh's hand briefly before going back to her seat. Miraya watched boys stuff USBs inside their socks. The class was chaotic.

When the bag-checking team of teachers came, Miraya was cool. She trusted the power of the invisiblily of that zip pocket.

But she was wrong to trust the one who hid it there.

"Shray? Come out, please," the teacher called.

Miraya panicked and glanced at Shray. It's okay, he mouthed, and went outside. She couldn't hear or see what was happening. She could catch phrases like Whose is it, tell the truth, I know you're lying, don't lie. Her class teacher was summoned and there was a tense discussion in the corridor right before her class. The students were all dying to get a glimpse of the drama.

Miraya watched Shray taken aside by the class teacher. They discussed something with their heads low and Miraya begged for a hint at what was happening.

She was freaking out. She had a strong feeling her notes were sniffed out but she didn't want to believe it yet.

Everything shattered when the class teacher suddenly turned and called her name. "Miraya. And Siddh. Please come outside."

At that moment, Miraya knew her life was ruined. She had managed to drag her name into the depths of hell just before she graduated. She was terrified of what was going to happen because she knew her parents were going to be called and blasted as well. She took a quick look at Siddh and found his face pale, fear conquering it. She didn't blame him. Miraya had experiences being yelled at in the Principal's room but Siddh was a pure innocent guy who hadn't done a single mistake except fall in love with her.

Just as they stepped out, the teacher said, "Shray, you can go back to your seat. Thanks for cooperating."

Shray wore the sincerest apology when he met her eyes as he walked past her.

Miraya knew it was over once they found the notes and read through them. There was no salvation. And that was why she completely understood why Shray had admitted the notes were Miraya's and Siddh's. It's okay, she said with her eyes. She didn't expect him to protect the two of them. She didn't blame him or hold anything against him for giving them away.

She really didn't.

What made her resent him was what she heard next.

"The audacity the two of you have to dump these disgusting papers in Shray's bag! You thought you would get away if you put it in someone else's bag? Is this the age to fall in love? The one job you have in this age is to study and the board exams are so close and here you are —"

That's when it registered in her mind.

Dump in his bag?

The pocket zip was small. The papers can only be stuffed inside.

And the notes were all they found. What about his cigarette?

The conclusion struck her like a shot of poison. Slow but sure to kill. It was as if Shray had taken an axe to her heart and cut out the biggest hole in it. She wanted to scream and yell and deny what she was hearing but there was simply no other explanation.

He had never hid the notes to begin with.

He set them up on purpose.

He let them get caught.

He let her life get ruined, shattering their over-a-decade friendship into meaningless dust.

Chapter 8

♥

Miraya slides down against the bathroom door and sits on the cold tiled floor, her knees pulled to her chest. She rests her cheek on her knees, feeling the tears slide over her nose and drip onto the floor.

It was a bad idea to relive the memory again. She always ended up in a pool of tears and regrets and anger. She could feel what she felt during that time. She was stuck in a triangular cage of cruel mirrors — Shray's betrayal on one side, losing Siddh on another side and her parents making her feel like she had committed the biggest crime in the world on the other.

"We had trust in you."

"We took care of you, let you study in the school you liked, bought you everything you wanted and is this how you repay us?"

"I can't even bear to look at you."

"You are our only child, Miraya. How can you do this to us?"

"The whole school is going to be talking about this. God, I can't even imagine what Sona's mother will say and spread to everyone she knows."

"You took down the reputation we built for so many years in one single blow."

"Do you even realise what you've done? What were you even thinking?"

"Look at your father. Has he ever told you not to do anything? Has he ever scolded you? He had so much trust in you. He works day and night trying to give you all the best things in the world. Look at him sitting there looking shattered. It's because of you."

"No phone for you. Sit and study for your board exams. And don't you even think of joining a co-ed college. You're going to a women's college, whether you like it or not. Find a course that is available there and study that. After you get a degree, we are getting you married first thing. "

At that moment, she seriously considered running away from her home. She had no one on her side, no one to understand what she was going through and no one to listen to her cry. She had never felt lonelier than that before. Hell would have been better.

Although, *Amma* was right about one thing. *Appa* gave Miraya all the freedom that she could ever want. She was allowed to go for overnight sports tournaments, hang out with her friends outside, come home at six in the evening, wear whatever she liked, get away with scoring average marks, and have a phone from seventh grade. A lot of her friends had openly told her that they were jealous of the relationship Miraya had with her family.

All that was flipped over in a day. Her freedom stripped off bare.

She was suspended from school for three days. And her parents told her to just stay home and study for her exams the rest of the week. She wasn't allowed to go to school by bus. She was dropped off at school by *Appa* just before her exam started and picked up right after it ended. It was horrible.

Miraya became a bird in a cage who had a taste of flying high. It was the worst punishment she could ever have been given.

Because falling in love had an age limit. If violated, it was con-sidered a crime.

As if love asks permission before pushing you off the cliff.

Over the years, her parents' anger reduced. At least enough to drop the horrific idea of getting her married after her undergraduate. She studied further, finished her masters and flew away to Germany. It was a good job offer so her parents couldn't say no. After she returned to India, Miraya had expected her parents to start looking for marriage alliances for her. But lucky for her, some god-like astrologer had advised their parents to stop looking until Miraya is twenty six years old.

But regardless, Miraya noticed that she can't even imagine falling in love again. It terrified her. It was almost as if she developed an allergy to it. Maybe that was why she wasn't interested in Kishore. The attraction wasn't enough for her to face her fear.

A knock comes through. "Miraya? You in there?" Fiya asks.

Miraya scrambles off the floor and wipes her tears on her sleeve. She glances at the mirror. Her eyes don't look puffy and red. There is a twinge of pink but she can use a lie to cover that. Her shoulder-length hair goes back to being presentable when she pats down the rogue strands at the back and weaves through the strands twice. Her lipstick is perfect.

"I heard you were sick. What happened?"

On second thought, her lipstick is *too* perfect. She grabs a toilet paper and wipes off the pink stain. Miraya flushes the toilet and unlocks the bathroom.

"You were fine a few minutes ago. What happened?" Fiya asks, taking her by the arm.

"I think the food didn't agree with me. I'll be fine tomorrow." Miraya gets into the bed and slips under the covers.

"Don't stress. Take your time. The interview isn't scheduled until Friday anyway."

"WHAT? He's going to keep us here for so long?"

Fiya kicks off her slippers and falls back onto the bed horizontally. Her body is splayed across Miraya's feet. "As if there's anything to complain about. Free food, free room, free trip, close to no work — this is what heaven feels like. Ashraf will be so jealous if I tell him."

Miraya can't wait to leave this place.

"If you're better by tomorrow, can we go into the city? I googled the best shops and the local food around here."

Oh, how she wishes she could revel in the perks of this trip. Instead, all she can do is curse and scream into her pillow about how stressful all this is.

"Miraya?"

"Yeah, sure."

"Do you need anything? Lemonade with salt? Soda?"

Miraya smiles. "No, I'm fine. If I want, I'll make sure to tell you. Now go out and click a hundred selfies in the same place like you always do. I know you're itching for some content for your Instagram."

"Are you complimenting me or calling me out for my weird selfie obsession?"

"Doesn't matter as long as you know it's weird."

Fiya makes a face as if she wants to slap herself. Miraya laughs and snuggles further into the bed.

"I fell right into that, didn't I? Now I understand why Ashraf always wins our arguments. I end up insulting myself in the end. Me and my stupid mouth," Fiya complains.

"I am pretty sure Ashraf wouldn't call that mouth stupid."

"Then what else will he call it? Dumb? Reckless? Chatty?"

Miraya blinks at her. "You know what? Forget I said that."

Fiya looks very very confused. "Honestly, I really don't understand. Why won't he — " Her eyes go wide. "Oh. *Oh. That.* "

Her cheeks turn pink.

"There you go. You got your answer. Now, let me close my eyes and peacefully wonder if you are the slow-brained one or if I am the humourless one."

She chuckles. "Sorry. Go to sleep. Text me if you need anything."

Miraya closes her eyes. And she drifts off to sleep.

□□□□□□□□□□□

"Miraya? Miraya?" Fiya's voice booms next to her ear.

She lifts her head from her pillow and rolls onto her back. "What?" Miraya's voice comes off as a croak.

"How are you feeling?"

Miraya throws the sheets back over her head and snuggles into her bed when she realises Fiya was here to make small talk. "Better."

"You won't believe what happened."

"What?"

"I met with *the* Shray Nivas!"

"What?" Miraya's eyes go wide after her sleepy brain actually processes her words. "WHAT?"

"That's a lot of Whats. But, I know right! Even though I knew I was going to meet him eventually, now that I did, I can't believe it. He is so sweet. And his voice is so —"

Miraya jolts up from her bed. She is aware that her hair must have a large resemblance to Albert Einstein's but she doesn't care. "You spoke to him?" she almost screams.

"Duh. And I told him about you. He said he looks forward to meeting you. It wasn't something he said out of formality, mind you. He really meant it. It might be because I spent three and a half minutes rambling away about how talented and precious you are but anyway, that's not the point. He invited us to dinner today."

Miraya almost falls off the bed.

"WHAT?"

"I thought you weren't starstruck when it came to celebrities. But you don't need to worry. He is very grounded. And–"

Fiya hides her head in her hands and gives her body a wiggle. Miraya spares her a revolting look. "And?"

"He hugged me!" Fiya melts into the bed like she's ice and the bed is a hot pad. "Ugh, he smelled so good. Like an actor but a sweet kind-hearted super-hot actor. Almost like a dream."

Miraya's never heard anything more absurd in life. Except for when she heard someone is selling toilet paper made out of gold for ten freaking crores.

"Don't forget about Ashraf," Miraya says instead. She doesn't know why she had to give that reminder.

"Oh, he knows. He is totally okay with me simping over Shray because he knows I can never get him. The faith he has in me is astonishing truly."

Miraya doesn't know how to feel about that. But she is not ready to eat food and make conversation with the destroyer of lives. Especially after reminiscing those sweet sweet memories a few hours ago, she definitely isn't able-bodied to eat with him.

She clears her throat. "Um, Fiya?"

"Yeah?" Her voice comes from somewhere below.

"I think I'm still feeling a little dizzy," Miraya begins.

Fiya's head pops up from her suitcase. "You said you were feeling better."

"About that..." She looks away. "I think I might have given my body too much credit."

"Miraya," Fiya drags the *ya* into a whine that resembles a dog's when he is denied his promised treat. "I told him you would come. I would look like a fool if I didn't bring you. Look at the bright side. It could be a prep-up for your interview so that it wouldn't be awkward that day. And you could get that voice note for your friend!"

Miraya panics. "You didn't tell that to him, did you?"

Fiya makes that face she has whenever she has forgotten a deadline.

"Oh my god, Fiya. I can't believe you. Why did you tell that to him?"

Miraya was thinking she can ask Fiya to pretend Dakshina was *her* friend and get that voice note from him. Her plans were ruined.

"Um, you didn't tell me not to?"

Miraya's eyes soften when she sees Fiya standing with a beautiful blouse clutched in her hand, ready to throw it away and wallow in self-pity.

Miraya runs her hand over her face. "I'm sorry. I am so sorry, Fiya. I didn't mean to yell at you."

"Did I do something wrong?" she asks meekly.

"No, absolutely not. It's not your fault."

"So, you'll come to dinner?"

Miraya couldn't say no to her. Not after scolding the poor girl for nothing.

She has faced Shray once. And walked out on him like a woman who doesn't give a shit about him. That's going to earn her some points, right? This is a work-related dinner and she's sure she can handle it. She's going to busy herself with food the whole time and keep the talking to a minimum. The night will be over and everything will go back to aligning with the itinerary.

"Yeah. I guess I'll come."

Fiya's eyes brighten. "Yes, thank you!" She thrusts the pale blue satin blouse and ripped jeans onto my face. "Does this say 'I'm having dinner with an actor but also not having dinner with an actor?"

"Huh?"

"We're going into the city. He might probably take us to a fancy restaurant. What if someone recognizes him and photographs him? We should dress casual but also fancy. You get it?"

"I thought we were having dinner in the resort. The food is good here. Why travel all the way there?"

"Miraya, can you stop complaining? Just let loose and try to make the best out of a free meal. I can live forever bragging that Shray paid for my food."

Miraya almost laughs at her words. "Fine. I'll not question any of your weird outlooks on life."

With that, she begins to dig in her suitcase, hoping Dakshina had packed something worth wearing. She almost calls her to ask her what to wear but she has a feeling she will emotionally blackmail her to wear the black lacy bra that she had needlessly packed into her suitcase. Miraya picks out a casual striped A-line dress that she pairs with a black knitted jacket and sneakers. She doesn't give a damn about what Shray thinks. He has seen at her worst (four-year old faded and worn out pyjama shorts with an unmatching hot pink hoodie).

"Don't you want to straighten your hair? You always do it when you attend parties or events," Fiya asks, lending her iron.

"Nah, I'll pass." That idiot is not worth the work.

Miraya looks at herself in the mirror. Her wavy black hair sits on her shoulders comfortably. Her winged eyeliner and pink lipstick makes her black eyes pop.

Comfortable yet classy. Achieved.

As they walk to the place where they'll meet Shray, Miraya asks, "How did you run into him anyway?"

Fiya stops meddling with her zipper in her jacket. "Oh, it's because of you actually."

"Me?"

"Yes. I asked if you'd like a lemon soda to drink, right? Well, after that, I was tempted to get one for myself. I got lost and walked into the bar which also had a lot of tables. And when I was about to turn around, there he came, charming as ever." Miraya rolls her eyes and Fiya chuckles, tapping on her chest twice to say she knows she's being too much and she'll stop. "So, Shray asked me if I was lost and I was speechless. It took a minute to get my mouth working and once it did, there was no stopping. My feet weren't even on the ground because I was so excited I almost died. So he made me take a seat and we talked."

Miraya frowns. "What was he doing in the bar?"

"He was getting a drink obviously. He had two glasses as we spoke."

The Shray she had known hated alcohol. He would rather smoke two packets of cigarettes than drink a glass of alcohol.

Seems like it wasn't only her who had changed over the years.

Chapter 9

♥

R ed. White. Blue. Green. Orange. Purple. Grey.

Now, why is Miraya listing all the colours?

Because she's trying to prove that the probability of Shray wearing a crisp black shirt that looks like it was tailored to hug his toned body is very very low. Out of the broad variety of existing colours, why oh *why* did he have to pick out the black one?

She squeezes her eyes close and opens them. Shray is standing before her in the damn shirt and jeans that look perfect on him, a smirk playing on his lips. And his eyes are on her.

He knows.

He knows that she finds him out-of-the-friend/enemy-zone attractive whenever he dons black.

Then that very slow bulb in her head lights up with a bling.

He knows because she told him.

It was ethnic day at school. Might as well call it Truth day after what happened.

Ethnic day means every guy was going to be eyeing a girl as if she's never been beautiful before and... vice versa. As for Miraya, she loved a sari but she didn't like the idea of going to school in a sari. At that age, she wasn't used to wearing one and her mother wasn't around to correct her dress if her draping slipped from its position.

And since she has to look grand, she has to wear long earrings and leave her hair loose to be on the same level with other girls. It wasn't as easy as it looked. That was why Miraya was glued to her seat, not even bothering to go to the canteen. She couldn't move.

She sent Shray instead.

The boys, for ethnic day, usually paired a shirt with a veshti, which was a white stretch of cloth with printed borders that should be wrapped around the waist and fastened in a... way she didn't quite understand. It was less complicated than draping a sari but she didn't know the technicality of it.

That year, there was a trend going on. Boys paired a black shirt and veshti together and somehow the pre-existing combination suddenly turned into the most appealing look for a man. And not surprisingly, her class boys decided to hop on that trend and colour-coordinate as well. She didn't think much of it.

But oh boy, she was in trouble when she saw Shray in it.

She blushed when he flicked her earrings and said they were weird on her. It was that bad.

And Miraya had a boyfriend.

Nothing made sense.

That was when she decided that Shray in black was dangerous to her well-being and inner peace. She refused to relive the three years she secretly pined for Shray under the security of the best friend label. That story was tragic and it was over and it was buried in the seabed of the Arabian Sea nice and deep with no chance of excavation.

Shray came back from the canteen with two ice lollies. And the end of his veshti was clutched in his hand, as if he was the nonchalant hero of a south-indian film. Good lord.

He placed the lollies on the table and picked up the other end of the veshti to fold it around his knees. His legs with fine hair were visible.

"NO!" Miraya blurted. "No, you're not doing that. Put the damn thing down or I'll complain about you to Meera Ma'am for public indecency."

Shray laughed. But he let the cloth fall back over his legs. "What? Why?"

"Just don't. It's... not nice."

"Is it that bad that you can't even look at me?" His voice was low and offended. Miraya knew he cared about his looks a lot.

She glanced at him. "I'm sorry. It's just... you are too distracting today. And ugh, it's so annoying and I hate it."

"Because of me?"

"Because of you in that black shirt," Miraya muttered.

Shray smirked. "O my sweet Miranda, my dearest soulmate, do you find me attractive?" His lips were pink from sucking the strawberry ice lolly.

She gave him a disgusted look. At least tried to. You see, Miraya was used to Shray's flirty banters but this time it made her heart skip.

"Come on," he pleaded. "I'll never bring up this conversation again."

She stared at him and sighed. "Fine, yes. You look very attractive. So do me a favour and don't wear black again."

"Even more attractive than Siddh?"

Miraya made a mistake. She got flustered immediately and stuttered for an answer. "I'm not answering that question," she finally said, swallowing.

"I'll never tell him what you said, I promise. Give me that ego boost please," Shray said. He knew her answer was him. But he wanted to hear her say it.

She framed her head with her palms and mumbled, "Yes, you are more attractive than Siddh. Now leave me alone."

It was too late. She had given him the satisfaction and he was grinning ear to ear. Clearly, her brain wasn't working.

Shray leaned closer and looked at her with dreamy eyes that stirred something inside her way too much. "O my sweet Miranda, are you finally seeing that you belong with me, your very own Ferdinand?"

Miranda blinked and then recovered only to grab the nearest notebook and smack him with it. "This is exactly why I didn't want to tell you."

He chuckled and took the notebook. He tore out a page from it.

"What are you doing?"

He put the pen to the paper and began writing. "What do you think? I'm writing a letter to the school to change the school uniform to black."

Miraya couldn't help but burst out laughing.

He still remembers.

"Miraya, right? I've heard a lot about you from your colleague. You look a bit familiar? Have we met before?" Shray asks, stretching out a hand.

Miraya wants to roll her eyes.

"It's a pleasure to finally meet you in person. You were different in the pictures."

"How so?" he asks, curious.

She knew he would fish for a compliment. *Ha, not this time, Ferdinand.*

"No, you looked better in the pictures. The wonders of editing, right? Technology is advancing rapidly." She laughs it off in the end.

"Miraya!" Fiya hisses, elbowing her.

"Oh, did I offend you? If I did, I'm sorry. I was just making an observation," Miraya adds to Shray. He watches her with amusement.

"You're just making this worse!" Fiya whisper-yells into her ears.

Shray shakes his head. "You didn't offend me at all. I like honest women. In the words of one such woman in my life, I look too attractive in black. I was hoping that would help my case."

Miraya openly glares at him. He smirks back.

That's how he wants to play it?

Fine.

Miraya takes a step forward. "Sadly —"

"Okay, let's keep some talking left for dinner, shall we? Now can we go, please? I'm a bit hungry," Fiya interrupts, her eyeballs going frantic, trying to ask Miraya what the hell was wrong with her.

"Oh, yes. Sorry," Shray says and climbs into the car. He is driving himself. Miraya assumed he'd sit in his car and be driven around by highly-paid men.

Fiya and Miraya sit in the back seat.

"Thanks for inviting us, Shray. It really means a lot," Fiya starts and Miraya sighs, looking out the window. The two, who apparently share a lot of interests, keep talking until he pulls up at the restaurant.

"Here?" Fiya asks, craning her neck to inspect the sage green and brown cottage-like cafe. It's very small and it appears to have only four or five tables inside. Even Miraya assumed they were going to have a fancy dinner. There were two-hundred-bucks-for-a-lemondade? kind of restaurants in Ooty. In fact, she has walked out of several of those very modestly after staring at the menu card for an embarrassingly long time.

"Yeah. And hey, don't judge the restaurant based on its size. It's the best Italian place out here. You two are okay with Italian, right?" Shray says, slotting the car between two others and killing the engine.

Italian. She loves Italian. She could live off it forever.

Miraya glances at Shray and wonders if he decided to bring them here on purpose or if it was a coincidence. And it's a work-related dinner, right? Who has pizza for a formal dinner? Shray meets her eyes and raises an eyebrow, making her quickly avert her eyes.

Maybe she is reading into this too much. It's just dinner.

They pick the table at the corner that doesn't have windows and Shray sits with his back facing the rest of the people. Somehow, Miraya ends up directly across from him and Fiya next to her.

Fiya dives into the menu, completely unaware of Miraya looking anywhere but Shray and Shray not looking anywhere but her. Miraya stares at the mosaic painting on the wall emptily and then counts the printed hearts on the tote bag that sits next to the lady in the table before her.

"What do you want?" Fiya asks.

"Anything," Miraya says. She doesn't want to be interested in this dinner. But in truth, the delicious smell of cheese and oregano makes her stomach cry. She is hungry.

Shray repeats Fiya's order to the waiter who stares at Shray like there's a really hard mathematical problem written across his face. He goes on to order pizza for both of them and chooses the one loaded with meat, just like she prefers it to be.

"Anything else, Sir?"

He orders soda. Then, almost as if he had forgotten, he adds, "Make the pizza without capsicums, please."

With an inaudible gasp, Miraya realises that him bringing them to this place is not a coincidence. He remembers her preferences for food and he brought them here because of her. She is unable to believe that he still cares enough to remember all this. Then why did he hurt her? Why did he throw away their friendship like it was scrap?

"You don't like capsicums? Miraya doesn't either. Even the smell makes her throw up," Fiya volunteers information like she has every right to.

"Oh, really? I didn't know. That's great, then," Shray says.

She is so tempted to rebel against the discussion and say she changed her mind about the damned vegetable. She wants to say she likes it just so she can wipe the smugness away on Shray's face. She would have if not for the terrible consequences that followed. She really despised capsicums. It was a nightmare.

Miraya doesn't know from where Fiya picks topics to discuss with Shray, but she is an endless stream of words and dramatic hand movements. Shray seems equally interested in their discussion. And Miraya looks around, bored.

"Miraya, have you seen all of Shray's films?" Fiya asks in an attempt to include her into the conversation. She has done this four times now and each time Miraya gave her only clipped answers.

"No."

"She wouldn't have watched 3AM," Shray says.

She whips her neck to stare at him in shock. "H-how did you know?" Miraya tries to cover up her stutter with her sharp look. That *was* the only movie she hasn't watched of his.

"It's horror, Miraya."

"So?"

"You hate horror."

Her thoughts disappear from her mind and all that's left is static noise. Miraya panics. It's confusing. Nothing is making sense to her.

"How do you know that?" Fiya asks, dropping her fork and propping her chin on her hand. Miraya can sense that Fiya assumed that Shray was speaking in terms of women in general and was trying hard not to pick an argument about horror and feminism.

She didn't know that he was stating a fact.

"I could tell that you didn't mind watching horror movies. But something about Miraya gave off the vibe that horror isn't really her cup of tea," Shray explains, tearing out a slice of pizza. "It was just a theory."

"Really? Miraya, don't you like horror movies?"

Miraya feels too stunned to grab the opportunity and say she loves horror movies. She would've made a fool out of him and his stupid confidence. But she doesn't say anything. She can't talk.

"Miraya? Are you okay?" Shray asks.

She looks up at him. He isn't grinning anymore. The worry is evident in his eyes.

"You look a little pale," he adds.

"She wasn't feeling well. She told me she felt better in the evening and that's why she came," Fiya says, placing a hand on her shoulder.

Miraya pulls herself together. It's hard and painful to shove away her confusion and hurt into some part of her mind and carry on like nothing happened but she does it anyway. She's used to it. She just needs a minute.

"I'm fine. I think I'm a bit dehydrated," she says, reaching for water. Shray pours her a glass and she forces a thankful smile.

Without a word, she takes a huge bite of her pizza and chews on it, smiling at both of them to show that she is alright.

They resume eating.

A few minutes pass quietly as the three focus on their food. Then, Fiya stands up. "I have to use the restroom," she excuses herself.

As soon as she is out of earshot, Miraya says, "I thought you had no time at all. Where did you find time for dinner with two people you usually don't bother to know the name of?"

"I've been shooting all night till 4 am into the morning. I slept for an hour and went right back into shooting an ad for which I had to travel up and down the hill to reach Coimbatore and come back. I slept for an hour again and did the dress fitting. It was evening already. Do you think I had the time to schedule something else in my agenda too?" he asks, his words coming off a bit snappy. After a pause, he sighs and runs a hand through his hair.

"I'm sorry I just thought — well, then why did you take us out for dinner? You could have chosen to stay in and get some rest."

Shray smiles fondly at her. Her heart is growing back the wings she had chopped off.

No, no, no.

Miraya adds the third item in her list of the dangerous things to her heart. Things to avoid at all costs.

Shray in a black shirt.

Shray's smile.

Shray wearing a black shirt and smiling.

It's just too difficult avoiding them.

"Miran– Miraya, I see my best friend after so many years and how can I not talk to her? I don't care for rest. You won't talk to me directly so I had to go about this another way and trick you into it in the name of a work. Then, and now, you make me do crazy things I've never done before."

Something flutters in her chest.

"But still. How can you last a day with only two hours of sleep? That's so unhealthy, Shray. You have to take care —"

She stops. She is supposed to be angry at him. She *hates* him. Miraya repeats the two golden sentences to herself.

He deserves to be hurt.

He ruined her life.

Shray leans closer with a smirk and his knees brush against hers. She quickly tucks her legs under her chair as if she was burnt. "I thought you didn't care about me," he whispers.

I *thought so too*, Miraya thinks to herself, clenching her jaws. *Seems like both of us were wrong.*

"I don't. Don't fool yourself," she lies instead and reaches for the last slice of pizza.

Shray doesn't let her take it.

"We can share it. Just like we did when we were younger," he suggests. Except when they were younger, there was a lot of yelling and trying to prove who was worthy of the last slice that preceded the compromise.

"Fine," Miraya says and tears out the crust for him and keeps the remaining for herself.

"See? It would be so nice to hang out together, Miraya. We can just go right back into it. It'll be like we were best friends all these years."

No, it won't. She can't just burn down the anger and grudge that she holds against him and act all smiley-smiley with him. He can't get away with it. She won't let it happen.

"No. Do you know how much I hate you, Shray? I can't just pretend nothing ever happened and pick up right where we left off. That's not how it works. Hell, you haven't even apologised to me. I hate that you are so infuriating. I hate that I loved you so much that it doesn't even let me hate you as much as I want to! It's like being stuck in a mental cage with nowhere to go."

Shray's back hits the back of his chair. He clearly didn't expect her to spill her guts out.

"So, just stay away from me. That's all I ask from you. You talking to me as if everything is sunshine and rainbows between us is confusing me and it's only making things worse. My mind is just not in the right place now. I feel like I can't breathe when you are with me. Let's keep this professional. I don't want to talk about us at all. I beg you. Can you do that for me, Shray?"

It's so quiet. Miraya bites her lip to keep them from trembling. And Shray... he looks broken. Like someone pulled his heart out of his chest and snapped it into two right in front of him.

He blinks thrice and then tucks in his lips. The light in his eyes is dead. Those eyes are not the starry night sky anymore. It's now a night sky that's been burned and covered in ashes. Something twists inside her when she realises she is the one who did it to him. She looks down at her lap.

"Okay," he says quietly. Too quietly.

Miraya looks at him.

"Okay, if that's what you want," he says, forcing a smile that's anything but happy. His voice is scratchy as if he is trying so hard not to break down. "Just... Please stop crying. I can't watch you cry."

She doesn't realise she is crying. Miraya touches her cheek and feels the teardrops. She takes the tissue Shray offers and wipes her tears.

She looks at the damp tissue in her hand and wonders,

What does her heart really want?

Chapter 10

♥

T here is no fan in her room.

The ceiling looks so empty without it.

At home, whenever she stares at the ceiling from her bed, the blades of the fan spin so fast that they lose clarity and blur out. Her mind is the fan and her thoughts are the blade. Spinning, spinning, blurring, blurring. All she knows is that she's running in circles, not making any progress at all.

But unlike the fan, there is no switch to stop her thoughts. At least not until she sleeps. And it is very hard to sleep with the noise inside her head.

For the past hour, Miraya has been stuck on that treadmill. She keeps replaying what happened at dinner to make sense of it and she comes to a few conclusions.

1. Miraya wasn't a person to hold grudges. Not for this long. But what Shray did to her flipped her life upside down and scarred her deeply that she simply refused to forgive him for it. And he hadn't even apologised! Or tried to. It's like he had forgotten what happened entirely. That hurt her even more. So, he deserves the cold shoulder.

2. She wants to confront him about it but the truth is, a part of her doesn't want that closure. She is scared that what he might

have to say or the meaningless excuse he might come up with will put her mind to eternal misery. That chapter of her life is closed. The most confusing character out of it had sneaked its way into her life and the best thing to do was avoid it. Confronting him means opening that book again and she will not do it.

3. If Miraya can still feel the butterflies around Shray after all these years, her feelings for him never died. She had just chosen to ignore it. And seeing him after a long time caused the warm fuzzy feelings to bubble right back to the surface.

Even though her heart wants nothing but to forgive him, walk into his arms and fall for his smile again and again, she won't do it. Because, if anyone's going to make her let go of her fears and jump off the ledge for love, it is Shray. She can't allow that. She can't let herself get carried away.

So, what is her action plan? Miraya can't figure that out. She would probably get the interview done as quickly as possible, maintain the fake illness she has and run for her life. Away from Shray, away from the source of all the complicated thoughts in the world.

But another part of her heart wants to stay here as long as she can and stare at Shray from afar because she can never afford to see him again.

Miraya hears giggles and the balcony door closing shut. "...defin itely will. And go to sleep. I know you have a big day tomorrow and no one's going to like cranky Ashraf. Get your beauty sleep now so that you'll wake up sexy tomorrow. Not like you already aren't," Fiya whispers the last line into her phone but in the dead of the night and with no whirring of the fan, it's clearly audible.

"I know what your profession is!" Fiya states, balancing her phone between her ear and her shoulder. "There is a high chance the students are going to pick you as their professor because you look like a dreamboat. And that's totally a good thing. Well, as long as you are mine."

Miraya shakes her head with a smile.

"Oh god, okay, okay. I am well assured of that. No insecurities. Gosh, that was a joke, Ashraf," Fiya says. Then she pulls away the phone and mouths to Miraya, *"he's so cute I can't handle it."*

Miraya laughs.

"Okay, goodnight. I'll kiss you but Miraya is right here and I don't want to make her gag. She's already bled her ears out after hearing our corny conversations," Fiya says into the phone. Miraya hears Ashraf's laughter.

Then, she hangs up.

"He is so sweeeeet," Fiya squeals and jumps into the bed, burying her face in her pillow and kicking the sheets.

"Marry him as soon as possible. If I was a student and I had a professor like Ashraf, I'd totally jump him," Miraya says. She watches Fiya's eyes grow wide and waits for a few seconds. Just like she expects, Fiya scrambles for her phone and calls her boyfriend again.

"I take back what I said. Don't wake up sexy tomorrow. And put on a mean face, don't smile and don't shake hands with anyone longer than two seconds! You are mine, okay? Only mine!" she yells into the phone, panic written over her face.

Miraya chuckles.

"Okay, godzilla," Ashraf says, laughing. There is so much fondness in his voice that a sliver of her feels jealous of Fiya. "I love you. Only you."

The gigantic smile and the embarrassingly deep plotch of red on Fiya's face is restored. "I love you too," she mumbles and then hangs up.

"Now that your lovey-dovey time is over, can we sleep, godzilla?" Miraya asks.

"Yes," she says, flushing, and switches off the light.

There is a long silence that squeezes itself between them. Miraya is aware that both of them are awake, revisiting the events of today.

Finally, Fiya whispers, "Today was perfect."

Sadly, Miraya can't agree.

□□□□□□□□□□

Miraya didn't get an ounce of sleep at night so she decided to sleep through the morning. She didn't have anything to do anyway.

Or that's what she thought.

"Miraya! Wake up!" Fiya barges in through the door and screams. Miraya screws her eyes shut and tugs on the heavy blanket over her face. It is so warm under the sheets. She wants to spend the rest of her life hiding under them knowing it's freezing outside.

"Miraya, you have to wake up. We have work!" Fiya comes closer to her and shakes her shoulders. "I wouldn't wake you if it's not an emergency. Miraya, you have to get ready now!"

"Why?" she whines, throwing her leg over the pillow and cuddling close. "Just tell them I'm sick. I don't want to be there during the photoshoot."

Fiya huffs and flings the blanket off Miraya. She hisses and coils into a semi-circle, clearly pissed at Fiya.

"You don't understand. The interview is happening in fifteen minutes," Fiya says.

Miraya bolts up from the bed. "WHAT?"

"Yeah, I just heard. It seems Shray's team has been ringing you for a long time but you didn't pick up."

Miraya grabs her phone off the table and almost dies when she sees 16 missed calls. They were from Shray's team and a couple were from Grace and Joyce.

Shit.

"But why? I thought they scheduled it for tomorrow!" Miraya says, jumping into her flip-flops and finding her toothbrush.

"You won't believe it."

She squeezes the paste on the toothbrush and shoves into her mouth. "Try me."

"Shray wasn't at his best during the morning shooting. He was very distracted and kept mixing up his lines. Ria called him aside and gave him a pep talk or something to help but he couldn't do it. It was an important scene and they couldn't afford to have many retakes because of the prop usage or something. Shray decided to not waste anyone's time and told he needed a day off. The director wasn't happy but he couldn't say anything because Shray rarely ever does this."

Miraya did not expect that. Shray— how— she can't understand. Is it because of what happened between them last night? Because of what she said? He didn't seem like himself during the ride back from the restaurant but she thought it was transitory.

Miraya feels guilty. But the next second, something inside her advises not to feel that way. It isn't her fault.

"Miraya? Hellooo..." Fiya waves a hand in front of her face. "Now that I notice, you've been awfully distracted as well. Did something happen? Did you two hit a nerve in each other during dinner?"

Miraya spits the foam in her mouth and laughs as if she was hearing something absurd. "Of course not. Why would we?"

"Well, I don't know. Your face seems to tell another story."

She gargles her mouth and shrugs.

"Miraya, what are you hiding?" Fiya asks.

"We don't have time for this. Get out. I have to take a shower," Miraya says, shooing Fiya out of the bathroom and shutting the door.

She isn't ready to talk about it. Not now.

Miraya tries not to get carried away with her thoughts in the shower and walks out of the steaming cubicle in a towel.

"Did his team suggest we finish the interview today or..."

"Oh, it was totally Shray's idea. He said he wants to get it over with since he is inconveniencing us by keeping us here. Honestly, I don't mind," Fiya says.

Oh. Great. He wants her to leave this place as soon as possible. He wants to get rid of her.

She feels horrible.

But she can't complain, can she? She really had no rights. She was the one who hurt him. She was the one who wanted each other to stay away.

Then why does it hurt when he wants the same?

"Miraya, we have five minutes. You don't have clothes on."

She snaps out of her thoughts. "Right, sorry."

Miraya grabs a red blouse and black formal pants to go with it. She doesn't have time to untangle the million knots in her hair so she brushes it on the shallow end to make it look decent. She colours her lip a dull red and hastily applies some mascara to make her eyes look less out of the bed.

Miraya doesn't have time to put anything on her face. She stuffs her feet in her flats and her bag which has the voice recorder and the notepad of questions.

Fiya runs to her with her jacket when she is out of the room. "Thank you," she says and rushes to meet Shray. As ironic as that sounds.

As soon as she reaches there, Grace shakes her head. "Did you drink last night? I heard you went out."

Miraya glances at Fiya and she shakes her head to tell her they don't know about their dinner with Shray. "I went out but I didn't drink. I am not that stupid."

"Why didn't you pick my calls?"

Miraya is annoyed with the tone the art director uses. "Hey, a woman can sleep dead to the world, you know. The answer is not always a hangover. Some people like to sleep with their phone on silent."

Grace rolls her eyes. "I shouldn't be surprised, I guess. You are always late."

With the day she is having, Miraya doesn't have the patience to put up with Grace's bullshit. She takes a step forward and glares at the woman with a fashion sense that stands opposite to her shitty personality.

"You don't get to be the judge of that, Grace. And don't take that I-am-one-post-above-you-so-I-can-be-a-bitch-to-you-and-get-away-with-it tone with me. You can have a higher position than me but I don't answer to you. I answer to Mrs Nandhini and the people she answers to. Not you," Miraya says through her teeth.

Grace clearly doesn't expect Miraya to stand up and fight her on this so she takes a step back. Fiya's eyes are the size of an Owl's.

Miraya turns around to see Shray standing by the door. When she catches his eye, he quickly wipes the brief smile on his face and walks inside the room.

Was that...was that a proud smile? It definitely looked like one.

"If you'll excuse me," Miraya says and gets inside the room.

"Fiya, stay here. I need to talk to you," Grace says.

"I want her there with me," Miraya argues.

"I'm sure you can manage a few minutes without her," Grace retorts. Miraya glances at Fiya for a silent confirmation if it's okay. She nods.

Miraya walks into the room and the door shuts behind her.

The walls of the room are painted sage green with white decor. It had wooden furniture, a nice big sofa and matching single seaters with white cushions that she imagines spilling something on and shudders. There is a brown vintage carpet spread out under everything, making a neat cosy room. And very expensive.

Shray is on the single seated sofa and when he looks at her standing awkwardly, he tips his chin towards the big one, asking her to take a seat.

He doesn't speak.

Miraya takes a seat. She pulls out her voice recorder, her notebook and her pen.

"Can we start?"

"Yes," he says, his eyes barely meeting hers. But when he raises his arms to push away the hair that falls on his eyes, Miraya gasps.

"Oh my god," she says and quickly comes over to his side. "You're hurt. How did you get hurt? You have blood on your arm."

The red stain was seeping through his white shirt. Miraya panics. The same way she did when Shray tore his ligament during one of his games.

"Should I call a doctor? What happened —"

"Miraya," he says.

"Is it hurting? Is it a gash? Can I look at it? It could get infected if —"

Shray peels her hand off his wrist. "Miraya, calm down, will you? And go take a seat there. It's nothing."

"I know you hate me right now. But just let me —"

"Miraya!" He almost yells at her. She backs away, hurt. Shray looks at her and then closes his eyes. She can see his jaws clench and his fingers run over his hair.

When he looks at her again, there is a barely managed calmness in his eyes. "You wanted boundaries and I am trying to give you that. It's fucking hard for me, Miraya. It's costing me everything but I'll give it to you if it's what you want. Just don't do something like this and make it even harder for me."

"Something like what?"

He lets out a weak laugh. "Like panicking over a fake blood stain on me and showing me that you still care about me no matter what you say."

Miraya doesn't know what to say to that. She feels terrible because he is hurting, fake blood or not. And it's because of her.

"Okay. I am sorry. I, um, did it out of habit," she says, attempting a laugh. It comes out as a heart-wrenching sound. She winces.

Miraya goes back to her seat and grabs her notepad. Just then, Fiya walks inside.

"You haven't started? Oh good," she grins and takes a seat next to Miraya.

Miraya feels restrained, like her heart and hands are tied. It is uncomfortable, tiring and wounding. When she glances at Shray, she can tell he feels the same way as well.

Chapter 11

"We've heard that you had a lot of support for your dream when you grew up. Who were your biggest cheerleaders?"

Miraya looks up from her notebook at Shray's silence.

"Do you want me to repeat the question?" she asks.

"No, I heard it. I... I just —"

"Oh, take your time. Or we can skip to the next question."

Miraya is now on the carpet, her notebook balanced on the tea table along with her voice recorder because the sofa had been uncomfortable and she had to lean forward to listen to him. Shray protested against it but Miraya had waved him off.

The only downside of her position is that she wants to get rid of her shoes because she can't fold her legs with it but since she didn't wear any socks, she is afraid her legs would freeze. So she has her legs spread out and her back leaned against the couch. Miraya was only a couple spaces away from Shray, who has been sitting in the exact position since the beginning of the interview. Fiya has gone to the washroom.

Shray fidgets with his fingers. He slowly speaks.

"My parents were a big support to me. They didn't cast aside my dream as a mere side effect of childhood. They encouraged me to chase it as long as I didn't lose myself in the process. And so I did.

Even at school, since there can be nothing done about the clothes since we had to wear uniforms, I spent a lot of time worrying about my looks and style. And though my teachers thought I was wasting my time, my friends understood. It meant a lot, you know," he says. His eyes meet hers. "Especially my best friend's support. It meant the world to me."

Time stops. Miraya stares at him. He stares back. There are no further explanations exchanged. There doesn't have to be. Because they know.

She wants to tell him that she is proud of him too. But she keeps it to herself.

The sharp ring of a phone pierces the tense atmosphere and Miraya takes a moment to realise it's hers. She tears her gaze away from his and digs into her back.

It's Kishore.

Miraya had called him late in the hours last night and he never picked up. His phone had been switched off. She needed to talk to him so badly.

And now he's returning her call.

She declines the call and keeps her phone on the table. "Sorry for that. Please continue," she says.

"I answered your question," Shray replies.

"Oh–oh right. Sorry," Miraya laughs again, internally facepalming herself for making a fool out of herself. "Who was your biggest inspiration?"

Her phone rings again.

Kishore.

This idiot. He should know she is in work if she declines his calls.

Miraya reaches to dismiss it again but Shray stops her. "It's okay. You can take it. It might be important if he's calling you again and again."

He. Shray saw the caller ID.

For some reason, Miraya wants to explain to him that Kishore isn't his boyfriend or anything.

But she nods and picks up the call, turning around for some privacy.

"Kishore! I am at work. I'll call you later, okay?" Miraya whispers harshly into the phone.

"Miraya *akka?*"

It isn't Kishore who answers. It's someone else. A girl.

"Um, who is this?"

Shray glances at her upon hearing her words.

"It's Kishore's sister. Radhi. I saw that you called last night. And Kishore didn't pick up because– because..."

Only when Radhi drags out her words does she catch the scratchiness of her voice, as if she'd been crying for hours. Panic rises in her. "Because what? What happened to him? Tell me, Radhi!"

"Is everything okay?" Shray asks, shifting from his seat to the one closest to her.

She doesn't answer him.

"Kishore...he is in the ICU," Radhi says, sniffling.

The picture of her best friend laying in a hospital room that could only mean bad news comes immediately to her mind, bringing tears to her eyes.

"What happened?" she asks, biting her lips to keep them from trembling. Her shoulders are shaking and she knows it because Shray wraps them with his arms.

"He met with an accident last night. His car rammed into a truck when he was trying to swerve around a careless bike. It's bad, Miraya *akka.* They've been keeping him in that room and we can't even see him. They've done two surgeries on him already and he's lost a lot of blood —" Radhi breaks off, sobbing.

On the other side of the phone, tears stream down her face quietly. She grips the phone tight.

"What did the doctors say?"

"They've said his recovery cannot be assured. They say there is a 50-50 chance."

Miraya steels herself. She wipes her tears and straightens her position. "Which hospital?" Her voice betrays her.

Radhi says the name of the hospital and Miraya repeats it so that Shray could remember it if she forgot.

"I'll be there, okay? As soon as possible. Is Aunty there?"

"Yeah. We've been here all night."

"Okay. Nothing will happen to him. Kishore will make it. He is tough. He will fight through. He always does," Miraya whispers, mostly to convince herself. But she knows it doesn't have any effect.

Miraya hangs up and her shoulders slump.

"How bad is it for your friend?" Shray says softly, rubbing her shoulders.

Her voice cracks. "Very bad, Shray. Very very bad. I can't lose him. He's all I have. I can't lose him." Miraya covers her face with her hand and cries.

So many images flash in her mind. Kishore teaching her German. Kishore saving her a seat in class. Kishore helping her move her things into his apartment. Kishore and her arguing over the best pickle to buy. Kishore hugging her when she cried watching *Me Before You*. Kishore smiling. Kishore laughing.

Kishore, Kishore, Kishore.

Kishore in a hospital bed.

She feels sick.

"You won't. You won't lose him," Shray whispers.

"How do you know?!"

"Because you said so. You said he is tough and that he will make it. Only if you believe your own words will others believe you. You've got to," he says, rubbing circles on her shoulder.

Miraya pulls away to look at him. She's really missed him so much. She missed Shray *so so so* much.

"Can-can you hug me?" she asks, her words cracking as her sobs squeeze through.

Shray doesn't say a word. He kneels down on the carpet and pulls her close to him. Miraya wraps her arm around him, clutching the fabric of his shirt as she sobs into his chest. Shray's hand is on her hair, smoothing it in some form of consolation and the other is on her back, patting her softly. His chin is on the crook of her shoulders and once in a while he kisses her hair.

Miraya's nails almost claw into the fabric of his shirt as she lets go and cries and cries and *cries*.

"Hey, I got you. I got you, okay?"

Miraya buries her head into his chest.

"Do you want me to talk about something else?"

She shakes her head. "Not this time. No."

"What do you want me to do?"

"Just hold me. Just hold me close."

And Shray does.

□□□□□□□□□□□□

What happens next is mostly a blur. Fiya comes in and almost drops her phone when she sees both of them tightly wrapped in each other's arms. Only when she comes closer, she realises Miraya is crying and Shray is comforting her. Shray explains everything to Fiya as he pours Miraya a glass of water. "It's very cold. Is it okay?" he asks before handing her the glass. Miraya doesn't get a chance to linger on the fact that he remembers that she hates cold water to drink. She simply chugs the water down and gathers her shit together.

Shray never lets go of her. When she is not pressed to him, his arms are around her. When his arms aren't around her, his hand is gripping hers. Fiya's eyes follow every movement. Miraya knows she has to remove herself from Shray's hold so that she doesn't have to explain their history to Fiya but she likes where she is. And even though Shray realises that this isn't appropriate, he doesn't let go. As if, if he can't show the world that Miraya is his best friend then he can at least show Fiya.

"Miraya? Do you want me to take over?" Fiya asks.

"Yes, please. There are two more questions. Just send me the recording later," Miraya says, standing up. Shray is on his feet too.

"Where are you going?" he asks.

"To explain the situation to others and pack. I have to leave." Miraya wipes her tears on her sleeve.

Shray glances at Fiya. "Can you let them know?"

She nods and leaves the door.

Shray takes her phone and tries her old passcode to unlock it. The old passcode was both of their birthdays.

It doesn't work.

Shray's face reads that he expected it but also hoped against hope that she didn't change it.

"It's 0315," Miraya mumbles.

As soon as he's unlocked it, he punches his number and saves his contact. "I know you don't want to speak to me. I respect that even though every cell of me is ready to beg you to change your mind. But if you ever need help, if you ever need me, call me. This is my personal number. You can call me anytime, Miraya. You mean a lot to me."

"Please don't lie to me like that," she mutters and takes her phone back.

"I'm not lying," he says sharply but he doesn't give her time to respond. "Where is the hospital?"

Miraya looks down and answers, "Coimbatore."

"I'll have you dropped at the hospital." She opens her mouth to deny help but he doesn't let her. "Don't put up a fight. I know you don't have a ride," he says, turning her by the shoulders to make her face him.

She really didn't have a ride. Her only option was to get on the soonest bus and she wasn't very fond of bus rides. She didn't know if there were cabs available in this town that made long trips. If she wanted to get to Kishore soon, she had to put aside her ego and accept all the help she could get.

"Thank you," she says.

"You don't have to –"

"No. Not just for the ride. For... everything." *I missed you. I missed you so fucking much. I don't know how I am going to survive the trip alone. I wish you were there by my side.*

"No problem. You can return the favour someday if it helps ease your mind."

"Yes. Yes, I will," she says immediately.

Shray shakes his head lightly and smiles at her. She wants to cry because she wants nothing but to hold onto him.

Fiya rushes in. "I spoke to Grace and Joyce. I told them you were done with the interview. They will inform Mrs Nandhini but they asked you to call her and speak to her personally as well."

"Thank you so much, Fiya."

"Can I hug you one last time?" Shray asks.

Miraya bites her lip. Mostly to trap the sobs inside.

She walks into his arms and breathes in Shray. It's easy to believe there is nothing but friendship and maybe some feelings between them. No feud, no betrayals, no one missing a chunk of each other's lives.

But, the ones easy to believe are the ones farthest from the truth.

"Take care of yourself, okay?" he chokes on a sob. He is crying. Shray is crying. When he presses his lips to her head, his tears drip onto her hair. Miraya squeezes her eyes tight and tightens her arms around him.

A second passes and Shray pushes her away and turns around so that his back is against her. She can hear sniffles. Her heart breaks.

"Goodbye, Shray," she whispers.

Chapter 12

Miraya applies for a week-long leave. She lies to her mother that her work trip got extended. She stays with Kishore.

It's been three days and he hasn't woken up yet. The only thing keeping her together is the doctor's statement. He said Kishore is out of danger.

Kishore's mother and sister convinced her to stay at their home for a while but she's only gone there to sleep. The rest of the time she lives in the hospital, napping on the couch in his room, holding his hand and crying silently. When Kishore's elder sister comes from Chennai, Miraya busies herself by taking care of her daughter Drithi. Kishore's mother refuses to eat properly and her daughters try to get some food inside her. People she doesn't know come to the hospital in tears and she watches them numbly as they enquire about the accident.

It's another night. Kishore's mother refuses to sleep at home while her son is lying in a hospital bed connected to a hundred tubes. But considering her weak health, her daughters plead with her to go home. Kishore's elder sister Priya has to take care of Drithi so along with her husband, they go home as well. Radhi hesitates to leave Miraya here alone so she offers to stay with her. But Miraya knows that Radhi is the one who takes care of her mother and her mother needs her at this time.

"It's okay. I can stay with him tonight. I'll call you if he wakes up," Miraya says, squeezing her hand.

"I feel so bad, Miraya *akka*. Please tell me if you're not comfortable here. It's not right to ask you to stay here."

"Kishore is my best friend. I want to stay here," she insists and watches Radhi leave after giving her her number and Priya's.

Miraya walks back into Kishore's room. Kishore lay there on the hospital bed with several tubes connecting him to beeping monitors. The ugly green colour doesn't suit him. His black hair is sprawled across the uncomfortable pillow, so in contrast to the white cotton and gauze wrapped around his head. Seeing him without his glasses is odd even though she has seen him like this every morning when they shared an apartment.

Every time she came from a late night at work, the television would be on with low volume and Kishore would have fallen asleep on the couch. When she wrapped a blanket over him, Miraya would notice that he slept like a baby. So innocent, so peaceful.

But as he lies still in the hospital bed, there isn't a glimpse of peace on his face. She's so used to seeing him laughing and smiling like a school boy that watching him not utter a word pricks her heart. Holding her tears, she reaches and takes his hand.

How many times has this hand held hers when they crossed roads together? How many times has this hand slapped hers away when she reached for too many chips? How many times has this hand held hers when he came with her to parties as her fake boyfriend because Miraya felt embarrassed to be the only one without a date?

Now it falls limp in her hand.

She touches her forehead to his hand and cries, her shoulders shaking as she tries not to make a sound.

"Kishore... wake up," she sobs. "Please."

Miraya cries herself to asleep. Later, much later, when the corridor is dark and lit with LED bulbs instead of tubelights, when there is less movement outside, she feels a hand on her hair. The hand caresses her hair in small intervals and her first instinct is to snuggle closer and bask in the comfort. When she does that, she hears a sound, almost like a breathy chuckle.

"When was the last time you washed your hair?"

Miraya shoots up from her bed.

Even though his familiar smile isn't back yet, Kishore wears something similar to that with the exact warmth in his eyes. Watching him watch her with his eyes open through a lens of mirth feels like someone popped a balloon inside her. A part of Miraya finally breathes, wiping off the sluggishness and replacing it with something positive. Her chest isn't heavy anymore. The tension inside her dissipates.

Kishore is alive and awake.

Kishore came back.

He came back to her.

Miraya tears up again and she scolds herself for being an embarrassing emotional animal. Kishore isn't alarmed. He knows what the tears are for.

"I missed you," she says, her words wavering.

He smiles at her. "I missed you too, roomie."

Miraya takes a seat on the bed and wraps her arms around him. He smells like rich antiseptic and there's the sharp twang of blood from his head wound. She doesn't care. All she feels is happiness because he survived. And she is so damn proud of him.

"Don't do that to me again," she whispers.

"I won't. It's not what I thought it would be anyway," he jokes.

"God, I missed you," Miraya says again and tightens her arms around him. "I was so scared, Kishore."

"I know," he whispers against her sleeve. "I'm sorry."

"I'll forgive you just this once," she says, the corner of her lips tugging up ever so slightly. She kisses his cheek and pulls away.

"What was that for?"

"For being a good friend and returning back to me. I'm just so happy right now." Miraya wipes her tears away and laughs. "Your family is going to freak out if they knew you were awake. Should I call them? Should I call the doctor? I should probably call the doctor first, right? But I promised them I'd call your family first if you —"

"You need to calm down first, Miraya," Kishore says. He has a fond smile on his face.

She exhales. "Okay, okay. Who should I call first?"

"Call the doctor. You can call my family in the morning. No need to wake them up now."

"Are you sure they would be okay with that? You don't know how scared we were. We thought you wouldn't make it, Kishore."

Kishore pleads with his eyes. "If you call them, they'd come right away. I don't want that, Miraya."

She sighs. "Fine. But if I am questioned, I'm going to blame it on you."

"And I'll take the blame like a gentleman," Kishore grins but it quickly morphs into a wince and he clutches his chest.

"Are you okay?"

"Yeah. I think I need to get my bandages changed," he musters as he strains against the tubes.

Miraya calls the doctor and they run a series of tests and ask Kishore a couple questions. In the meantime, she goes to get some coffee. Miraya checks her phone and there is the usual voice message from her mother asking her not to skip her meals or work too much into the night. There is one from Fiya enquiring about the situation. She has been checking up on her everyday. Miraya hasn't called her directly yet because she is afraid she would ask her about her interaction with Shray. She wasn't in the state of mind to explain to her. Nor does she ever want to.

That brings her thoughts to what happened that day. Miraya feels like an idiot. How could she so shamelessly ask him for a hug after she told him explicitly to stay away from her? Shray would have thought that she was just using him. She didn't mean to. At that moment, she didn't have time to process things. Or see things clearly. Miraya was selfish because she desperately needed that hug no matter what he thought of her. And it kinda saved her.

Shray and Miraya didn't hug in school. They weren't allowed to. The rule wasn't written anywhere but it was implied with every judgemental glare from the teachers. The first time they hugged was during Shray's birthday. His mother met with an accident on the same day and was paralyzed from the waist down. He had cried in his arms when she went with him to the hospital. After that, they hugged whenever they could — movie marathons, after hanging out in shopping malls, study sessions. Shray's hugs were addictive in its own way. Miraya can't explain it any better than calling it a warm tent with no connection to the outside world. It was just him and her, and for that moment it was the only thing that mattered.

Even after so many years, Miraya felt the same. His hug never lost its power. She could stay right there in his arms for the rest of her life.

If only he hadn't put a knife into her back.

Another thought-provoking question pops into her mind: What if Shray had been in the position of Kishore? What if she almost loses him and regrets wasting so many years of her life over a stupid grudge?

But is her grudge really stupid? Isn't she allowed to be angry at the man who had destroyed her relationship with her parents and forced her to give away her freedom altogether? Isn't he responsible for all the hurt and pain she has felt in the past few years? Isn't it worth making him suffer a little bit even though she suffers along with him?

All the years of frustration and pain was compressed inside her chest until it turned into bitterness and grudgery because even though she had Shray to blame, she didn't watch him take responsibility for it.

He was out living his life, becoming the best version of himself while she learnt the art of lying to her parents' face and tried not to drown in the ocean of her lies before she could be where she wanted to be.

Miraya's fingers hover over Shray's contact. But they don't press it.

No matter what her heart wants, he is nothing to her but a heartbreak and a goodbye.

Chapter 13

♥

THREE MONTHS LATER.

Leave it to Dakshina to sneak liquor into her dressing room on her engagement night. "I'm nervous, okay?" she reasons when Miraya gives her a pointed look.

"Daksh, you will be fine. You look like a daydream. The only thing you should be nervous about is jealous men sending daggers at Ranav for stealing you before they get a chance," Miraya says, fishing a *jalebi* from the sweet box and biting into it. "Mmm, these are good."

"You're not the one about to stand in front of five hundred judgemental eyes!" Dakshina says, sipping the drink until she gets the very last drop.

Miraya shrugs. "I am not the one who signed up for this."

Dakshina throws her head back and groans. "Okay, now we're doing makeup. Then clothing. Then jewellery. I have to finish it in two hours."

"Your father is not coming?"

"He said he wanted to even though he has work. I told him not to. He can come for the wedding. There's not much going to happen tonight anyway. All these lavish decorations are only for the photographs and presents."

Miraya pushes the rest of the *jalebi* inside her mouth. "I admire you, you know, Daksh. I can never stand independent and do the things you do. Planning an engagement party for five hundred people on your own and partly funding it out of your own pocket, doing makeup and styling by yourself — I can never."

"It's not like I did it on my own. I had Ranav backing me up. I had your help. Without you, I wouldn't have been able to book a good photographer. You helped me pick out the ring and tell me the customary traditions to be followed. It might seem impossible when you think about it but when you're forced into such a situation, you could do it too, Miraya. I say this from experience so trust me on this: If you have someone supporting you like Ranav, you'll be surprised how much you can do," Dakshina drops her makeup brush and turns to look at her. "All you need is one person to trust you more than you trust yourself."

Miraya doesn't believe her.

She wants to be independent and she is trying to be, but a part of her is scared to stand alone. She needs people. She needs her family's opinions no matter how in contrast they are to hers. There is a constant need for validation. Someone has to keep telling her, *You are going in the right direction. No, that's not the right thing to do. You need to choose the other one.* She wants to make her own decisions but it isn't as easy as it sounds.

Or maybe she isn't trusting herself enough.

"Are you sure your parents would be okay with me not inviting them? I feel bad about it," Dakshina says.

"Oh, trust me. You will feel worse if they come." Miraya grabs a tissue to wipe her hands.

"But still..."

"I'll be honest, Daksh. My mother doesn't like you. I don't think my father even remembers who you are. So, drop the subject."

Her best friend puts her hands over her chest. "Ouch. Your mother was always nice to me."

"Oh, she is nice on the outside. But eh, not so much on the inside. She thinks you are a bad influence on me." Miraya didn't want to tell this bit of information to Dakshina ever but there was no point hiding it from her. She knows how naggy her mother can be.

"Double ouch." Dakshina stares at her reflection in the mirror with her nose scrunched as if something is wrong with her.

"Don't worry about it," Miraya says, wrapping her arms around her shoulders. "I love you and you are perfect."

Dakshina blinks.

"What?"

"Um, Ranav hasn't said something as sweet as this to me. Should I call off this wedding and marry you instead?"

Miraya laughs. "He wouldn't expect that plot twist."

"I know right," she says, smiling at Miraya. "But seriously, I love you too and you are perfect despite what you and your parents think of you. You'll always be the perfect girl who I had a crush on in college."

"Aww."

"Wait, does your mother know I am bisexual?"

Miraya shakes her head. "She will personally drag me out of the apartment and find a new place for me if she knows. It's better if it's a secret, trust me."

Dakshina is used to the appalled Indian aunties who overreact when they learn of her sexuality. Lalitha Aunty, who lives next to them, had stared at her like she'd grown a new head when she had caught Dakshina holding hands with her ex-girlfriend and pecking her lips quickly. The news had spread through the apartment like forest fire and Dakshina was ever since treated differently. For a while, there were whispers about Miraya as well, theories about both of them sharing a room. It was disgusting that the old men and women were so invested in their lives.

Dakshina would joke whenever she caught some of them giving her the eye. "Imagine if I married a woman and invited them to my wedding? I want to see that look on their face."

"I'm sure you wouldn't have the chance to. They'd run," Miraya told her.

For Miraya, this was more the reason for her to look up to Dakshina. In such a narrow-minded homophobic society, it really takes a lot of strength and resilience to stop caring about what people say and be unafraid to be yourself. Dakshina did it. She had learnt to get back up after the numerous times she cried and attempted to take her life. Slowly, she trained herself to look at others' unwanted opinions of her as mere jokes. Now, Dakshina would laugh it off and walk away because she knows they don't have the power to destroy her.

There is a knock on the door. Miraya answers it.

"How is she?" Ranav asks. He is still in his sweatpants and t-shirt. It's hard to believe he will be the centre of attention in the event in a few hours.

"Yeah, she is alright. And partly naked," Miraya says. The comment doesn't make him blush like she expected it to.

Ranav sniffs the air and scrunches his nose. "Did she drink?"

"Wow. Does it smell?"

He laughs. "Yes, Miraya. Now, scoot. Let me talk to her."

"Does that translate to 'Get out of this room so I can make out with my girlfriend'?" She crosses her arms against her chest.

"If I say yes, will you move?"

"Ranav!" Miraya chides and he ruffles her hair in apology. "Fine. It's not like it's the first time you two are making me feel hopelessly single."

"That just means it's time you get a boyfriend. Talk to Kishore and let me know. Maybe we could get married on the same day," Daksh calls out from inside. Miraya turns to glare at her and in reply she makes a funny face.

Miraya steps out of the room and travels through the decorated stage and hall, milling with busy people running to and fro to make the event perfect. Miraya spots Ranav's parents talking to the caterers and then moving onto the people arranging the chairs. They catch her eye and smile at her. She smiles back.

On the first chair in front of the stage, Ranav's brother is sitting with his daughter asleep on his shoulders, his arms coming around her to type something on his phone. She can't find his wife. She must be somewhere making sure the event will run smoothly.

Miraya goes over to him. "Hey. Want me to hold her for a while?"

"Would you?" he immediately asks and a chuckle escapes her lips. "I'm sorry. This work is really important and my right arm is so close to falling asleep."

"It's okay. I'll gladly hold her." He transfers the sleeping baby to her. The little one, clad in an uncomfortable but cute pink silk skirt and blouse, has drool all over her chin. She puts her thumb between her lips and settles in the crook of Miraya's neck.

Miraya takes a walk with her and then she gets a call. Kishore.

Ever since his accident, Miraya and Kishore talk daily. He knows her work schedule by heart and she knows his. They always make sure to call each other or if not drop in a text about their day.

"Hey," she answers.

"What are you upto?" There are sounds in the background as if someone is crinkling cheap candy wrappers.

"I have a drooling baby asleep on my shoulder and I'm taking a walk in a decorated hall. What about you?"

"Oh, fancy. I decided to clean my couch and guess what I found?"

"Um, dirt?"

"That and a hoard of candy wrappers. Ring a bell?"

Miraya's eyes go wide. "The-the one I stuffed inside?"

"Exactly. Did you even know where the bin was while you lived here?" he asks.

"Sorry?" Miraya offers. "I was lazy, okay? Plus it was fun shoving the wrapper inside and never finding it again."

"Well, I found it."

"Um, congratulations?"

"Miraya!"

She laughs. "I'm sorry. Are you taking your medicines?"

"No. I stopped last week. When will you stop worrying about me? It's been three months."

Miraya balances the phone between her ear and her shoulders and pats the baby's back when she moves. "Forgive me for caring about your wellbeing."

"Okay, then allow me to worry about you. Did you call Shray?"

Miraya sighs. "No. I won't call him. There's no reason to."

"Come on. You miss him. You think of him everyday."

"That doesn't mean that I should call him."

"So, you agree that you miss him?" There is the sound of smirk in his words.

"Ugh, I hate you!"

He chuckles. "Look, Miraya. I know what he did to you was horrible. I know how much you've suffered. But I also know that you have feelings for him. You like him and miss him a lot and after meeting him again after so many years, the feelings resurfaced stronger. You can't let that mean nothing. It's okay to give up a few years of grudges to be with someone you love."

"What's your point now?" Miraya is a little annoyed. She doesn't want to hear it.

"Do yourself a favour and call him."

"No."

"Fine."

"Bye."

"Bye!"

Miraya hangs up and groans. Shray has become a sore subject in her life. Her feelings have been in constant fluctuation, switching courts like a ping pong ball. She hates thinking about it or trying to make sense of it. It only gives her a headache.

She had written her best article about him, crying in the night and cursing herself during the process. Mrs Nandhini loved the piece so much that she hugged her and said she was proud of her. Shray's pictures were a big hit. Her favourite one was him laying on the dewy grass wearing a white turtleneck and ripped jeans, squinting at the sunlight with a heart-melting smile on his face. It was decided that it wasn't cover-worthy but there was something about that picture that made Miraya's heart beat differently.

Fiya had figured that talking about Shray was not a great move. She had asked if she knew him and Miraya had smiled weakly and said she used to. That was the end of it.

After the September issue was out, Fiya had bought two copies and gave one to her. "I know that you weren't so sure about buying one for yourself. But it's something you should be proud of," she said.

The issue had sold moderately well and everyone was impressed with what the Chennai unit could do. She lost the employee of the month to Grace but Miraya wasn't worried about it. She was genuinely happy because Grace had stayed there and supervised everything on her own. She deserved it.

Although the past three months have gone back to the same monotonous work-eat-sleep cycle with a few ups and downs here and there, she carried with her the messy impossible knot called Shray. She is scared to touch it or attempt to untangle it. It is just there... in a corner of her heart.

"Thank you for holding her." A voice from behind. She turns around to face Ranav's brother.

"No problem. She's so cute," Miraya says, caressing the little girl's hair before handing her over to her father.

Just before she goes back to Dakshina's room, a text from Kishore pops in her phone.

I'm sorry. I'll not talk about him again. Truce?

Miraya texts back.

I'm sorry too for being snappy (and for the candy wrappers). Will call tomorrow.

Chapter 14

Miraya is back at the beach. The sun has set already, much before she reached. The sky is carelessly splashed with hues of pink and violet above the sleepless waters, bleeding into a dark blue upwards. A cold breeze wavers in, coaxing Miraya's orange skirt into a slow dance. Her hair unravels from her claw-clip. She walks on the sand in her shoes, feeling the sand pour inside every time she presses a step forward. Miraya's going to have a hell of a time getting every grain of itchy sand out of her shoes later but she doesn't care. She is just happy the beach is open again after the rainy week.

Miraya loves rain. Be it the heavenly smell of the first few drops hitting the ground, or the strangely comforting drumming of raindrops on roofs and window panes, the blur of buildings and roads or the stormy grey clouds finally letting go of their burden. She loves it all.

But rain is also an inconvenience. Footsteps are wet, floors are slippery, there is water leaking from holes on walls you never knew existed. Everything is damp and the dampness reeks after a while.

The past few days had been ambushed by incessant rains, causing quite the havoc in the city. Drainage has always been a problem and no matter the steps being taken to control flooding, the same situation arises every year. Thankfully, this year is much better than the last one. The rains have stopped early. Work has resumed. Schools and colleges have reopened.

Traffic is also back, unfortunately, but Miraya doesn't care.

She feels nice today.

She wants to savour it.

Miraya tips the newspaper cone in her hand sideways to let the masala-tossed puffed rice fall into her palms. She throws it into her mouth and chews. Her lips curl around her teeth when she bites into a chunk of raw mango, the sourness of it quickly balanced by the blandness of the boiled peanuts. The view for her eyes, the burst of flavour on her tongue and the lull of waves on her ears — Miraya hasn't done this in a while and she realises how much she missed it.

Sometimes, feelings like these cause a stir inside her. Makes her remember every little thing that has caused her happiness and be grateful for it and feel happier. Usually, the things she draws happiness from is from the people around her.

Dakshina is engaged.

Fiya and Ashraf are going strong.

Kishore has fully recovered from the accident and landed a new job with a higher pay.

Miraya's youngest cousin Anjali got her first period three days back so her parents have gone to their hometown to pay her a visit.

MIRROR's December month's issue was published two weeks back. The piece she had written about Samantha's new fashion line received good feedback. Fiya's story about the oldest bakery in Hyderabad was just in time for the Holiday season, catching quite the attention.

The blinding Christmas sale in her favourite stores is another reason for her happiness. All Miraya eats these days is cake. It makes her feel giddy.

Her phone rings.

Miraya already spoke to her parents in the morning so it wouldn't be them.

She frowns when it's Fiya. Her colleague rarely calls her at this time.

"Hello?" Miraya answers, popping the last bit of her snack into her mouth and balling up the newspaper in her hand.

"Miraya! Have you heard?"

"Heard what?"

"Actress Ria and her fiance Vinay were going to get married soon, right? She suddenly called off their marriage."

"What? Why?"

Vinay was a producer in the film industry and he was well-reputed and dare she say, hot. Miraya has watched him in award shows and always admired him for his humble nature and down-to-earth personality.

Ria was a very popular actress as well. She earned a lot of fans with her debut and has never stopped since. A lot of people were shocked that within a few years in the industry, she decided to get married.

But Vinay and Ria were cute together. People slowly got used to them being a couple and began rooting for them, the endless fan pages on social media being enough proof.

It was heartbreaking that they broke up.

"That's the problem. Reports are pinning it on Shray."

"What?" Miraya's voice comes a little too high-pitched. She bites her tongue.

"I know. It's so absurd. But they have managed to link it all together. You have to read the articles, Miraya. They are portraying Shray as the bad guy. That man would never do such a thing," Fiya vouches for Shray as if she's known him all along. Miraya is mildly irritated by that but she shrugs it off.

"Okay, I'll read them now. Bye," Miraya says and hangs up. She googles Ria's name and a series of articles show up on the web page.

She clicks on one which has mentions of Ria, Vinay and Shray in it.

ACTRESS RIA AND PRODUCER VINAY SANTHOSH BREAK UP; HERE'S HOW SHRAY NIVAS IS INVOLVED.

July saw quite a number of engagement announcements and wedding bells among celebrities. One of them, and the most loved couple, was Ria and Vinay Santhosh. Earlier this afternoon, the actress took to her social media to officially announce that the couple are splitting. The reasons weren't mentioned.

Fans are shocked at this sudden development.

Amongst the fervour of this news, to add on to the fire, pictures of Ria and Shray Nivas looking quite cosy on a hiking trip have been released on the internet. The source hasn't been identified yet but these pictures are taking the internet by storm. The Orange actress is all smiles as she latches on to Nivas' arms as they walk down a hiking trail. The actor isn't any less happy.

Fans have been enraged at Shray for breaking up their most loved couple. They blame Shray "for stealing Vinay's woman," as one user commented. Some fans have expressed that Ria is better off with someone like Shray Nivas. The internet is torn but there's one thing we are undivided on. Chocolate Boy Shray Nivas's reputation is bruised and has taken quite the hit because of this scandal.

None of them have commented on this issue yet.

Actress Ria and Shray Nivas are starring in the murder mystery Room No 3, *which is set to hit the theaters this January.*

Miraya stares at the pictures. Shray is laughing, his mouth ajar like he doesn't have a care in the world. Ria isn't holding his hand. Her hand is on the crook of his arm, which could easily come under friendship. From what she'd observed on the day she met both of them, they were good friends. And Ria had mentioned something about her fiance blowing her off again.

Online articles use meaningless hooks to invite a person to click on the link. This could be one of them. They have exaggerated the pictures and to any other person not familiar with the business, their justification might seem logical and true. But not to her.

Or maybe Miraya just doesn't want to believe it. Maybe she doesn't want it to be true.

There is a strong feeling in her gut that says that whatever this was isn't Shray's fault. It cannot be. Shray is not a person who will steal another man's woman. Miraya remembers that one time when he almost cried after he broke up with Shanaya. He is a gentleman.

But you also thought Shray was your best friend. Look what happened.

Miraya closes her eyes.

Confusion. Haziness. Darkness. The feelings return back to her as soon as she thinks about him. It's as if her relationship with Shray is a stubborn cloud hanging in her sky, hiding the sun. She hates it. She wants clarity.

Kishore says Miraya will only get it if she talks to him.

She doesn't want to.

She wants to be angry with Shray a little longer. If she meets him again, she knows she will break. As much as she wants to be strong, she knows she isn't.

Afterall, one of Miraya's weakness is Shray.

"Congratulations!" Miraya screamed, running towards the team as they climbed down from the bus that took them to the inter-school game. She had been asking her PE teachers non-stop about their progress in the competition and she had barged into their classroom and announced it when she heard they won.

Her eyes skimmed over every black head in the crowd but she didn't find Shray. She paused on Suriya. "Where is he?" Miraya asked.

He knew who she was talking about. "Shray hurt himself."

"What?"

He lugged his bag over his shoulders, sweat dripping from his head. "He hurt himself when we had five minutes left. It looked pretty bad at that time. Everyone told him to sit it out but you know Shray, right? He said he's fine and carried on. When we won, he couldn't move. He was just laying there on the ground, screaming. The teachers took him to the hospital."

Miraya's eyes were already wet. "Which hospital?"

"David's."

"I have to go see him," she said, her breath falling short.

"We have one more period left. I am going there after school so I can take you if you want," Suriya offered.

But she couldn't wait one hour. She asked permission to use the restroom and slipped out of class. Miraya beelined for the staffroom, found the Maths teacher, Padma, who was also her aunt, called Amma through her phone and explained the situation. Amma called the school and let them know that Miraya will be leaving school with Suriya.

She spent the next few minutes crying in the bathroom. He shouldn't have hurt himself when she wasn't there. He shouldn't have hurt himself at all.

As soon as the bell rang, she ran to Suriya's car and couldn't sit still until she stepped out in front of the hospital. She saw Shray's mother in her wheelchair and his father seated in the waiting area.

"Miraya, you're here." His mother laughed lightly. "Shray told me you'd come rushing in soon. He also told me to tell you not to panic. He is alive and well."

Miraya couldn't smile back. "How is he?"

"He tore his ligament. If he wants to continue playing sports and perform heavy physical activities, he needs to get surgery done. Otherwise, he is advised physical therapy," Shray's father explained.

"So, he won't play again?" Suriya asked from behind.

"No. He chose not to. He said it isn't fun anymore."

Suriya rolled his eyes, probably thinking he could convince him later on to keep playing. To Miraya, it wasn't a surprise. Shray had already been talking to her about quitting the team.

"There he is," Shray's mother pointed to the left. Her best friend grinned, walking towards them in crutches. Her heart squeezed.

The nurse asked if he wanted help, but he charmingly waved her off.

"Did you cry? You cried, didn't you?" Shray teased as he stood before Miraya.

"Man, you should've seen her. Big fat crocodile tears. My car seat is soaking," Suriya intervened.

Miraya kicked him. "Shut up." The two of them laugh at her but she had none of that. She flung her arms around Shray.

"I hate you. How many times have you made me worry about you just this year?" she mumbled. Miraya would've hit him if his parents weren't sitting right before them.

"I don't know. Thrice?"

"Don't scare me again. If something happens to you, I'll kill you."

"When did you become such a romantic?" he whispered into her ears and she almost smacked him.

Almost.

Instead, she held him tighter.

That was the moment she knew.

If Shray is hurt, she is too. He is her weakness and will always be.

And that's why the article angers her so much. She wants to scream that it's not true. She wants to hold Shray close to her because she knows that he is somewhere under the same moon, drowning in worry over the risk of losing his career.

Chapter 15

♥

A week passes and Ria's scandal is still as hot as it came. In the course of seven days, a few more pictures have been released. They are pictures from the set, and honestly speaking, it looks completely non-romantic. The most talked about is the one in which Ria flicks something off Shray's hair. She can understand that it can be misunderstood to be cute and lovey-dovey but it's natural for friends to do that too. Miraya has done it multiple times at school.

She is pissed at how Ria isn't bothered to comment about the issue. What is she thinking? Does she want people to think Shray and her are together? Is it a cheap idea for their movie promotion? Is that what this is?

Miraya tries not to think about it but she has read every trash article about them and stared at the pictures a million times. She reasons that it might be because she wants to know if she is right about Shray. Or know if he is really in a relationship with Ria.

Mrs Nandhini and the other directors of the office are in a meeting in the cabin room. Miraya is sitting in front of her computer, editing a troublesome piece on aesthetic culture. She can't help but feel Mrs Nandhini glance at her through the glass windows once in a while. Miraya is worried, already making a list of all her mistakes to try and find which one she is going to be whooped for.

1. She had accidentally knocked Mrs Nandhini's cup of coffee when she went to submit her file but had quickly cleaned it up and blotted out the stains on the paper.

2. Miraya had been very late last Thursday because her car broke down (She slept through her alarm).

3. She had sent an email to the main quarters without attaching the file, only to realise it much later. That was the fourth time she pulled that shit.

4. Miraya had also been late yesterday because of traffic (Dakshina had forced her to drink hence she woke up late with a hangover).

She can remember only so much. Or was there more?

Miraya slowly slips off to the pantry to help herself to a cup of coffee. Yes, a beautiful life-saving coffee machine was installed and a refrigerator too. Priscilla was in charge of maintaining the pantry and refilling the sachets. She was a gem.

Miraya adds no milk but an extra sachet of sugar before leaning on the counter and sipping the hot liquid. Fiya was on leave today so Miraya was missing the usual chatter. On one side, she was a bit happy because she can push in a lot of work without getting distracted but on the other side, she felt bored.

Giri walks in. "Hey, Mira. How's it going?" He always wears collared t-shirts. Most of them are striped, the others solid-coloured. Polka dots are a no-no. He prefers darker shades.

"Just the usual. What about you?"

"I am actually preparing to pitch an idea for the next issue."

Miraya pushes herself off the counter with her hip. "Oh, that's great. What's it about? Maybe I could be of some help."

Before he can answer, Priscilla barges in. "Mira, Mrs Nandhini called you to her room immediately."

Oh, here it goes.

The coffee loses its magic and instead swirls inside her stomach uneasily. She has a feeling that whatever this is isn't anything good.

And... she is right.

Mostly.

"Take a seat, Miraya," Mrs Nandhini says.

She does.

There aren't a lot of papers on her desk unlike the usual. Her son's picture frame on her table is accompanied by a new one she hasn't seen before. It's a picture of Mrs Nandhini, her son and his wife. It must have been taken at the wedding.

"I'll get to the point immediately," Mrs Nandhini begins, weaving her fingers together and resting them on the table. *Oh, thank god.* "We've received a request for a story."

Miraya frowns. "About what?"

"A story on Ria and Shray's friendship."

"What?" Miraya almost gasps.

"Wait before you react again. They have specifically asked you to do it."

Confusion.

"Why? I mean, who?"

"I don't know about the why. I do know the who." Mrs Nandhini pauses, taking a deep breath. *Oh, can she ever be less dramatic for once?* "Shray Nivas has specifically requested you to do the story."

Her heart thumps fast. "B-but, we don't do these kinds of stories."

"I know. But the superiors think it might be good for the magazine because Shray will be addressing the issue for the first time through MIRROR. That's why they've decided to publish it online as a part of the Friday weekly-upload. If it is published in the magazine, by the time the issue is out, the topic of the scandal will be dead."

Oh, alright. This would not be good for the magazine. It would be *great*.

But Shray asking for *her* to do it is suspicious. What is he after this time? Why did he pick her? What is his intention?

"It's a good opportunity. And he has specifically asked for you. That should be flattering," Mrs Nandhini says, smiling. But Miraya doesn't react. "The superiors want you to take this up, Miraya."

Miraya doesn't want to. She knows that if she does, it will be the end of her dream of avoiding Shray for what he did to her. But she can't deny the fact that she is also curious as to why he chose her specifically and about what he has to say about the issue. Plus, it will bring in a lot of attention to MIRROR. Maybe this time she will be able to bag the employee of the month award.

"Okay," Miraya says, slightly defeated.

At this point, she is going to close her eyes and let the wind carry her to wherever she has to be. She is tired of fighting, fighting, *fighting*. Her life is determined to take her places she doesn't want to go and she doesn't have the energy to be the stubborn kid again and demand they go elsewhere. It is what it is.

"I'll pass on the details to you," Mrs Nandhini says.

Miraya nods and leaves the room.

A lot goes on her mind as she sits through the day and pushes some work in. She wants to talk to Kishore about it but she already knows what he will say. *Talk to Shray about what he did back in school.*

It was a touchy subject. Even thinking of it brought back the distinct fear and shame she felt when her parents hung their heads down as they listened to the Principal go on and on about how Miraya broke the trust they placed on her and how much of a disgrace she is to the school and the family. Top it with the sting of betrayal and the blossoming hatred for Shray. It was a bad mixture of emotions to feel. It was dangerous, like poison. Spreading through her body slowly, painfully, effectively enough to leave behind large traces of it to survive years and years of forgetting and creating good memories.

The feeling lingered like bad perfume.

Talking to him about it is like giving life to it. Allowing it to spread again.

She doesn't want that.

Miraya is going to talk to him about Ria and Vinay and nothing else.

She is out of her office as soon as she can and drives hastily to her apartment to try and get some sleep. Her thoughts are consuming her, telling her to do two completely opposite things at the same time. It is exhausting. She needs to shut off her brain for some time.

Miraya tries the radio. She tries flipping stations to find something that is catchy enough to distract her.

She isn't distracted.

Her thoughts go back to Shray.

Is he okay? Is he terrified? Is he trying so hard to keep his calm but losing it on the inside?

Shray is a person who isn't overly affected by things that happen around him. He doesn't butt into things or make other's problems his own like she does. But if it is something involving someone or something he loves, he becomes sensitive. He becomes emotional. He loses his temper, his composure cracks and he acts like he has lost everything in this world.

Miraya hates that she is worried about him.

Did he ever worry about her in the past few years? At least once?

She parks the car and punches the button on the elevator.

Miraya's phone rings.

Amma.

Great.

It takes three deep breaths and a few clenches of her fist to prepare her to answer the call. "Miraya, have you reached home?"

"Yes."

"Okay, okay. Your *Paati* is coming to Chennai for a week. I thought I should tell you beforehand so you can clear your schedule. Take her to the temple as usual," she says.

"Okay."

Miraya doesn't argue because she loves *Paati*. She is the only one in her family who treats her like an adult and lets her make her own choices. Whenever she comes to Chennai, both of them visit the temple near her parent's home in the evening, catching up during the walk back. The childish excitement in *Paati*'s eyes when Miraya takes her for their ritualistic mani and pedi session is something she can never get tired of watching. *Paati* makes her special *gulab jamun* for her, lets her know of the recent developments in the family, their history and a few fond childhood memories of hers. Miraya loves sleeping in *Paati*'s lap and listening to her talk beautiful Tamil with her soft voice, as she cards through her hair lovingly.

With a smile, she steps out of the elevator, her thoughts clinging to her grandmother.

It is the sweetest distraction.

Chapter 16

♥

Miraya is asked to meet Shray in his house through a god-damn text with a period. When she is questioned by the nosy security at his gate, she almost rolls her eyes. She is pissed that Shray is acting like he rules the world. Maybe when people become famous, they're more susceptible to arrogance.

She is let through when she says her name and mentions why she is here. Miraya wants this interview to be in a formal place. Nothing that will allow her to get too comfortable. But as soon as she steps inside the house, she flushes her thoughts down the toilet.

Shray's house is beautiful. He has chosen a basic colour palette: Black, grey, white. There is a parking shed for his car on the left, beyond which is a well-maintained lawn. There are no potted plants but there are bushes with pretty flowers and fancy-looking climbers creeping up the grey walls. She smiles at that. Shray never liked potted plants. He preferred plants to be rooted in the ground.

Miraya walks to his house and before she can knock or ring the bell, the door opens. Shray's in a navy shirt and cream-coloured trousers. His hair is fresh out of the shower, not dripping but drenched. He smells like soap and musk.

"Hi," he says.

"Hi," she responds.

Shray opens his mouth to say something but decides against it. He scratches the back of his neck and opens the door wider. "Come in."

Miraya suddenly feels self-aware and conscious. Almost shy. Stepping into his house seems like invading his privacy but she tells herself it's okay. It's not like she is uninvited.

She sits on the incredibly soft couch, her back stiff. She wants to lean back but she doesn't.

"Can I get you something to drink? Coffee or Hot chocolate?"

"Coffee, thanks."

This is so awkward. She doesn't understand why. Miraya has been friends with him for years and was casual and authoritative when they met three months back. What's gone wrong?

She takes the time to look around the house. Minimal art frames on the wall. Grey curvy-striped rug on the floor. Furnished tea table in black with a glass top. Grey couches with white cushions. A cushioned rocking chair, the colour of cement. White marble floors and white walls. A shelf full of DVDs.

But there are some things missing.

No TV in the living room. No grand chandelier lights. No home decor. No clock.

She glances at the kitchen. The only thing visible to her is Shray's arms resting upon the black marble counters. There is one other room on the ground floor, just next to the winding stairs. She has a feeling his room is on the top floor. The last time she had seen his room in his parent's house, it had colourful movie posters and pictures of popular actors, a pokemon laundry basket and a Popeye-themed cloth hanger.

Their favourite cartoons were Popeye and Ben 10. Cartoon Network was their world after school. Every evening after school, she would go to Shray's or he would come to her place and they'd do their homeworks quickly so that they could stay glued to their seats in front of the TV for the rest of their evening. Thinking about it brings a certain warmth to her heart. She feels fuzzy.

"Here," Shray says, handing over a pastel green mug of coffee.

Miraya takes a sip.

"Is the sugar okay? I know you take extra sugar but I wasn't sure if you still liked it that way," he says.

"It's perfect, thank you." The sugar is a bit too much but this was the first time Shray was making her coffee so she didn't comment.

"How have you been?" Shray asks, sitting on the couch across from hers.

"Well." Miraya places the mug on her lap. "What about you?"

"Do you want me to be honest?" he asks, leaning back against the couch.

"Who doesn't like honesty?"

"The media. The story-spinners on the internet," he offers. Miraya doesn't expect that. "I feel horrible, Miraya."

Her name sounds strange on his lips. When he called her that three months ago, she wasn't clear-headed to register the feeling of the sound. Now that she does, she doesn't like it. It's different. She has to get used to it.

"Do- do you really like Ria? Are you in a relationship?" Miraya asks slowly.

Shray sighs. "No. She's my friend." He looks over at her. "Shouldn't you be recording this?"

"You can talk to me... as a friend, I guess. Just for now. I can write it objectively later on. I want you to feel comfortable sharing things," Miraya says. "And... I promise I won't misuse your situation for the profit of MIRROR. I won't reveal information you don't want to either."

The surprise on Shray's face is evident. "Do you know why I wanted you to be the one doing this?"

"I was saving that question for the last."

"I'm here to collect the favour you owe me. I hoped it wouldn't come to that but here we are."

Ah. The favour she promised in return for the ride back to Coimbatore when Kishore was hospitalised. It's kind of a blow in the chest that he didn't pick her because of her talent. "What do you want?"

"I'll tell you later."

Miraya wants to protest but she nods anyway.

"How are you dealing with it?" she asks, zeroing in on the topic.

He pushes away the hair on his forehead. "It's hard. For both of us, actually. Ria is already grieving over her relationship with Vinay because she really loved him. These pictures couldn't choose a worse time to circulate. People are bashing both of us. They say Ria likes to jump from one man to another. They call her a slut and other disgusting names. They say I stole her from Vinay to get revenge on him for a reason I don't know myself. And I am the bad guy in this love triangle. There's so much bullshit on the internet. On top of this, the PR team says to go along with it because it will do us good for the movie. Apparenly, bad publicity is still publicity. It's so stupid."

"Media has always been like that. You knew what you were getting into when you decided to be an actor."

"I did, Miraya. But it's not any easier when it actually happens. It's... fucking with my head." Shray's expressions betray his anger and frustration and worry that he is clearly confining inside of him. He is suffering on the inside.

The rise to fame is like walking through a rose bush. You wonder if you'll survive the thorns but suddenly find a rose hidden among them. When you keep your head down and follow the rose, one leads to another, and you'll see the obvious path before you.

But one mistake, one wrong step or one innocent laugh could strip you off the roses, erase your pathway, and leave nothing but your ugly scars for the world to see. It'll dissolve every good thing you've done in your life, peel away the pride and praise you've harboured and flip your life upside down. All it takes is just *one mistake.*

Rising to fame is delicate and slow. Defaming is harsh and in-stant.

Shray knows it too. He is scared of it and she can see it on his face.

"You brought me here to undo that. Let's talk about your friend-ship with Ria. I'll try my best to write a catchy article that makes everyone want to believe that you two are best friends and nothing more," Miraya offers.

Shray's lips tug upwards and he mumbles something she doesn't quite catch.

"Let's start."

Shray doesn't open up immediately. Clipped answers are what Miraya gets for the first few questions as if he is scared to even talk about Ria. He takes time easing into a comfortable exchange. Sometimes, Miraya makes dumb jokes to get him to laugh or asks questions she already knows the answer to just to get him to open up. Everytime he locks eyes with her, she feels a storm building in her chest. A storm of butterflies. An accumulation of suppressed feelings.

She is an expert in holding grudges but with him, her powers are nothing. They are twigs dangling off the branch amidst a storm. Her love and affection for him keeps overpowering her hatred.

Miraya wants to shake it off but it sticks. Clings to her soul even after a decade.

Miraya has to remember what he did to her over and over again to keep her from smiling too much during the conversation. She doesn't want him to think that she is on the road to forgiving him already. Or that she is warming up to the idea. She doesn't want to accidentally suggest the possibility of becoming friends again. He hasn't even apologised yet, for god's sake.

"There's really nothing between Ria and I except friendship. We really gel well together. Besides, during the shoot, everytime she was upset about Vinay, I would be the one to cheer her up. We get along well and share a lot of similarities, especially with the way we were brought up," Shray says.

"Do you know what caused their fall-out?"

"Yes, but it's really not my place to comment on that. One thing I can confirm is that it is not because of me."

Shray is getting frustrated and worried by the second. Miraya senses it. His lips are pressed together, so firmly that all she wants to do is kiss away the worry. Upon closer inspection, she can see that Shray hasn't slept well for days. There are black rings around his eyes and his lips are chapped. He hasn't been taking care of himself. Miraya wants to bring him close to her and hug him tight. She wants to make him food and stay over to make sure he is getting enough sleep.

"Okay, this is enough. Do you have a picture we could use to promote your friendship?"

"I think so."

"Please send that to me."

"Okay."

Shray and Miraya sit there in silence. It's heavily layered with awkwardness and tension. She wants to reach out to him so badly but Miraya ties her hands together. She can't. She won't.

She distracts herself by tracing the rim of the coffee mug, not ready to leave him yet.

"You have a nice house."

"Do you want to stay for another cup of coffee?"

Both of them say it at the same time. Miraya's fingers torture each other in her lap.

"Um, you go first," she says.

Shray repeats his question and she nods, taking up his offer. She doesn't want to leave him when he is like this, low and vulnerable. There are a lot of thoughts running through his head and she can see it in the way his eyes wince.

Shray is hurting.

Miraya watches him get up to go to the kitchen. She can't hold herself back anymore. "Shray?"

He turns.

Miraya stands up and walks over to his side. She takes his hand. It's cold, rough. It's familiar. Her fingers weave through his.

Shray stares at her, his black eyes curious and surprised and relieved at the same time. Miraya touches his cheek and he leans into her palm. "It's going to be okay. Trust me. You'll be okay."

Shray's eyes tear up. His lips tremble. In one swing of his arms, he pulls her close and buries his face in the crook of her neck. Miraya gasps. She doesn't mean to. The feeling of having his body pressed up against hers, moulded together like wax with his strong, almost crushing grip, syncing their heartbeats together — it makes her feel exhilarated. As if she has found something she lost.

His shoulders shake. Miraya's arms hold him tighter. Her fingers come up to his hair, caressing the soft curls in a form of comfort.

"Thank you," he whispers. "Thank you so much."

Chapter 17

♥

After Shray decided that it was enough soaking Miraya's sleeves with his tears, they pulled away from each other. It was evident in his eyes that he didn't want to. She hated that she felt like that too. But Miraya walked straight into the kitchen and started striking a conversation about his refrigerator. Shray followed, preparing two cups of coffee again for both of them while she explored his kitchen, occasionally pausing to appreciate his choices. She was impressed that Shray cooked for himself on most days.

Small talks and lame conversations ensued while they sipped their coffees together.

And now, Miraya and Shray sit next to each other on the couch, their coffee mugs empty.

"Did you ever think of me? At some point in your life?" Shray asks.

She lets out a laugh. There's no joy in it. "I tried not to, if that counts. But it's hard when your face is everywhere. Those were the times I wished you weren't as popular."

Shray winces. Miraya does as well after hearing her own words. She was having a normal conversation with him a few minutes ago. Where did the bitterness come from?

"Was it that bad?"

"Yes."

Miraya shifts away from him without intending to. Shray notices. He volunteers and creates a bigger gap between them. Miraya, upon realising what she had done, wants to tell him that he misunderstood. But she doesn't.

"Miraya."

"Huh?"

"Can you look at me for a moment?"

Miraya does. That's when she registers that Shray is wearing a worn-out ugly looking bracelet. It's black and braided with five little cubes that spells 4EVER. Her eyes widen. Why does he still wear this bracelet? Did he put it on today just because he was meeting her?

Shray sees her gaze on his hand and twists the bracelet around his wrist. "Why are you staring at it like that? You gave me this, remember?"

"Why do you still have it?"

"What do you mean? Of course, I still have it. I even have the fancy hair clip you told me to safe-keep but never got it back."

But why? You can't stab me in the back like that and just pretend it didn't happen! She wants to scream it to him but something stops her. A warning. An alarm. Asking questions like that are not really the best way to go if she doesn't want to discuss the past. It was self-inflicted pain. She's had enough of that.

Miraya swallows the question and starts afresh.

"Do you have problems sleeping?" she asks.

Shray gives her a look that says *I know what you're trying to do and I don't like it.* But he gives in and answers her question anyway. "I do. My head is loud, always filled with thoughts and what-ifs and this adding onto my decreasing self-worth, my mental state is not exactly looking pretty. It's bad. I'm trying to cope. I tell myself this is close to nothing in the film industry. I have read about worse scandals myself and people forget about it in time. I tell myself this too will pass. But it's as if the days are suddenly moving in slow-motion. And not all the celebrities who were caught in such scandals are exactly flourishing in the industry. Some have gone off the cinema radar. They've become... no one. What if I become like them? What if my career ends before it even begins?"

"It won't. You'll be one of those who are resilient. You'll be back in the game in no time. As you said, this too will pass," Miraya says, squeezing his fingers briefly. She pulls her fingers away but he flips his hand and holds onto them.

Her eyes are on him.

"Miraya." It's just a name. But it does something to her. "Tell me why."

"What why?"

"Tell me why you won't talk to me like you used to. Why are you so angry at me? Did I do something wrong?"

Miraya almost scoffs. She snatches her hand from his grip. "I can't believe you asked that."

"From the moment you told me not to talk to you again, I've thought about every possible reason you might be angry with me. But I can't find anything, Miraya. The closest I can think of is losing contact with you."

"Oh really? Then, by all means, please tell me why you lost contact with me?"

"You changed your number. You wouldn't give it to anyone, not even to me. I came by your house so many times but your parents didn't let me see you. They told me not to visit. I tried, Miraya. I even asked my father to ask your father about you. The bits and pieces of information I got is how I kept track of you. I heard that you took up journalism. That you landed a job in Germany. Came back to India and joined another magazine. There wasn't a day I didn't think of you."

Miraya stands up. She was fed up. She was tired. She was angry. "You know what? The critics were right. You are a brilliant actor, Shray, especially now that I'm seeing it firsthand. You thought of me everyday?" A bitter cruel laugh. "Funny. Guess you've learnt how to lie fluently as well. In school, you were so terrible that I can see right through you. Now, your skills are next level. Amazing. Good for you."

"Miraya, what the fuck are you saying?" He is on eye-level with her.

She glares at him. "What the fuck are *you* saying, Shray? I know what you did. Don't you feel the least bit of remorse for what happened? You ruined my life, for god's sake. Does being an actor entitle you to a life without basic manners and human emotions? You think you can just act your way into my life again? Well, fucking think again, Shray. You are a horrible person. Don't you even try to play the game you're planning to. I am not that naive school girl again who trusts you blindly. You are an arrogant asshole. You are —"

"Shut up. Just *shut up*, Miraya. I have no fucking clue what you're talking about. You think I'm acting? You think I'm faking my feelings? I thought you were the only person in the world who could understand what I was going through. I thought you knew me better than anyone else. That is why I had you brought here. You are the only person I trust to convey my feelings precisely as I feel it." Shray's left hand is on his hip. The other is pointing fingers at Miraya. Accusing, *enraged* fingers. "And you are insulting my career now? You know how much acting means to me. You know it and you still made that comment. Just because I've been in love with you for eleven fucking years doesn't mean that you are entitled to say whatever the hell you want and expect me to be okay with it! Actually, it hurts even more. You are killing me!"

Miraya is dumbstruck. Her mind is nothing but a blank space. No thoughts, no images, no symbols. Not even a dot. Her tongue is twisted, mouth dry and heartbeat rising like crazy. She feels like she might pass out.

Shray runs his fingers through his hair and tugs at the strands like he wants to pull them out. He steps forward. "Tell me one thing. What are you even expecting from me? You give me no hint, no clue as to what I did. If you won't even tell me what's bothering you, how can I solve it? Because I want to, Miraya. I so badly want to. I want you. I've been wanting you for years. Help me out."

Her voice cracks. She chokes out the words. "I c-can't." It's barely audible.

"Why?" Shray's feet are touching hers. He's so close. He takes her hands. Squeezes them. "Tell me why."

Miraya's breathing quickens. Her lungs are shrinking. She wants air. She's run out of it. Her chest is heaving. She doesn't know what to say. She doesn't know what to do.

She's already turning around when she says, "I c-can't. I just can't."

Miraya walks around the table and grabs her bag. She slings it over her shoulders, stumbles as she stuffs her feet into her strappy flats, not caring to buckle them tight. Miraya is at the door.

But Shray grabs her before she can keep her foot out.

"Miraya, wait. I just bared my heart out to you. Help me out here, please," he begs. Shray never begs. But at that moment, he was very close to falling on his knees.

But her mind is exploding. It's too much information. It's too much emotion. She can't handle it.

"I'm sorry." Tears spill out of her eyes.

"You owe me a favour, right? I want an explanation. That's the favour I need."

She swallows a sob and shakes her head. "Anything but that. I can't. I can't do it. I'm not ready. I don't think I ever will be."

Shray looks devastated. As if everything in his world is breaking apart. As if he is losing grip on all the ropes he's tied them together with. Miraya frees her arm and is about to leave when he pulls her back. She turns to him to beg him to let her go. But this time, she sees some flare of determination in his face. Like he has a plan.

"You said anything."

"What?"

"You said *anything* but that. And I want this. I want you to give me a chance."

With that, he tilts her chin and presses his lips on hers.

Chapter 18

♥

Miraya is completely still under Shray's touch.

Time stops. It really does.

She feels every minute movement of his lips, every little shift in the temperature, the increasing weight of his hands on her. She feels it as she freezes in the moment with wide eyes, a heart racing against light and feet struggling to stand. Miraya's fingers claw his shoulders to keep her from crashing to the ground.

Shray interprets that as a sign of encouragement. His arms wrap around her waist, pinning her close to him. He angles her face without breaking the kiss so he can kiss deeper.

Shray's lips are warm, inviting and tempting. If she thought Shray's hug was the best, his kiss was a staircase to heaven. Maybe she was feeling this way because she has never been kissed before. Or maybe she is feeling this way because she has wondered too many times what it might feel like to kiss Shray.

Oh, it feels good. So good.

Miraya is nervous and self-conscious. She doesn't know what to do. She is afraid she might ruin it. That's why she stays perfectly still while he kisses her and tries not to melt in a gooey mess.

But when Shray licks her bottom lip with his tongue, teasing her as if to say *you know you want to,* she gasps. His hands grip her hips tighter. It hits a switch inside her, unlocking all the pent-up feelings she has stored inside her for him. Hate and love. Love and hate. A cruelly delicious mixture of both.

She gives in and kisses him back. Miraya surrenders all control to him and allows him to guide her. She moves her lips against his. Slowly, then with a little bit of confidence, and then hungrily.

Drenched in pleasure from head to toe, she forgets the laws she has made up in her head. She forgets everything and doesn't care about it because she feels her neurons bursting with an overload of sensations. There is a blackout in her brain.

Shray backs her up against the door. Neither of them break the kiss. It's almost like a competition, an extension of the argument they were having. They aren't ready to lose.

Shray's fingers trace the sliver of skin just beneath her shirt. He doesn't slide his hands under the piece of clothing and make her burn with his touch like she wants him to.

Oh man, she has lost it.

Her mind has given up on her. There is no one to tell her to stop.

Shray presses his lips to her one last time and pulls away, breathless and panting, staring at her like she was the eighth wonder. "You like me too. You have feelings for me. Miraya.... since when —"

Reality hits her like a brick flung at her face. She pushes him away. "No. No, I don't."

His lips are on the way to becoming a bruised red. The flushed look on his face, his breathless state, his chest heaving and a swollen lip from kissing is a painting Miraya would sell her kidney for. But it is also criminal evidence she wants to destroy.

Miraya should have pushed him away when he kissed her. She gave in to him despite her obvious hard feelings towards him that she has conveyed several times. Her actions don't align with her words, her words don't align with her thoughts, her thoughts don't align with her heart. It's a stupid meaningless cycle. Miraya is guilty of what she'd done. She is ashamed. She had given in to some twisted want buried inside her like a fool. An idiot. That's what she is.

She doesn't bear to look at him anymore. "I have to go," she mutters, her eyes never meeting him.

"Miraya..."

Her eyes squeeze close. "Please. Don't." She is the one begging now.

Miraya opens the door and shuts it as soon as she is out, non-verbally asserting that she doesn't want him to follow her.

He doesn't.

She runs.

□□□□□□□□□□□□□□

Dakshina would've called Miraya insane if she knew she was taking a cold cold shower in the midst of December. But Miraya didn't know of anything else that could wake her up from this dream-like nightmare she was stuck in. She keeps feeling the heat of Shray's hands on her, her skin bending to his touch like the rubber pencils she was obsessed with in fifth grade, his breath on her skin, his lips on hers. No need for a time machine. All Miraya had to do was close her eyes. She was back in the moment, reliving each and every bit of detail in the scene. The kiss was haunting her. Can finally getting something that she had wanted for a long time make it cursed?

Shray and Miraya had been best friends for more than a decade. They have touched, hugged, hit, elbowed, slapped each other numerous times. Touching was a part of normalcy. But now, a small brush from his fingers elicited a million sparks from her body. Did a few years of complete ignorance of each other starve them altogether? Is that why any form of touch between them is beautiful and bruising? Is that why she hadn't been able to hold herself back when he had kissed her?

Or was that to do with the confirmed feelings they had for each other?

Miraya simply cannot comprehend that Shray had feelings for her all this time. Eleven years, he said. He has loved her for eleven years. And she hadn't known it. He hadn't shown it. Why?

If he had told her, she would've loved him with every single cell in her body. She would've given him the world. None of this might have happened. Maybe they'd still be together. Maybe she would've watched him become the star he is, not from the side-lines but from the luxury box with the clearest view. Why didn't he just tell her?

Why didn't you tell him?

She sags against the cold tiled-wall. Miraya assumed he wasn't interested in her romantically. She had no clue of his feelings nor did he suspect it because he was always checking out the junior girls, telling her who was his type and who wasn't. He went after Shanaya and he went after Eshita.

But now that she thought about it, it was him who'd broken up with both of them. Never the girls. When she asked him why, he'd said the relationship didn't feel right. Miraya had even made fun of him for that.

Now she knows.

Everytime he patted her back when she choked on water, every-time he hugged her close, everytime he had ruffled her hair, everytime he shared his earphones with her, everytime he acted possessive — he *loved* her. And the countless times he had flirted with her. Miraya had thought it was out of playfulness, a kind of a jolly friendship. She had wished every time that he meant those words but he actually had. Shray had flirted with her because he wanted to. He had just chosen to cover it up nice and clean with friendship.

Another thought pops into her mind. It might be arrogant and cynical of her to assume that of Shray but she has a feeling that it could be right.

Did Shray tattle Miraya and Siddh out because he was jealous of them? Because he finally snapped and decided he'd break them apart?

Now that she recalls, Shray had always been possessive. He liked knowing his favourite people's favourite was him. He is a tough guy who doesn't express his emotions a lot but he is soft on the inside. Whenever Shray's mother fed her food when she went to their house, he wouldn't have it. Shray would demand that she feed him as well. He liked attention. And he *loved* the attention of the people he loved.

And Miraya hadn't given it to him in the way he wanted it.

Maybe he became bitter and lost sense of what he was doing.

The more and more Miraya thinks about this, the more and more her head spins. Her chest grows heavier with time and she just wants to rip it out of her chest and throw it away.

And how did he find out about her feelings? Was she too transparent? It should've been evident in the way she kissed him. Stupid, stupid, stupid. She should've pushed him away and snapped at him for being so thoughtless. She should've hated his touch or the way he gripped her hips and caressed her body like he was born to do it. She should've hated the kiss. She should've hated him.

But she *loved* it. She wanted to kiss him again.

His kiss was poison but she was addicted to it from the very first sip.

Miraya crouches down under the shower and screams. Why is this so hard? She can't breathe, she can't think, she can't even function properly.

Tears roll down her cheeks. Sobs wrack through her body. The cold water tries to wash her worries away but it's no help. The water is not cold enough to drown out the hotness of her tears because it is all she can feel. It is not cold enough to freeze her nerves and her brain so that she could never think again.

"Miraya?" A voice from the door.

Miraya slaps her palms against her mouth to trap her loud sobs. Her shoulders fall up and down. They quake as she tries to calm herself down.

"Miraya? Are you in there? Are you okay?"

Ranav.

He is worried. She has to answer him or his worry will turn into fear.

Miraya flips the shower off and dries herself. Her hands are shaking and the tears don't look like they're going to stop.

"Miraya, if you aren't answering, I'll have to call Daksh."

"Coming," she chokes out, wrapping the towel over her wet hair. It doesn't stay. It keeps unravelling and she gets frustrated. Throwing on her t-shirt and shorts, she slowly opens the door. Her hair is dripping wet. Her cheeks too. She is a mess.

Ranav is sitting on the edge of her bed, tapping his foot impatiently. He stops at the sight of her and his eyes soften into genuine concern.

"Oh, Miraya," he says, standing in front of her in two quick strides. "Come here."

She stays still, her eyes down. She is so lost. Looking up and meeting Ranav's eyes is hard. Wrapping a towel around her hair is hard. Thinking of Shray is hard. *Everything* is hard. She wants a temporary break from life. Somewhere she can do nothing, her brain and body void, just floating idly in the air all day.

Because, at this moment, it's too much.

Miraya doesn't know where to start.

Ranav pulls her into a hug. He pats her shoulders in a steady rhythm and tightens his arms around her as if she can squeeze out all the pain inside her.

"Why are you here?" Miraya asks.

"I came to pick up Daksh's laptop. She said you would be home. I bought lasagna on the way so I thought I'd let you know. You were in the shower but I heard screams. I was scared, Miraya."

"I'm sorry," she mumbles.

"You don't have to be sorry for anything. At least you vented it out. It helps."

Miraya wraps her arms around him.

"Please don't tell Daksh. I don't want her to worry about me. She already has a lot on her plate."

Ranav doesn't agree immediately. "Miraya, I have to know if it's something you can handle on your own. Because if you need help and you're shutting us out because you think it would be trouble for us, then I can't. I have to tell her. She is your bestfriend. I can't do that to her."

Miraya wipes her tears on his shoulders and shakes her head. "No, I can definitely handle it. I can."

"And if you need any help, whether venting out, or someone to listen, advice or help —"

"I'll let you two know."

Ranav pulls away and wipes her tears. "Get some sleep. It will help you clear your mind. And don't starve yourself. I'll put the lasagna in the fridge. Heat it up later and have it. Okay?"

"I promise."

Ranav smiles and ruffles her hair. "Sleep, Miraya."
She takes his advice to heart.

Chapter 19

❤

It's after seven in the evening. Miraya is on her bed, a bowl of lasagna licked clean sitting on her bedside table. She is trying to sleep but she is mentally incapable of it.

Miraya pulls out her phone. The light flashes on her face, making her squint and distance the phone away from herself. She clicks on Shray's contact and the keyboard pops up. Her fingers hover over those twenty six letters, trying to find the best combination of them to start the conversation.

Hey.

Backspace.

You awake?

Backspace.

Can we talk?

Pause. A deep breath. Send.

Miraya chews on her lips as she waits for Shray to respond. Staring at her phone, waiting for texts and refreshing her notification box every minute is something she hasn't done in years. It's a strange and foreign feeling to keep waiting on someone, praying the message turns 'read' as soon as possible. But she does it anyway.

Three minutes pass but for Miraya it feels like three hours. The three dots appear on his side of the chat and her ankles cross in anticipation.

Yes.

One word. He typed those three letters for such a long time.

Can we meet? She sends.

Now?

Yes.

Where?

Miraya thinks. Shray can't be seen in obvious places and they need some peace and quiet to untangle the mess of feelings. A place comes to her mind.

The ground we used to go for our morning practice?

Okay. Be there in twenty. Fine with you?

The conversation is so formal and awkward that Miraya wants to run away.

Yes.

Just as she is about to exit the messaging app, her eyes pause on Shray's profile picture. It's an image of him and his brother Vidyuth against the backdrop of lush green tea estates. Shray has Vidyuth in a headlock and his brother looks at him from below. Both of them have wide grins plastered on their faces. Miraya zooms in on Shray's face. There is light in his eyes. Something that wasn't there when she last met him.

Shaking her head as if that will dissolve all the conflicted thoughts inside her brain, she puts on her sweater, exchanges her shorts for her jeans and walks out of her room with her car keys. Dakshina isn't home yet so she locks the door and runs to her car.

The public ground that they were meeting in was the ground Shray and Miraya had practised in every morning. Sometimes Vidyuth joined them during their morning runs. Suriya was a lazy bum so he wasn't very consistent with his practice. He would show up once in a while. Most of the time it was only them. It was the place where Miraya and Shray used to talk a lot. They talked about their class and their families, discussed secrets, vented out to each other, cracked jokes and made a lot of memories. She remembers the time Shray tried to do a push up with her sitting on him. He'd managed three before he had cursed and pushed her off him.

No one would be there at this time of the day so it was a safe place to talk their feelings out without being self-conscious.

She parks the car and walks up to the steps to wait for him there. When the chilly air greets her with a generous welcome, she shivers. The sweater won't do it. It's *not enough*, she thinks. *She should have worn the black jacket.* Huffing and blowing on her hands, she sits on the cement steps, hoping her butt won't freeze off.

Time is ticking. Twenty minutes gone. No sign of Shray.

Thirty minutes. She can feel the iciness bite her skin.

Thirty-five minutes. She decides to go back to her car.

Thirty-six minutes. A black car parks itself next to hers.

Shray hops out and sees her standing next to the steps like a loner, shivering in the cold. "You waited *outside*?" he asks, hinting at how stupid she had been to do so.

"Yes."

"You should've waited in the car."

"I was going to now." She didn't meet his eyes. "I thought I could manage it because someone said twenty minutes." Miraya shouldn't be talking about punctuality but unintentionally, the words slip out in bitterness.

"Got caught up in traffic," he mumbles, stepping closer to her and removing his jacket. Shray drapes it over her shoulders and pulls it close so that it hugs her snugly. His fingers brush her palms and he pulls back immediately. "Shit, you're freezing."

Shray takes her hand like nothing ever happened between them. He sandwiches them in between his palms and rubs it to thaw the coldness. All Miraya can do is stare at him.

He is beautiful under the moonlight. His dark hair falls against his forehead in adorable curls, his eyes glazed with shine, his nose pink from the cold and his lips almost red. She guesses he must've been chewing his lips all day long. Like her.

Shray is a dream. No wonder every girl wants him for herself.

He blows on her hands and ushers her to go back to the car. But she shakes her head. Miraya wants to walk with him.

She stuffs her hands into the pockets of his jacket and tips her chin towards the open ground. He understands.

"So..." he begins.

"I just want to figure out why you didn't tell me you loved me all this while," Miraya says, not beating around the bush.

Shray sighs. "I wanted to. So many times. Every second I was with you, I wanted to."

"But why didn't you?"

He rubs his forehead. "Miraya, what would have changed if I had told you?"

She whips her neck to the side to look at him. "Everything, Shray. Everything. I loved you back then too. I loved you so much that I thought I would go crazy."

"Why didn't you tell me then?" Shray crosses his arms across his chest.

"Because I thought you weren't interested in me like that. I was worried that if I told you, we would drift away. You know you were the most important person in my life. I couldn't risk it," Miraya says.

His finger taps the air in front of her. "Exactly why I didn't tell you as well. There's no pointing in blaming each other for what could've happened. I guess we were both good at hiding our feelings." Shray shrugs. "It doesn't matter. It's not too late, Miraya. It's never too late. We could be together now. If only you wouldn't push me away."

Miraya shakes her head. "It's not that easy, Shray. And..." she swallows the rock in her throat, "I don't want to be with you. I don't love you anymore."

"Oh, please, Miraya. The way you kissed me —"

"It was the heat of the moment. I couldn't think straight. It just happened. Just because I kissed you doesn't mean I have feelings for you, Shray. You're not that good of a man."

He laughs. Almost a scoff. "Oh, wow. Now are we rating each other's morality and goodness?"

"Don't make this funny. It's not. I just came here to tell you that I acknowledge and respect and understand your feelings for me but I cannot reciprocate it. I don't feel for you that way," Miraya says.

"Miraya, if you want time, you can have it. I'll gladly wait. Don't reject the idea of us altogether. It isn't fair."

"You don't talk about what's fair and unfair, Shray. What —" She catches herself before she can utter another word that will open a doorway for her past. "The point is, I can't do this because I don't have feelings for you anymore."

"Are you seeing someone else?" The apprehension in his voice is quite evident. For a second, Miraya considers saying she is seeing someone else and if he asked, she could just say it's Kishore. Because Shray knows him and has watched her weep so openly when he was hurt, it would be all the more convenient. Kishore is in Germany now and Miraya can say they are in a long-distance relationship. They cannot meet each other even if Shray demands it.

The deceptive story spins in her mind so quickly, clearly, considering all possible threats and offering solutions to each. That is how her brain has been trained to react to such a situation. All these years, whenever she is met with some situation or question she doesn't know the answer to or doesn't want to be honest with, the lies slip out of her lips effortlessly. It's become a habit. A habit she isn't consciously controlling.

But this time, with Shray, she catches herself before lying. Her lies won't work on Shray. No matter how perfectly they are spun and crafted, with his mysteriously beautiful dark eyes, he could see right through her like she was a sheet of glass.

"No. I am not seeing someone. And I don't want to be seeing you."

Shray takes her hands. "Miraya." Just her name. Her heart sings at the sound of it. "Miraya, please. I love you. I love you so so much. I can't escape it. I think about you every single day. I wish that you are happy every single day. I want to be with you, Miraya. I want to hold your hands whenever I want to, press them to my chest so you can feel my heart and watch your face when you realise it is beating for you."

Miraya's palm rests against his chest. She can feel his heart. She knows it wants her more than anything. Her lips part but there isn't a word that comes out. "I want to press my lips on your knuckles, kiss your fingertips and trace the lines on your palm. I love you so much, Miraya. Please don't do this to me. Give me a chance."

Tears. She feels tears trickling down her cheeks and she doesn't know what it is for. Is it because she has finally heard the words she has most yearned for in her life or is it because she has to forget these beautiful words were ever uttered and let him go?

"I'm sorry," she whispers. "I'm so sorry, Shray."

Miraya's heart breaks when she sees his face. It's so torn and helpless, like the world has turned an ugly grey and the cement is melting, running like water, and every brick is falling apart, crashing down.

"Why?" His voice is so pained, wounded and parched.

"I just can't."

Shray doesn't say anything else. The silence is deafening, so loud that it eats away her sanity.

"You don't have to worry about the article. I won't let personal feelings interfere in my work," Miraya says and with that she is turning around and walking back to her car.

She takes one last look at him, standing in the empty, barren field, like the world has given up on him. She stifles the throaty sob that climbs her throat with a whimper and reverses her car out of the ground.

Only when she is back in her apartment and Dakshina compliments her new jacket, she realises that she'd forgotten to return it to him.

And when Miraya cries herself to sleep, the smell of his jacket envelops her in a selfless hug, something she never knew she craved.

Chapter 20

Not a week later, Miraya's life falls apart.

It is humiliating enough to have a picture of yourself broadcasted without your knowledge. It is *mortifying* to have your picture circulated among others and commented on. But what happens to Miraya is worse.

A picture of Miraya and Shray being intimate with one another is stamped on every entertainment headline in the state. There is one of Shray draping his jacket over her shoulders, one with her hands pressed to Shray's chest, one with Shray kissing her hand. She feels invaded, insecure and destroyed. She isn't stepping out of her room. Her phone is blaring with calls, most of it from Shray and the rest from *Amma.*

Her life is ruined. All over again.

If the pictures were blurry and vague, she could have easily come up with lies stating that it wasn't her. She could have asked Shray's PR team to not put a name to the face next to him. But her face is vivid, as if shot in broad daylight.

As if that's not embarrassing and life-threatening enough, Shray's fans were quick to match her face with her name only to find out she was the one who had written the article about Shray and Ria's friendship. They are linking up one another, spinning cute romantic history between them or making up nonsense stories of how they met.The article she had written is blowing up, bigger than before. MIRROR is calling her. Fiya and Mrs Nandhini are calling her. Kishore is calling her, no doubt having heard about it from Dakshina. Dakshina and Ranav are taking turns to convince her door to open up.

Everything is a mess. A fucking mess.

She wants to run away.

The knocking on the door stops.

"Miraya, you better open the door or I am breaking this down." *Amma.* She is here. She is furious. Miraya cannot face her again.

"Aunty, please. Let me talk to —"

"Dakshina, you don't have any idea what is happening, do you? She just uprooted what's left of our family's dignity by getting herself photographed in the night with an actor. Do you even know what that means for us? No one will ever want to willingly propose marriage to her. Because now, the whole world knows she is the type of person to spend late nights with men. They know she is having an affair with an actor. Who will ever volunteer to marry her now?"

"But still, Aunty. Miraya is hurting. She clearly didn't know —"

"You stop talking, *kanna.* I know all about you. This won't seem like a big deal to you because you are used to fooling around with men. I know what kind of woman you are. We are not from that kind of a family."

There is not a word from Dakshina after what Amma says.

"No one cares about your opinion of Dakshina. I am her fiance and I know her and love her for what she is. That's all will ever matter," Ranav says.

Miraya closes her eyes. Amma is making things worse. She is hurting Dakshina and Ranav. Because of her.

"No one taught you to speak to your elders with respect?" Amma asks.

"I have no respect for someone who treats the woman I love the way you did," Ranav retorts.

"How dare —"

Miraya opens the door. "Stop it, Ma. I know you are angry but you have no right to insult my friends."

Amma glares at her. "You have no right to talk. You are the one creating problems everywhere you go."

Something bubbles inside Miraya. Like lava inside a volcano ready to burst. She wants to open her mouth and scream that it's not her fault. That she didn't do anything wrong. She was twenty-five years old, for fuck's sake.

But Miraya cannot.

She keeps quiet. She suppresses the anger inside her. Shoves it deep so it can never surface.

"You are not staying here anymore. Let's go home," Amma says and walks out. Appa is standing outside her apartment, devastated. He is the picture of disappointment and regret. Regret for leaving Miraya out of sight.

At that moment, Miraya knows that she is going right back into that cage.

The trip back home is painful. Miraya hasn't endured such a torturous silence in her life before, not even when she got yelled at in the Principal's room.

Appa takes a seat on the sofa. *Amma* sits next to him, a hand on his shoulders. Both of them are tired, the lines on their faces more prominent than ever. *Appa* hasn't dyed his hair recently so only the tip of the strands are black. Grey climbs up the roots.

He looks at his wife and then shakes his head as if he has no idea what to do anymore. Miraya is ashamed even though she didn't do anything wrong. She wants to kick herself for even suggesting the idea of meeting at night, in a public place. She should have driven to Shray's house at least. Miraya should've pulled her hand away when Shray took it. She shouldn't have accepted his jacket. She should've checked if someone else was using the ground at that time.

Should've, should've, should've. So many excuses.

"What were you thinking?" *Amma* starts. "This is why I didn't like it at all when you wanted to major in journalism. Once you step into the media, things like these are bound to happen. Your *Appa* was the one who supported you and it was because he wanted you to study whatever you wanted to. Look where that led to. You just destroyed our reputation overnight."

Reputation. Reputation. Reputation.

In this country, the scales tipped differently. Men who cooked deserved a trophy of self-sufficiency but women who worked deserved a slight to the status of the family. Speaking fluently in a foreigner's language won you more beaming smiles than speaking in your own native tongue. Wealth was greater than happiness. Shame stung more than loss. Greed was more a powerful fuel than the pricking needle of conscience.

But above all stood the damned reputation.

People feared a stain on their public image more than the weight of the truth itself. *What will others think of me?* was the constant, never-ending and *never-tiring* question cycling through each person's mind. They were terrified of others thinking of them as poor, incapable and pitiful. They did everything they could to iron out the creases on their image, polish it with just the right amount of— if not more— showcases of well-being and see the glitter of great family prestige wink at them.

Reputation ruled the minds of people. Over humanity. Over kindness. Over sincerity. Over love.

Because what people perceived and were made to perceive was a wicked game everyone was caged in. And there was no way out.

Miraya's sick of it.

But Miraya doesn't say a word against her. She knows it will equal to adding oil to the flame.

"From when is this going on? Between you and Shray. I thought both of you weren't in touch."

"We're not. In a relationship, I mean. And I met him for work and we got to talk. I was only helping him," Miraya says, regretting ever agreeing to help in the first place.

"Don't lie to me!"

"Ma! I am not lying."

"It doesn't look like you two are friends. Which friend touches you, kisses your hand and meets you in the dark?"

Miraya sighs. "It's a long story."

"What? I won't understand? Is it too complicated? Well, make me understand, no? Make it simple."

Miraya's eyes fall shut and she shakes her head. What was happening between Shray and Miraya wasn't an easy knot to remove and be done with it. It was a mess. It can't be put down into words. It is too hard to even process it. She can never make her parents understand.

"Everyone has seen you with him. Tell me. Who is going to marry you now? Huh? He is touching you in the picture. Out in the open at dark. The whole world has seen it."

Only silence from Miraya's side. And a few unabashed tears.

"Do you think Shray will marry you? You know how men are. Women are like clothes to them. They'll wear it one day and throw it aside another day. It's so easy for them. But for women, you're thrown away for life. Your reputation goes. Your life gets ugly. What were you thinking, huh? You are twenty-five years old and don't you know the consequences of your actions?" Amma chides, giving her a stare that says *if you weren't my daughter you'd be dead.*

Silence lingers again. Miraya's legs are aching from standing but she won't dare sit down. Pain is good.

"Why not?"

Miraya's eyes shoot up from the puddle of tears on the floor.

The words were from Appa. It was the first time he said something after the disaster.

"What do you mean by why not?"

"Why won't Shray marry her? They love each other. They have known each other for a long time. And we've known him since childhood. He is from a good family," *Appa* says.

"But...he is an actor, dear."

The way she says the word actor makes Miraya wince. It's so natural to admire and laud an actor's performance and looks when you watch them on the screen. But when you see them as a fellow human being, you tend to attribute the worst qualities to an actor.

Drinking. Smoking. Women. Arrogance. Media. Exposure. Publicity.

As if other men don't have these qualities at all.

"So what? Your daughter is in the media too. Let them do whatever they want. Once she is married, she will be his problem."

The fact that the words come out of her father's mouth shatters Miraya. Appa was her everything when she grew up. He was her hero. He was her role model. He was her rockstar.

Now he has lost hope in her. He has given up on her.

"But..."

"Talk to Shray's family. If they are okay with it, let's get the engagement done secretly. You can tell our relatives that since he is an actor, we wanted to keep it quiet. This won't be a problem if they're engaged."

"*Appa*, we aren't —"

"You can get married whenever you want after that. But this is the only way to salvage your life and our family's reputation."

With that sharp answer, *Appa* stands up and disappears into his room.

Chapter 21

The air is thick with tension. There's no room to breathe.

"Ma..." Miraya's broken voice comes, slicing through the tension in an attempt to receive understanding.

"Don't talk to me. Whatever your *Appa* said is the right thing to do. I have to call Shray's mother at once —"

Amma's phone rings. She sees the caller ID and her eyes widen. "It's Mala."

Shray's mother.

Miraya's heart feels like it's standing on the edge of a cliff, an inch away from plummeting to its death.

This is really happening. Miraya's mother and Shray's mother are going to have a talk about marrying off their children. Her and Shray.

This can't happen. *This can't happen.*

Amma puts the phone on speaker.

"Revathi, how are you? How is your husband?" Shray's mother asks. Her voice is chirpy and bright. It makes Miraya's stomach coil.

"I am fine, Mala. Jeevan is fine too. We are just dealing with a lot right now."

"Oh, I understand. Miraya and Shray didn't tell us about their relationship at all. I mean, how unfair is this? We got to know about them through the media as if we are some third person to them. I am so bummed they didn't feel like they could tell us about their relationship. Shray tells me everything, you know. He says I'm his best friend. And yet, he hid this from me. I didn't expect this at all."

Amma replies with a nervous chuckle. "Yes, yes."

Miraya has always felt a little jealous of Shray because of his parents. He had the best relationship with them. They were so understanding, being married by love themselves. Independence and freedom were perfectly balanced in Shray's life.

She knows it's wrong to compare her parents and his. But every time something like this happens, Miraya can't help but do it and feel so bad for herself.

"I wanted to talk to Miraya. I rang her but she didn't pick up the call. So, I naturally had to call you."

"Actually, Mala, we were just discussing that."

Miraya falls to her knees next to her mother and shakes her head. *Please, no,* she begs silently. *I can't get married to him.*

All she receives in return is a helpless nod. *Amma* switches off the speaker option and walks off to her room so that Miraya can't intervene.

She clenches her jaw to keep the sobs away but the action only brings more tears to her eyes. Miraya plops on the sofa and hides her face in her palms. How is any of this possible? She had gone to meet Shray to put an end to whatever feelings and confusion remained between them, not to grow them into something more. She was the unluckiest human being on the planet. It was as if the universe was plotting against her to make her life miserable than it already is. Whatever she didn't want, she was granted generously. Whatever she wanted, she was given but with a horrifying catch that again became a worry. How excruciatingly unfair is this? What did she do to deserve this treatment?

Nothing in her life is going according to her plan. Nothing. The one thing she had wanted out of her life was Shray and now he is *everywhere*. Work, family, relationships, friends, love. Every part of her life had Shray involved in it.

How come there was no trace of him in her life for all these years and suddenly, as if planned, he appears everywhere all at once?

Amma steps into the living room again. "Shray's family is more than glad to have you married to their son. They say he doesn't have a better match."

No, no.

Miraya remembers all the times she'd visit Shray's house and Mala Aunty would comment that she'd be the happiest person in the world if Miraya ended up becoming her daughter-in-law. At that time, though Miraya faked objection and claimed Shray and her were best friends for life, the idea seemed so right and good on the inside. Young Miraya had thought it was a dream to marry Shray. But now, everything has changed. Even though she has feelings for Shray, it would be a self-inflicted struggle to marry him after he had stabbed her in the back.

"But they can't make decisions for Shray so they will discuss with him and get back to us. I'm sure he will agree to it. It's not like marriage affects a male actor's career anyway."

There is a high chance that Shray might actually agree to it. He admitted that he has loved her for eleven years. Why would he ever pass up an opportunity like this?

"I can't marry him," Miraya says. "I *won't*."

Amma rolls her eyes. It makes Miraya so angry. "You should've thought of that before you went and fooled around with him. Is this why you didn't want to move back home? To stay out late with him?"

"Ma!"

Anger flares through Miraya. Her mother's implication in her words is so insulting that she can't take it anymore.

"You will marry him, Miraya. If Shray agrees, they will get back to us. We will fix a date to officially discuss and decide a date for your engagement as soon as possible."

Miraya knows there's no point arguing with her mother.

She has to talk to Shray.

Miraya grabs her bag and storms out of her house.

As soon as she is in her favourite coffee shop, she digs through her bag for her phone and immediately calls Shray.

"Oh thank goodness, Miraya. I've been calling you since morning," Shray says, annoyance and relief fighting for control in his voice. "I am so sorry you got dragged into my shit. You don't deserve this. You don't know how much I regret it. It's my fault. I am so sorry, Miraya."

"It's not your fault. It's mine. I asked you to meet me outside when I shouldn't have hesitated to meet you at your house. I should have known which one was the bigger risk," Miraya says, her anger and frustration about her situation at home easily taking a backseat. The concern and panic in Shray's voice makes her want to comfort him. Both of them were victims here. She was sure he must be having a tough time too. Two scandals in a row? That's a big blow to his reputation.

"All I could think of when you called me was to see you and talk to you. I didn't think of anything else so it's my fault."

"I actually did think of it, you know. But I assumed no one would be using the field at that hour. I didn't even bother to check. I am so sorry."

Shray sighs. "I think we'll be owning up to this blunder forever if we continue this."

"Yeah, you're right." Miraya was chewing her lip at a pace she never has before.

"Miraya?"

"Yes?"

"I want to see you so badly."

Miraya closes her eyes shut. She wants to see him too. At times like this, Miraya wonders if her mind and her heart will always remain at war. When will they ask for the same thing? When will she not have to weigh the pros and cons of everything she wants, think and overthink repeatedly and tire herself out trying to make the right choice?

"I want to meet you as well. There are things we need to discuss and I'd prefer to do it directly. But wouldn't it be too risky?" she asks meekly.

"I can slip out of my house. We just need a safe place where we will be undetected."

Miraya thinks. It wouldn't be too long for the media to sniff out her apartment and her parent's house. Her phone was already filling up with emails and messages asking her for an interview. The only other places she can think of is Ranav's place and Fiya's home. Fiya has been looking after her grandmother all by herself because her mother is on a Europe trip so she can't trouble her. That leaves Ranav.

"I think I know a place. Can I get back to you?"

"Yeah, sure."

Ranav immediately offers to let them meet at his house. He gives her instructions as to where the spare key is as he has work. Miraya cries a million thank yous to him but he shushes her.

She sends the location of Ranav's house to Shray and takes an auto rickshaw there with one thing in her mind.

This marriage cannot happen.

<h1 style="text-align:center">Chapter 22</h1>

♥

Miraya doesn't know how Shray manages to slip out of his house but he reaches the spot a short while after her. He is in a muddy brown hoodie that says *Out of Coverage* and Miraya laughs inwardly at how relatable it was to the situation at hand. Shray pairs that with denim shorts which falls upto his knees. His legs are hairless and smooth, glistening under the sunlight.

"Miraya."

She tears her gaze away quickly.

"How is the situation at home?" he asks, as he removes his shoes at the door.

Ranav's house is double-storied with interiors that don't stick to a strict colour palette. There are paintings of the sea on two walls — blue and white waves pounding the rocks on the one behind the wall-mounted TV and a beach scene on the other. Ranav's sister is an artist who sells customized paintings so Miraya suspects she might be the creative hands behind the artwork on the wall.

"It is really bad. You must know. Your Mom must have spoken about it to you."

Shray sits on the pastel-blue couch and Miraya sits right next to him, one of her ankles under her thigh.

"Yeah. I am sorry. My mother is excited about this idea. To be honest, she has been excited about getting us married from when we were kids," Shray says.

"I know."

"So... what are you going to do?" he asks, curious but nervous black eyes looking up at her.

"I honestly don't know. I don't want to get married."

"Right now? Or to me?"

Miraya doesn't say anything. She doesn't know the proper technique to tell him that he was her problem.

Shray's eyes look like they've lost a war. Miraya hates this look on him. It doesn't feel right with her. She feels this uncontrollable urge to engulf him in a hug and say it was going to be alright.

But she had no right to when she was the one hurting him.

"It's okay. I understand," he says.

"What about the situation on your side?" Miraya quickly changes the topic.

"Thankfully, people have decided to drop the idea that Ria and I are in a relationship and that I caused her to split with Vinay. They've accepted that both of us are dating and have been at it since school." Miraya raises her eyebrows at that. "A lot of our school pictures were shared by an anonymous source," Shray explains.

"Bet it's some money-digging asshole from our class," Miraya mutters.

Shray smiles. Miraya catches that and for a second she feels happy that she made him smile.

"You have no idea how fast these people are when it comes to snooping around others' lives. Did you know we are trending on Twitter? They call us Miray."

"You checked?"

"Don't blame me. I root for us too, you know," Shray says, punctuating it with a grin. Miraya wants to rip her shallow heart and throw it out. "But anyway, my PR team thinks the news of us dating is doing me more good because the spotlight on me has become positive. There is also a rumor that you are doing a cameo in Room No 3."

"What?"

"Yeah. Apparently there's a photoshopped picture of us together on set circulating around."

"Can't you or your team make an official statement that the rumors are false?"

Shray shakes his head. The black waves on his head also move along his forehead. "I told you. My team thinks it's a good promotion for the movie. They want us to keep at it."

"Dating?"

"Yes."

Miraya rubs her temples with her fingers, feeling the headache creep in. "We are in so much shit," she says with a loud, defeated breath.

"So... what should I tell my mother about our marriage?"

"That is what I wanted to talk to you about," Miraya says, sitting back up straight. "You have to stop this marriage, Shray."

He pauses and then whispers, "Do we really have to?"

"Shray..."

"Come on, Miraya. We'll be great together. Look at this as a sign to consider the possibility of us."

Miraya closes her eyes shut. She rests her head on her hand.

I know! she wants to scream. *I know we'll be great together.*

Miraya had envisioned them getting married so many times and they were all happy dreams. She knew that with Shray she would be loved and understood. And yet, the wound in her chest is not ready to heal. It's barring her from flinging her arms around him and never letting go.

"I'm sorry, Shray. I can't do this."

Shray leans back against the couch harshly, letting out an exasperated sigh. There is a helpless look on his face that is painful to watch. His hands are running through his hair and his lips are pushed slightly to the side as he chews on the insides of his cheek.

"Okay, now what do you want me to do?" His tone makes her wince.

"I— I want us to break up."

He raises his eyebrows as if to ask if she understands herself.

"My parents want both of us to be engaged as soon as possible. You have to tell your parents that it can't happen immediately. You can use me as an excuse. Say that I want this engagement to be a very private affair and amidst the chaos and the rumours now, it won't be possible now. So ask them to postpone it. My parents will consider if your parents talk to them."

Shray shifts slightly closer to her. "Then?"

"We will pretend to date as much as we can between your busy schedules so no one is suspicious. My parents might become more understanding of the situation as time passes so by then, we will fake a big argument, blame each other for it, cause a scene and break up."

"Something is not adding up."

"The break up should be something significant. What I accuse you of should make my parents think that you are not the right guy for me and it should make them hate you. That will make it easier for me to convince them to call off this arrangement. You can also cook up a story and make me the villain to convince your parents that I won't make you happy. We will go our separate paths after that. I know this isn't the best plan but this is all I can come up with. "

"When did you learn to lie and scheme like this?" he asks.

That question hits her like a spear to her heart. Miraya wasn't ashamed that she lied her way through life to get what she wanted. She has accepted it and gotten used to it. But the question coming out of Shray's mouth out of all feels like someone is twisting a knife in her wound, cutting her up again.

"Is— is this okay with you? Are you in?" Miraya's voice shakes with something unknown to her but she manages to keep her calm.

"What's in it for me?"

Miraya frowns. "What do you mean?"

"Why should I do this? Play along in your little skit?"

"Funny how you ask that with so much judgement when acting is literally your job."

Shray rolls his eyes. "The whole thing caters to benefitting you and only you. What's in it for me, Miraya?"

"Do you want to be married to a woman who didn't choose you as her husband? Do you want to destroy her life and yours?" Miraya shoots back.

"It's not appealing enough for me to commit to your request," Shray says dismissively, making Miraya more irritated by the second. "I don't care if it's you who is destroying my life."

"What do you want then?"

Shray grins as if he has heard the words he had craved all along. "Two things. One, date me publicly so that it helps my promotion. Two, promise me that you'll give me a chance. Give us a chance."

Miraya shakes her head immediately. "No. No way."

Shray weaves his fingers together and rests it on top of his knees. "Then, the deal is off."

"But... this is too much. I clearly told you I can't —"

"I'll play by your rules when you play by mine, Miraya."

She wants to punch his shoulders for being so clever and aggravating at the same time. Giving them a chance is a sure shot way to strengthen her feelings and make her fall irrevocably in love with him. There is only so much self-control she has. Encouraging the idea of them isn't a good idea. Nor is appearing in public together.

But to escape this marriage, this was the only way. She can't mess this up.

Miraya didn't want to lie to Shray at all but he is adamant on making it difficult for her. So, she makes her best genuine face, the one conveying defeat and sincerity at the same time. "Okay. The deal is on."

Chapter 23

♥

It took two more days for Shray to convince his parents and for them to convince Miraya's parents to delay the engagement. Begrudgingly, everyone understood that their engagement ceremony cannot be done anytime soon. This loosened the tight grip Miraya's parents have on her.

The people at MIRROR have been treating her differently. There are whispers near the pantry, discussions about her lucky love life across bathroom stalls and subtle glances chasing after her. Miraya can't comprehend if the others know she can hear them and feel their attention on her and if they are doing it purposely to rile her up. Because Miraya wasn't the sweetest person in her workplace who strived to please everyone. She had a lot of underground enmity and rivalry going on between a few of her colleagues beneath thick skin and fake smiles.

Her apparent love life being broadcasted on every media source was like hitting the lottery for them.

Especially Shree.

"I heard Grace Ma'am saying that when Miraya was interviewing Shray, she took a very long time and they were alone. The night before, both Shray and Miraya weren't there at the resort." Pause to giggle like an amateur hyena. "And Miraya was late the day of the interview. Maybe something happened," she whispered to Midhuna while Miraya was next to the printing machine.

How conveniently they had forgotten that Fiya was there with her during the interview. As time passed, Miraya only wanted to laugh at how ridiculous the stories turned out.

The only person who didn't make a comment was Fiya. She didn't even talk to her. There were occasional smiles and information spat out about assignments and articles but there was not a word more than that.

Miraya guessed that it might be because Fiya felt betrayed that she hadn't shared the details of her relationship with her when she was very open about hers with Ashraf. The only reason Miraya didn't tell her was because whatever was between Miraya and Shray was too complicated to put in words. She didn't want to lie to Fiya because Miraya trusted that girl like she did Dakshina. The problem was that she wasn't ready to explain it again.

Miraya owed Dakshina and Ranav an explanation because she was using his home to meet Shray from time to time. It was their hideout for the moment. But Miraya couldn't bring herself to recall the events that happened in school. She had vaguely hopped around it, only mentioning that Shray had betrayed her and that was what made her parents strict.

They didn't prod into it much and Miraya was grateful for it. She explained what happened from the moment she first met Shray in seven years.

"Shit. Here I was, asking you to beg Kishore to be your boyfriend when you had a whole ass dramatic love story going on with Shray Nivas. Fucking hell," Dakshina said. "I can't believe I was such a dumbass roommate. How did I not sniff that out?"

Ranav shushed her. But Miraya was more impressed with the fact that Dakshina understood why she hadn't told her about it. She wasn't angry that she had hid it from her.

"But come on, I would have cooked you Italian double the times if I knew you were going through so much heartache, you bitch."

Dakshina, Ranav and Miraya stayed up the whole night talking about her and moving on to lighter discussions. At four in the morning, when their eyes were fighting against sleep, they were talking about how cartoons in their childhood were so much better than the shit kids were watching these days. They fell asleep mid-conversation, Dakshina and Ranav cuddled in the right side of the bed while Miraya curled up in the left.

She had taken an off the next day and stayed at home, playing video games with Dakshina and baking strawberry cupcakes.

Now, she is licking off the icing that sticks to the bowl she had refrigerated her cupcakes in. That's when Shray calls.

"Yeah?"

"What are you doing?" he asks.

"I took a day off today. I baked cupcakes," Miraya says.

"Let me guess, chocolate chip?"

"Nah. Strawberry."

"Last I remember, you weren't a big fan of strawberries."

Miraya swipes the last bit of icing and puts it in her mouth. "Yeah, but I developed a liking for it. Dakshina loves strawberries so I had no choice."

Miraya and Shray had long phone calls, getting to know each other all over again in case there came a situation in which they had to prove their love or some shit. Dakshina had snatched the phone and introduced herself to him the previous day and ever since then they have become best friends.

It was unbelievable that only a few months back Dakshina was begging her for his autograph because now they were calling each other *Bro*.

"What are you upto?" Miraya asks, balancing her phone on her shoulders and rinsing off the sparkling clean but sticky bowl.

"I had a meeting with my team about a new ad campaign. They asked if I could rope you in but I said no. You aren't interested, right?"

The bowl falls from her hand with an annoying clang. "Hell no!"

Shray chuckles. "I thought so. They asked me to convince you but I clearly told them that no amount of convincing can make you join the shoot."

"Good. I mean, asking me to be seen with you in public is one thing but this... this is taking it too far," Miraya says, plopping on the sofa. She rests her head on the arm of the sofa and slips her feet under the chequered blanket. "What was the ad anyway?"

"It was for Cafity. That coffee candy."

"Why did they want me?"

"I only skimmed through it. The ad was about a high school couple. It involved one of them slipping them this candy with a note saying *Coffee date?*. I guess they wanted to bring in romance like what Dairy Milk does for their chocolates."

"Ah, cute."

"Because our high school pictures are trending on the internet, using us for the ad would have been quite the jackpot for the company."

"Well, too bad," she says.

"Miraya?"

"Hmm?"

"Did you really mean it when you said you'll give us a chance?"

Miraya stops shaking her legs. She slowly pushes herself up to sit.

"You didn't, did you?" he asks.

"Shray..."

"I am not going to lose you again, Miraya. Not again. I am pretty sure you can fall in love with me again. But it can only happen if you allow yourself to. Everytime I catch you letting go of those inhibitions in your head, you quickly put those walls back up again. You won't tell me what happened or give me anything to work with. I don't know what else to do other than beg."

"Drop this conversation. You don't know what you're talking about."

"That's exactly what I am saying, Miraya. *I don't know.* So, tell me."

"I can't, Shray. I just can't. Will you stop bringing this up again and again?"

He sighs. There is a long pause.

"Okay. I am sorry. But if you ever decide to tell me, even at two in the morning, I'll be ready to hear you out."

Miraya answers with silence.

"And I'll make an alternative request. If giving us a chance is too hard for you, give me your word that you'll allow yourself to open up to me. I need you to at least try because this, the awkward semi-formal conversations we are having right now, is killing me slowly. I want to share things about my day that I know will crack you up, watch you laugh and tease me with that lopsided smile of yours and listen to you talk animatedly with those wild gestures I love. If we can't go back to the way we were, I at least want a part of it back."

Miraya's eyes tear up. She wishes for everything that he said too. But not all wishes come true, does it?

She closes her eyes and that one lone tear slides onto her cheeks. Miraya can't bring herself to say No to him. Not after what she heard.

All he wants is for her to open up. Tear down her walls a little, just a *little* so he could see the surface of what's inside.

Miraya can afford to do that.

"Okay. I will try. But I can't promise you anything."

"That's all I want. You trying."

Chapter 24

♥

"I'm scared, Shray. Can I skip this one?"

"You skipped the three other events I suggested before. My team is not happy, Miraya. We have to be seen together in public. And this is the perfect opportunity because Ria will be there too. If the cameras catch both of you having a fun conversation, it will only strengthen our fake relationship," Shray explains through the phone.

Miraya throws open her closet. "But it's so sudden! I haven't prepared anything and I don't have clothes that are appropriate to wear to a trailer launch event," she says, scrunching her nose at the number of t-shirts, solid-coloured blouses, formal pants and jeans she has. Miraya doesn't invest in party wear since she rarely has a reason for one.

"You don't have to worry about your clothing. I'll take care of it. The question is, can you be there?"

"I can sit back in the audience quietly through the event, right?"

"Yes, and right after the event concludes, Ria, you and I will meet. Sounds okay?"

Miraya doesn't like it. The only person she will know in the event is Shray. Even though she knows he will do anything to make sure she is okay, she can't help but feel anxious about it. It's a different environment. A different world. Miraya is pretty good at conversations but still there is a fear of being judged lodged in the back of her mind.

Last night, she came across a comment stating that Miraya doesn't deserve Shray and she is not even beautiful. Being a part of the media industry, she knows how these audacious comments work. She shouldn't let it affect her. But still, it does. Miraya is a secure person who is aware of her flaws and strengths and views herself as a strong, efficient woman. Comments like these become cracks on her self-confidence and she is worried the comments might make it shatter soon enough.

She can't let Shray know about it. He had specifically asked her not to read comments or any articles related to her and Shray. But she had gone and did just that. She can't let it show that her emotional grit is becoming more of a facade.

"Okay."

"During the event, if anyone recognizes you or surrounds you, don't react or respond to questions. Just make sure you show support to both Ria and me so that in case you are caught on camera, you'll only prove to them that we are tight-knit."

"Shray, what if I mess this up? I don't want to bring you more trouble," Miraya says.

"You won't. I'll be at your place tomorrow noon with the dress. Don't overthink it. Get some sleep. It will all be okay. You'll be amazing."

Somehow, Shray's words calm her down. They give her the exact type of assurance she needs even though he doesn't say anything extraordinary. It's just the usual combination of words thrown carelessly around to make impossible promises. And yet, why do they have so much power over her?

"So... I'll see you tomorrow."

"Yes," Shray says over background chatter. "Did you eat?"

"Yes. Yes, I did. Um, you?"

"I'm going to. Call me if you need anything for tomorrow, okay?"

Miraya's voice simmers down to that of a petted cat. "Okay. Bye."

The next morning, Miraya wakes up before her alarm because she is an anxious bundle of nerves. So many possible embarrassing situations might occur in the event. One slip and it will all be all over the news. If it only harms her, she would close her eyes, bite her teeth and get through it but her mistakes affect Shray as well. She feared she might bring bad publicity.

In fact, Miraya might already be doing so. She accidentally read another comment accusing Shray of having standards that are knee-low.

At noon, she sits in front of the mirror, in her towel, straightening her hair. She hoped the makeup techniques she knew would be enough to make her look at par with the other attendees.

The doorbell rings, signalling Shray's arrival. Miraya wraps Dakshina's bathrobe around herself and answers the door. "Hi," Miraya says, but it comes out as a miserable squeak.

Because what she sees robs away the strength in her voice. Shray looks like he walked out of Hollywood, minus the stereotypes and fake accents. His charming smile takes her breath away but Miraya doesn't mind. She wants to drown in his eyes, his smile and the dimple on his cheeks.

Her eyes run over him. His black suit is tailored to make him a walking thirst trap, fitting him like a glove. Wavy black curls looking glossy on his head. His jawline is perfect.

God help her keep her hands and thoughts to herself.

"Miraya." He chuckles. She wants to drown in his laughter too.

"Huh?"

"You're staring." He says it softly, *fondly*, as if he loves that she is staring at him. The words are like a caress, a gentle hair-tuck behind the ear.

Behind him, a door opens to the opposite apartment and Shilpa Aunty walks out with her trash bag. Miraya's eyes widen when she locks gaze with her and Shray turns around to see what's causing her diversion. Just a second before Shray fully faces Shilpa Aunty, Miraya grabs him by his crisp, shiny and expensive coat and drags him into the apartment.

She shuts the door with a bang.

"Thank God, she didn't see you," Miraya breathes.

"Who is she?" Shray asks, placing a brown bag of brand-new clothes on the couch.

"Shilpa Aunty. The Gossip Aunty of this building. She is always snooping around. Especially after she caught Ranav coming in late at night to the apartment. Also, she spread rumours about both of us being gay couples so Dakshina had practically slapped her with the invitation to her engagement."

"Wow. Did she attend?"

"Of course, not. I would have thrown her out myself if she had come," Miraya says, eyeing his clothes. "I am sorry if I got wrinkles on your suit."

Shray pats the fabric down. "Don't worry about it. Try on the dresses and pick one to wear tonight. You can keep the rest." He tips his chin at the bag.

"How many are in here?" Miraya peeks into it.

"Five. I didn't know if your preference is the same as all those years ago so I took a few guesses and picked out what I thought would look good on you."

Miraya's heart wavers. He has no right to be this sweet.

"Okay. I'll be back soon." Miraya heads to her room. "You can help yourself to some coffee or whatever you want from the kitchen. I think there are a few homemade red velvet cookies in the tin in the top shelf, second row."

"Got it," Shray says, standing up.

"And Shray?" Miraya pauses right before her door and turns around.

"Hmm?"

"You look— um, you look perfect."

Before she can see or hear his reaction, she slips into her room.

The first dress is a wine-coloured A-line dress reaching below her knees with a triangular open cut in the back, exposing her hip. It hugs her in the right places and it makes her look leaner than usual. As she walks out of the room, she thinks she can match it with her favourite pearl earrings.

Shray isn't in the living room. There is noise in the kitchen so she goes there to find him snacking on the chocolate crisps Dakshina is obsessed with. "How is it?" she asks, making Shray turn around.

The crisps in his hand fall down.

Miraya turns to the side and asks, "Yes or No?"

"God, Miranda. You look so fucking beautiful."

Crimson dusts her cheeks. She tries to roll her eyes but the smile on her lips is stubborn. "You aren't allowed to call me that," she says.

"You're my girlfriend. Can't I have a nickname for you?"

Miraya gulps. He says the words like he means every single syllable of it. "*Fake*. Fake girlfriend," she reminds.

"Semantics." He waves her off. "Try the pink one. Pink always looked good on you."

"Why, isn't this nice?" There is a twinge of disappointment in her voice.

He chuckles and steps closer to her. His hands press on her shoulders. "I am scared somebody might steal you away because you are so pretty. Let's try the pink one."

Mirays glares at him. "No. I like this dress. What's wrong with it?"

"Ah, the rebel in you is back. Come on, Miranda. There are so many other events lined up for me to attend. You can always pick this one for later."

Miraya pushes him away. "Other events? I am not stepping out of this house for any other event of yours again. This is the first and last time."

"Fine. Will you just try on that dress?" Shray says, turning her around and pushing her into her room.

"But I will wear that pink one only if I like it. Otherwise, I am wearing this one."

Shray mumbles something and locks the door behind her.

Miraya picks out the cover with the pastel pink one and gasps when she realises what it really is.

A *sari*.

It is a heavy-embroidered pink *sari* with a black velvet full-sleeved blouse. It is the most gorgeous *sari* she has ever seen. Miraya wonders how much it costs.

"It'll take some time!" Miraya calls out to Shray at the other side of the door.

"I know. I'll be waiting."

Miraya can't deny that she is enjoying trialling on beautiful clothes for him. His expressions and his compliments make her feel mushy and confident at the same time.

But to her *amazing* luck as always, the hooks in the blouse are at the back. And she can't fasten more than one hook. The blouse is a little tight on the arms so she can't really twist herself to hook them.

With a sigh, she leaves the blouse on however it is and begins to drape the *sari*. The material is flowy so it is obedient under her fingers. In a few minutes — and with a lot of safety pins — she is done. Now the blouse...

Miraya bites her lip. She obviously needs help with it but she is too hesitant to call Shray. *This isn't what fake boyfriends do for their fake girlfriends!*

But she can't leave the house like this.

"Um, Shray?"

"Yeah, come out, na? I want to see," he says.

Miraya squeezes her eyes close and opens them, exhaling through her teeth.

"I need help," she says. "With the blouse."

Footsteps.

"Can I come in?" His voice is so close. Just outside the door.

Screw this.

Miraya opens the door.

Shray steps in and takes in the room. Then, he looks at her.

"Um, the hooks in the back... can you—"

"Miraya, stop being so shy. It's okay. I would close my eyes if you want but then I can't really help you with the hooks."

Miraya shrugs her shoulders and smiles nervously. "Right. Okay." She turns around.

The worst part is that some twisted part of her brain is regretting not wearing that lacy black bra.

Shray tries not to touch her skin when helping her but the one time his knuckles kiss her skin, feather-light, it sends hot shivers up her body. She presses her eyes close and forces herself not to lean back into him.

He places a hand on her shoulders. "Yup, all done. Are you comfortable?"

"Huh?"

"The sari. Is it comfortable? Are you okay walking in it?"

"Yeah, why?"

He smiles fondly. "The last time I saw you in a sari, you wouldn't move out of your chair at all. You ordered me around all day, remember?"

Oh, she remembers.

"I am used to it now. I like wearing it. And this one is really nice. So beautiful, too," Miraya says, standing in front of the mirror and running a hand across the fabric.

Shray looks at her through the mirror. "Yes, so beautiful."

Miraya is in the front and Shray is behind her, not touching but close enough to feel his presence. She can see him through the mirror. Their gazes meet. Shray takes a step closer, just an inch but that is enough for Miraya to come to her senses and move away from him. "So, how is it?"

"Gorgeous. Do you like it?" he asks, smiling.

Miraya smiles. "I do. I think I'll wear this and save the wine-coloured one for later."

He smirks. "Told you. *For later.*"

Her eyes go wide. "No, that's not what I meant. I just —"

"Chill, it's okay, Miranda. These few slip-ups of yours will keep me going. Don't apologise for that."

With that and a gentle pat on her shoulders, he walks out the door. "Get ready soon. We have thirty minutes."

Chapter 25

♥

Miraya finds herself enjoying the event.

"I have to take a call. I'll be back. Will you be okay?" Sasmitha says, holding her phone to her chest.

"Of course."

Sasmitha nods at her and rushes outside, the phone pressed to her ear. She was Shray's publicist's wife, who offered to accompany her and keep her company throughout the event. She was sweet, with a very feeble voice that was impossible to hear over the roar of the crowd.

From her seat Miraya can see the back of Shray and Ria's head, sometimes huddling close to whisper something to each other. The directors, producers, cinematographers, music directors, lyricists and the other cast members were all seated in the first few rows as a lady anchor hosted the event. She has to give it to the anchor for keeping the audience very entertained and patient till the trailer was screened publicly.

In the chaos of the event, no one has recognised her. Miraya was just another audience with a fairly better seat than the rest.

Applauds fill the air and Miraya watches Shray walk up to the stage. She sits up straight.

Under the fancy lights, Shray shines like the star he is. When he climbs up the stage, he smiles and Miraya's heart flies to him. The twinkle in his eyes and his well-groomed attire makes him swoon-worthy. Miraya hears raging squeals from the audience seated in the deck above her and approves. Shray Nivas is worth all the hype.

The lady on the stage congratulates him as the trailer looks spectacular (it really did) and wishes him the best for the movie. But she traps him with questions about his next movie, his most awaited one yet. Shray confirms that he was indeed working with the popular director alongside a prominent star in the film industry.

"I am really excited to work with both of them. The shooting is scheduled to start next month so that's something I am really looking forward to," Shray says. His suit enhances the gorgeous planes of his shoulders, tailored to be just tight enough to make women drool.

"We heard you are not single anymore. Fans are craving some information about your new relationship directly from you," the lady asks. Okay, now Miraya hates that lady.

For a second, Shray's eyes falls on the side where she is seated and Miraya panics. But he quickly averts his gaze and smiles. "We really wanted to keep things private but because people want a peek into my life so badly, they have taken that liberty away from me. I don't want to bring more attention to it. But I can tell you one thing: I am happy and I am doing well in my life. I am grateful for the love my fans shower me with and the messages I receive everyday. Thank you so much."

After a concluding speech like that, the lady doesn't dig more into the subject or ask new questions. She wishes him and the entire team the best. When Shray walks down the stairs, his eyes find hers. He doesn't smile, scared that he would bring attention to her but she knows the meaning of his gaze. You did well, she mouths. Shray purses his lips to confine the smile edging on his lips and takes his seat.

Ria walks up on the stage and the lady begins making conversation with her. Miraya zones out for a few minutes but her focus draws back in at the question thrown at Ria.

"How was the experience of sharing screenspace with Shray? People are already claiming you have great chemistry."

"Shray is fun. The film has a serious and mysterious tone to it but while shooting, we were always making jokes and laughing. He is one of the sweetest person I have worked with and we have become really good friends. He has been a massive support to me as well and I appreciate it so much. He is almost like a little brother to me."

Miraya hides her grin. No better way that destroying a rumor of a romantic relationship other than naming their bond as that of a sister and brother. It was brutal and honest.

"Do you want to comment about the recent allegations about your divorce?"

Ria scoffs. On stage. Miraya doesn't know where she finds the guts to do that. A sudden respect for Ria blossoms inside her. "Why will I want to? It seems that others know my story better than me these days. I wouldn't ever wish to ruin the people's fun of spinning crooked stories about me, please. And besides, what I have to say isn't going to erase all the slanders posed against me. Why bother, right?"

Ria laughs it off so the spite and anger in her words isn't heavy. The lady laughs with her to break the tension and moves on to the next question.

But Miraya cannot move on. What Ria did was amazing. She scolds herself for ever being angry and jealous of her, even for a second.

The event goes on for another hour. Sasmitha begins to tell the story of her marriage to Shray's publicist and though Miraya could only hear pieces of it, she manages to realise the whole story. She also goes on to tell her that Sasmitha insisted to her husband to not use Miraya as a publicity prop but he didn't take her advice. Miraya says that she has come to terms with the arrangement so it's not a problem anymore. When Sasmitha asks her how Miraya became friends with Shray, Miraya expertly diverts the topic to the event.

When the event is over and the crowd filters out, Miraya stays in her seat and watches Shray interact with the members of their team. With the way he talks casually to most of them she can tell that he has been using a lot of his charm lately. The producers and the directors leave and slowly the other cast members also follow. But Ria and Shray walk towards where Miraya is seated.

"Finally he lets me meet you," Ria says, reaching for a hug. Miraya hugs her back. "He never once mentioned you. With a woman so beautiful as you for his girlfriend, how did he stay quiet, I don't know."

"The topic never really came up," Shray says, joining Miraya. "And it was this beautiful woman's request that I don't go advertising my relationship anywhere. I had to comply." He slides his arm around her waist and pulls her to his side. His fingers graze the bare skin on her hip and she feels her neurons combusting one by one. It shouldn't feel so great but it does.

"But I should have known it wouldn't last," Miraya comments.

"Everything has a downside to it. Stardom is not easy as it looks," Ria sighs. "Sometimes I just want to quit and have a peaceful life in some English countryside."

Miraya smiles empathetically. "But what you said up on stage? I really respect you for that. It isn't easy to be so vocal about the issue. Usually, it is advised to bury the issue and pretend it didn't happen. I am so glad you stood up for yourself."

Ria casts a sideways look at Shray. "I like her."

"It'll only be a surprise if you don't." Shray's eyes meets Miraya's and she knows that every word that spills out his mouth and every action that he does is intentional and real. He means everything. That makes her die a little.

"Alright, lovebirds. I would love to continue this conversation over coffee but I got to run. My niece demands my presence and a bucket of chocolates so I better be on time before she decides I am the bad Aunty," Ria says, looking over at the entrance to nod at her assistant. "Nice meeting you, Miraya. Bye, Shray. Take care."

Ria hugs both of them, leaving her floral perfume on their clothes.

Then, she disappears through the door.

"You think anyone might have caught that on camera?" she asks.

"Look around," he whispers, leaning in closer than usual.

Miraya subtly takes a sweeping glance around and notices a few people videoing them and some whispering to each other, pointing at them. Miraya feels uncomfortable. She wants to hide behind the huge pillar of concrete right before her.

Shray senses it. "I am right here," he says, squeezing her hip a little.

"It's just...so invasive. I feel like I am exposed," Miraya whispers, turning to him. "Does it always feel like that for you?"

Shray smiles and tucks a strand of hair behind her ears. "It does but I got used to it. That's the only way to be unaffected by the cameras."

"Can we leave?"

"There'll be more cameras outside. Will you be okay?"

Miraya bites her lips. Being recorded feels like someone is owning a part of you that you never gave them. It brings back the memories of when the article about Shray and her came out with their personal pictures. She thinks about the people whose private pictures get leaked online, exposing them to thousands of creepy eyes across the world. Miraya feels naked when she is clothed perfectly but what about the people whose nude pictures get circulated online? She can't even imagine how they were feeling.

Shray's publicist calls Shray. Miraya knows she is overthinking and stalling so that she doesn't have to be photographed. "I hate this," she mumbles at last.

"I am sorry, Miranda," Shray says softly. "It'll be quick. You don't even have to look up or glance at the cameras. If you still don't want to do it, then we'll not. It's up to you."

Miraya takes a deep breath. "Will you hold my hand?"

Shray's arm slips from her waist and intertwines with her fingers. "Always."

"Let's go."

<h1 style="text-align:center">Chapter 26</h1>

♥

One thing that Miraya has always remembered about Shray is that he joined her in whatever trouble she got into. In school, Miraya was a nosy person, butting into problems and volunteering solutions for others just because she enjoyed the idea of 'saving' others. In some cases, she didn't get directly involved in the problems and stood as a reliable advisor or support but in some cases she was badly tangled in it.

On the other hand, Shray kept to himself. He only involved himself if something concerned him personally. Like for example, when Miraya got into trouble. At first, she argued against him hopping onto every problem of hers but a few years later, being scolded together became natural.

She remembers this one incident clearly. It happened during eleventh grade.

Miraya had this vicious English teacher who had a case of horrible mood swings. One moment, she would be nice and forgiving and the other, she would be the incarnation of the devil.

Most of the time, Mrs Kavitha had a soft spot for Miraya and Shray. She would often pick them to read out the dialogues in the play and give the class a free hour if Miraya and Shray requested her. English was the one subject Miraya scored well in and Shray did well in every subject so they assumed they were immune from her mood swings and the occasional show of wrath.

But they were wrong.

"Has everyone finished the homework I gave you last Thursday?" Mrs Kavitha asked.

Miraya looked around and then at Sona. "What assignment?" she hissed.

"Character sketch of Prospero and Alonso."

"What? When did she even give this? Was I absent?"

Sona looked unsure. "I think you were there..."

"Shit," Miraya cursed and went back to scanning the class. Everyone was nodding and taking out their sheets to submit. "Shray! You finished?"

Shray stopped flipping his book and stared at her. "Why, didn't you? I sent you a text the day before."

"You send more than twenty texts everyday. You should have sent it in capital letters so that I didn't miss it!" Miraya wanted to pull out her hair. Mrs Kavitha definitely did not look like she was in a good mood that day. There was no way she could shimmy her way out of this.

"Wow, this is what I get for going out of the way and reminding you. Next time, why don't you just ask me to do your assignment?" Shray bit back.

"You will do it?"

"God, Miraya." Shray shook his head at her. "Try talking to her. Maybe you'll get lucky."

Miraya wanted company. It always helped to be yelled at together than alone. Siddh was a perfectionist so there was no way he wouldn't have done it. Sona and Priya went to tuitions together so they would have done finished it. To her bad luck, even that idiot Suriya had a side of the paper written. Even though it was less than *a page, at least he had written something. Miraya had nothing to submit.*

Fisting her hands and propping them on the desk, she stood up guiltily.

"Why didn't you finish the homework, Miraya?" That 'why' scared the shit out of her. The teacher's eyes were rounding in on her, anger already rising slowly inside her. She definitely cannot afford to use the 'I left it at home' excuse. She would be directly sent to the Vice Principal.

"I didn't do it, Ma'am."

"You don't even have any excuses?"

The problem with this question was that it had no correct answer. If Miraya gave excuses, she would be yelled at for not taking responsibility for her actions and making false excuses. If she didn't give excuses and admitted the truth, it would lead to a derogatory remark thrown at her as well. Why bother answering?

Miraya simply lowered her gaze.

"I know you are very capable of completing the homework, easily might I add, but you have become way too lethargic, Miraya. Focusing on extra curricular activities and sports is okay but your marks are the only thing that's going to speak in the end," Mrs Kavitha scolded. Miraya glanced at Shray sideways and caught his discrete snicker. The number of times Miraya had heard that statement in life was innumerous. She always mocked the teachers and joked about it later on with Shray. "You are in your eleventh grade. One more year until you graduate school. It's about time you start becoming serious about your academics."

"Yes, Ma'am. Sorry, Ma'am."

"Get out of the classroom and finish it. Show it to me at the end of the hour."

Miraya glanced at Shray. Beg her, you idiot, *he mouthed.*

"Ma'am please, Ma'am. I'll be careful next time. I'll do it and submit it tomorrow for sure," Miraya tried.

"Get out, Miraya. Don't waste my time."

Miraya bit her jaws and grabbed papers, Shray's pen and her textbook. She walked out of the class. Oh, she was used to being punished but being yelled at to get out of the class in front of Siddh made her feel pathetic. He would probably think Miraya is a dumb girl. Miraya groaned and slid down onto the floor.

A few seconds passed and Miraya picked out the page numbers. All of a sudden, Mrs Kavitha was yelling at someone again. She peeked inside to see who was being blasted and her jaw dropped when she saw Shray at the receiving end, his gaze low.

Another sharp Get out came and Shray joined her outside the classroom. "What the hell is wrong with you? I thought you finished your homework."

"I did," he shrugged, dumping it on her lap.

"Then, why did you say you didn't?"

"Class is boring without you. And it's peaceful here."

Miraya wanted to smile, laugh and cry at the same time. But all she did was smack his shoulders. "You're an idiot."

"I know. Now copy my homework before she comes out and checks if we are fooling around. She knows we are capable of that."

Miraya rolled her eyes but she started writing. Then paused. "Do you think Siddh might have thought I was dumb?"

Shray sighed and leaned back against the wall. "If he did, he'd just prove my theory that he is a pretentious asshole."

"I hope he didn't," Miraya pouted.

"Shut up and write, Miranda.

"What are you thinking about?" Shray asks, jolting her out of her thoughts. The car is on standby because of the traffic signal.

"Nothing," Miraya says, turning away to the window. She catches the eye of the driver's quizzical expression through the rearview mirror. "Actually, I was thinking of the time you got kicked out of the classroom just so you can join me outside even though you did the homework."

Shray cracks a smile. "Oh, I remember. Mrs Kavitha's class, right?"

"Yes. I can't believe I didn't know then that you loved me."

Shray is mildly shocked at her words. Miraya never speaks about their feelings when they were alone. But the point is that they aren't. Only belatedly Shray realises that Miraya is creating a scene for the driver to eat up and spit it in someone's ear. *Of course,* he thinks to himself. Though it is a clever move, it causes a wave of hurt inside him. To cover up the wince, he takes her hand and gently tugs her toward him to make the gap between them smaller.

"What can I say? Both of us were dumb," Shray says, grinning. Miraya looks into his eyes and tries to hide a smile. Instead she lays her head on his shoulder and he places their intertwined hands on his thigh.

By the time they reach Miraya's apartment, it is dark. Miraya untangles her fingers from his and only then does she realise Shray is asleep. She was so caught up in the feelings bubbling inside her that she barely noticed his even breath.

Miraya taps his shoulders. "Shray?"

Two more taps on his cheek gets him awake. "Where are we?" he says, his voice scratchy.

"In front of my apartment."

Shray sits up and his hands immediately go to his hair, trying to perfect it. It has become a habit for him. "I am so hungry. You didn't eat as well. Should we go out for dinner?"

"Again? Through the traffic? No thanks," Miraya says, already getting out of the car.

"Maybe I'll order you something? I don't remember you eating anything from noon."

Miraya sighs. It's true that she was starving. She was surviving the day on a bunch of nuts and a nutella-banana smoothie she had whipped up in the morning. "Get out of the car," she says.

"What?"

"You haven't eaten either. Let's eat together. Come on." She walks towards the gate. She hears Shray saying something to the driver and then shutting the car door. Miraya smiles when the sound is followed by Shray running towards her.

They stay silent in the elevator. Miraya unlocks the door and switches on the light in her apartment. When she removes her heels, she crouches down and inspects the skin that's peeled off, slowly turning red. At the same time she feels an acute pain in her stomach which could only mean one thing. Her period was already two days late. And it chose a very bad time to come. "Shit, shit, shit," she mutters under her breath and walks straight towards her room.

Before Shray can say anything, she shuts the door.

Shray removes his coat and pops open the first button on his shirt before plopping down on the sofa. He pulls out his phone and scrolls through the food delivery app, trying to guess what Miraya would be craving right now. Safe guess was Italian but they've been having too much Italian together.

The door to Miraya's room flings open at the same speed it shuts and Miraya marches out of her room. She stands with her back towards him and says, "Hook."

"Oh, right," Shray says and fumbles with it. He could feel the tension in her body. Once he unclasps the hooks in her blouse, he puts a hand on her shoulder. "Miraya. What's wrong?" he asks.

"Nothing. Just leave me alone," Miraya says and vanishes into her room. Once she disrobes her sari and hangs it over her chair to let it air-dry, she steps into the shower.

The events of the day had been very stressful and her heart and mind was in a state of unsettlement and discomfort. She wasn't feeling the best but back in the car, with her pressed close to Shray, it felt manageable. Now, topping it all with her period and the fucking shoe bite which stung under the hot water, she was pissed and frustrated, just wanting to unleash all of her emotions on something and slip into sleep.

Miraya does a few breathing exercises as she puts on a t-shirt and her sweatpants. She opens the door.

"Okay, what do you want? I say, we try Lebanese tonight. Have you tried Leba—"

"Please, Shray. I don't have the energy to do anything. Just pick whatever," Miraya says, joining him on the sofa and massaging her forehead.

But Shray simply loves to annoy the shit out of her. So, he does the opposite. He makes her talk.

"Tell me what happened. Are you still uncomfortable from the attention you received today? Are you not well? Do you need something?"

"Shray, I'm tired and stressed and hungry and to top it off, I'm on my fucking period. Just leave me alone!"

His eyes widens and then he nods. "Okay, I'll check if there's anything in the fridge." With that, he stalks to the kitchen and leaves her alone.

Miraya closes her eyes and releases a sharp breath. A few minutes pass.

"What is this?" Shray asks from the kitchen. Miraya opens one eye and finds him holding a cylindrical glass container of red chutney.

"It's *Kaara* chutney. We always have that in stock here."

"Do you have Dosa batter?"

"Why?"

"For what else? Making Dosas."

Miraya groans. "I don't have the energy to make Dosas now, Shray. I don't think I can even–"

"Who said you're making it?"

She frowns and sits upright to look at him. "*You?* Do you know how to?"

"Did you think I lied when I said I cook for myself?" Shray asks, crossing his arms and leaning against the counter. He looked so hot, his chest slightly pushed to the front, his shirt tightening around his arms and his hair a little dishevelled. "Yes, of course I know how to make Dosas, Miraya."

"The big bowl-like container in the top. It has the batter," she says.

He grins. "Just sit and relax. I'll make sure you have food in your stomach in a few minutes."

Chapter 27

♥

Curiosity nags Miraya.

From the living room, she can only hear the mannerless hissing of the pan when he pours the batter. Miraya wants to see if the circles are masterful and effortlessly made, if Shray has rolled his sleeves up or he has left it as it is, and if he has bothered to wear an apron.

Deciding she wasn't going to pass up the opportunity of watching Shray with a spatula in his hand. Miraya walks to the kitchen and hops onto the counter.

Shray grins and passes her a plate. She takes it without protest.

As Miraya watches him, she can't help but observe how his eyes are focused and the skin between his eyebrows are pinched together in concentration. If someone had told her to imagine Shray flipping Dosas in his expensive suit, she would have called it absurd and laughed it off. But, at this moment, standing beside him as he pours white circles on the pan, there is nothing funny about it. All she can think of is how fucking hot he looked. It blew her mind, really.

"Are you admiring me or the perfection of this Dosa?" he asks, flipping it onto her plate.

"Neither," Miraya answers but there is a smile in her voice.

Shray pours the batter again and allows it to cook. In the meantime, he grabs the chutney and serves her a generous dollop of it. Standing in front of her with his elbows resting on the marble counter leading to the sink, he watches her eat.

"I think you'll be flipping Dosas for a while," Miraya says. "I am starving and this, surprisingly, is tastier than usual."

Shray leans forward and boops her nose. "That's because it is served with love."

Miraya swats his hand away and stuffs another piece into her mouth. "No, but seriously..." she begins, chewing, "will you be able to stand here and make me how many ever Dosas I want?"

"Why do you ask that? How many do you want?"

Miraya calculates in her head. "Maybe ten?"

"You got it, Ma'am. I'm on a mission." He salutes and places the next Dosa on her plate just after she finishes the previous one.

Five more Dosas come to life and vanish. "Are you a little full?" Shray asks, serving her some more chutney. There was only a little more left in the container.

"Why? Are you tired already, you weak puny man?" She pokes his arms with her finger.

"No. Watching you eat is so tempting. I want to taste it as well," he says. "Can you give me a bite?"

"Of course," she says, stretching out the plate towards him.

"Just a bite. Feed me, no?" he says, attending to the Dosa.

Her hand automatically breaks a piece of the Dosa, dips it in chutney and raises to his mouth but midway, she freezes. Miraya hesitates. She also realises how she might not have paused to think even for a second if he had asked her to do the same back in school.

Shray's teeth trap his lips and let loose. "It's fine, don't worry. I'll wait to taste it. After all, the wait only makes the taste better." He tries to laugh it off but there is hurt in his eyes.

"No, I am sorry. I was thinking about something else."

Shray doesn't believe her lie. But he doesn't say a word and opens his mouth. "Thank you," he says and the sincerity is brimming in his eyes and his voice. Miraya's heart crushes. The small act of love towards him makes him so happy as if the darkest parts of his life have finally been shed some light and warmth. Has she been too harsh on him all this time?

Miraya takes a bite herself and then feeds him again.

"No, it's okay. I just wanted to taste—"

"I know you are hungry and you are dying to eat. Open up," she says, stuffing a piece in his mouth.

Shray doesn't argue after that.

They alternate bites and the whole time Shray spouts some random rubbish to make her laugh. "I am not even kidding. This happened!" he says.

Miraya shakes her head. "I wish I could believe you but no."

"Come on, Miranda," he sings and Miraya stuffs a piece in his mouth to shut him up.

"I think I am done. I am full. Move around. It's my turn to show you my dosa-making skills," Miraya says, hopping down from the counter and dropping the plate in the sink. She washes her hands and places another plate in Shray's hands.

He eats only four which makes Miraya question her cooking skills but Shray reasons that he really was full.

"I never imagined I would enjoy making dosas for someone so much as I did today," Shray admits, plopping on the couch.

Miraya doesn't say anything because before she could, her phone rings. Shray picks it up from the table and gives it to her.

It was Kishore.

"Hey," Miraya says, sitting on the other chair.

"What are you doing?"

Miraya bites her lip and looks at Shray. "Um, I am with a friend," she says as quietly as possible.

"Friend? Which friend that I dont know of?"

Miraya places a hand on her head and dips her head down. "It's Shray," she mutters through her teeth.

"Oh. That *friend*. I get it," he teases. "Is he nearby? Is that why you are too shy to say his name?"

"Shut up."

"Oh wait, it's almost eleven in India, isn't it? What are you doing with a friend so late at night, huh?"

"Kishore, I'll kill you if you don't shut up." With that, Miraya awkwardly excuses herself and walks off to the balcony to get some privacy.

"Too bad we are many hundred thousand miles away."

"You are so annoying sometimes, do you know that?"

"Oh, I know. So, are you confessing your undying love for him anytime soon?"

"Stop it, Kishore. I swear to God."

He chuckles. "Okay, okay."

"So, what's up with you?"

"I know you are busy ogling your man so I'll call you sometime later and tell you. Alright?"

Miraya leans against the wall and sighs. "Fine. Take care, okay?"

"Yes Ma'am. And you have fun but don't forget to use protection. I am not ready to become the cool Uncle for another kid just yet."

"*Kishore!*"

Miraya hears a booming laugh before the call ends. *Idiot*, she murmurs and then smiles to herself. Leaning against the balcony railing on her palms, she takes in a deep breath and watches the stars above. The moon isn't on her side of the balcony today so she tips her head up and closes her eyes.

"Hey," she hears a voice from behind her.

"Hey."

Shray joins her, their shoulders almost touching. "You never told me about Kishore."

"Oh, right. He's my best friend. I met him in German class..." She rambles on and on about Kishore bringing up their daily silly arguments in the apartment and their mad schedules. Shray listens to her patiently, smiling occasionally.

"Seems like he is very close to you."

"He really is." She looks at the sky, a grateful smile tugging on her lips.

"You always spoke about me like this. In school, I mean. I used to love it when you introduced me to someone," Shray says randomly.

Miraya turns to him and before she can tuck in the hair that dances in the air, Shray reaches forward and pushes the hair back gently. Shivers creep her body.

"I really loved you back then. Of course, I made you seem like the greatest person in this world," she says, turning away. "I loved showing you off."

"I loved showing you off too. You were the best thing that happened to me so how could I not? Suriya would always tease me about it but I never cared."

"Did Suriya know that you loved me?" Miraya asks.

"No. That idiot has a big mouth. He simply can't keep secrets, you know that," Shray says, stepping backwards.

He stretches his arms upwards and his shirt rises, cuffing him in the right places. At times like these, Miraya just wants to wrap her arms around his torso and rest her head against his chest. She wants to feel the planes of his chest, the warmth of his body... and the taste of his lips. Again.

She wants to *love* him.

But can you love someone without forgiving them? Can you love someone when you also hate them for what they did to you?

"I am happy you were by my side today," Shray says, interrupting her thoughts.

Miraya blinks to clear her dazed gaze and nods. "Me too. It wasn't the best experience for me but I am not sure if I would've survived if you weren't with me. Are you sure this will work?"

"It will. The media will eat this shit up right away. I know it's not something you are accustomed to but I am sorry to have you do this."

Miraya shakes her head. "Don't be. A deal is a deal. I gave you my word so I have to hold onto it."

Shray leans back and sighs. "I think I should get back. It's pretty late and I am tired. I have to hit the gym early in the morning."

"Oh."

Miraya doesn't know how to respond without showing her disappointment. Shray catches the emotion that passes her features and smiles fondly. "I'll call you tomorrow."

Miraya nods.

Shray heads back into the living room to get his coat.

"You know, why don't you crash here?" Miraya suggests, biting her lip.

Shray stops and turns around.

"Here?"

"Yes. You can sleep in my room and I can use Daksh's room. She won't be back for two more days."

"Are you sure?"

Miraya nods. Being in Shray's company is like being addicted to slow poison. You know it is bad and it will hurt you in the end but you like it anyway. You refuse to let go.

"Just a minute. I'll tidy my room a little so you can get comfortable there," Miraya says and disappears into her room. When she comes back, Shray is on the phone with someone.

"Yes. Five-thirty in the morning," he says. When he notices her, he smiles and gestures to give him a minute. He goes back to his call, what she hears sounding like instructions.

Once he is done, Shray asks if he can get a change of clothes and Miraya brings back a t-shirt and sweatpants from Ranav's shelf in Dakshina's room.

"Just ask me if you need anything else, okay?" Miraya says before putting on a kettle of warm water.

"Okay."

A few seconds pass. Shray speaks again. "Oh, I need something."

"What?"

"A hug if it's available."

Miraya's eyes shoot up from the kettle.

Shray slowly makes his way to her. "I miss our hugs, Miranda. I still remember the first time you hugged me. When Ma was in the hospital. I think of it sometimes and I realised that that hug meant a lot more to me than you can ever imagine. It kinda saved me."

She bites her lips and does not make eye contact with him. If she does, she will break. She hates deep conversations with Shray for a reason. It reminds her of what they were and what they could be and it's painful. Miraya wants to beg him to stop, talk about something superficial like his first time riding a horse or his trip to Vietnam. But Shray continues.

"And when I tore my ligament and you cried in my chest, hitting me and hugging me at the same time. At my birthday party. The favourite gift I received every year was that tight hug of yours. There's something healing about it. Medicinal, even. Do you ever feel the same?"

Shray is close to her and she is sure he can see her lips tremble against her wish. Miraya tries to focus on the kettle but she can't. Not when every word he says hits her in the chest like thunder.

"At least, *did* you ever feel the same?" he asks.

She glances at him, teary-eyed and nods. "I did and I do."

"I think we deserve a hug after today," he whispers quietly. Shray opens his arms and Miraya walks into it. As his arms close around her, she sighs and places her own on his back. When he tightens his hold, her palms clutch his shoulders tight. Shray smells great – like an exotic mixture of luxury and ordinary. The smell of home.

Miraya finds herself burying her face in his chest. He rests his chin on her shoulder. "I missed this so fucking much," he whispers. "*God*, Miraya. I wish we could reverse time and be stuck in a period when it was the two of us against the world."

"Me too, Shray. Me too," she whispers back and pulls away. She wipes a tear quickly and turns around. "But too bad time machines don't exist."

Chapter 28

T he next morning Miraya wakes up to a note stuck on Dakshi-na's lamp. She almost doesn't notice it as both the colour of the sticky note and the lamp is yellow. She peels the note off and reads.

I am leaving for the gym after which I'll head back to my house. I didn't want to wake you so I borrowed a fresh towel from your closet and the spare toothbrush from your cabinet. I hope you don't mind. Thanks for letting me crash here. I'll call you sometime later.

Shray x

P.S. You still sleep with your fingers tangled in your hair. Cute.

A smile stretches on her lips as she stares at the note. Waking up to such a sweet note from Shray feels like someone filled her heart with hot chocolate and marshmallows.

Miraya makes Dakshina's bed and pads over to her room to get ready for work. Everything is as she left it yesterday, except for the well-made bed. Of course, Shray had tidied up before leaving the room. He was such a neat freak.

She showers quickly. When she steps out of the bathroom, her phone rings. It is her mother.

Miraya presses the phone to her ear. "Hey, Ma."

"You didn't tell us that you'll be going to the trailer event with Shray. Why are we always finding out things through the internet?

We are your parents. Don't you think we deserve the right to know of your plans?" *Amma* says.

"Ma, it was a last minute plan. And I wasn't supposed to be seen. I was somehow captured by the cameras. I was just there to support Shray. I had to do it for him," Miraya explains.

"At least give us a warning next time. And where did you buy that sari? It was so pretty. You looked so beautiful in it, kanna."

Occasional compliments from her mother were Miraya's favourite because she rarely ever got them. "Thanks, Ma. Actually Shray bought the sari for me."

"He has good taste. And he is kind. Your Appa and I were talking and we realised that we haven't met with Shray at all since your schooling. I discussed it with Mala and she invited us for dinner with them."

"Oh. When?"

Miraya places the phone on her table and puts on the speaker while she readies herself for work.

"Today. Mala just called me. She said she checked with Shray's manager and found that he was free tonight."

"Tonight? I mean, you are telling me now?"

"Why? Do you have work to do?"

Miraya paces in her room. Can she get a break? At least for a day to go back to her normal life and recharge to be fake?

"No. I was just surprised since it's on such short notice."

"It's just dinner, Miraya," her mother deadpans.

"Okay. I'll talk to Shray."

With that, she hangs up.

As if cued, her phone lights up with a message from Shray. *I'll not be free for the next one week. Let's hang tonight?*

Oh boy, he didn't know that they already had plans made for them by their parents. *I suggest rechecking tonight's agenda with your manager :)*

Three dots popped up and disappeared only to show up a few minutes later. *When did this happen? Dinner with your family? I am freaking out!!*

You have all the reasons to be. Sorry.

What if they question us?

Highly likely considering my mother's paranoia when it comes to my life. We'll have to have a solid storyline, when we lost contact and when we reconnected. I'll come up with a plausible story and send it to you. Just memorise it, Miraya typed out and hit send.

Okay. Help me out today please.

Miraya responds with a thumbs up emoji and a pink double heart. Only after the message is delivered, her eyes shoot wide at the blunder she had made. A heart? A fucking double heart? *Seriously, Miraya?* She wanted to curse herself out. The apprehension and anxiety she feels when the three bubbles pop up again on her screen is out of proportion. She wants to die.

The bubbles keep bouncing for an extra minute or two and then she receives a single pink heart in return.

Her heart thuds. What does that mean?

Miraya wastes a good amount of time decoding that emoji and when she checks the time she drops the phone on her bed and rushes to apply her makeup. "Fuck, fuck, fuck. I can't be late again!" she curses under her breath. She skips breakfast and drives rashly to work.

And of course, to no one's surprise, Miraya reaches her office seventeen minutes late.

□□□□□□□□□□□□□□□□

Miraya is strapping on her sandals when Shray leans over her and shoves his phone in front of her face. "How is this for my wallpaper?"

Miraya takes his phone. "I don't remember seeing this picture at all," she says.

In the picture, Shray was in his football jersey, looking glossy under the sun as he was drenched in sweat. Miraya was standing in her uniform, on the third step in the sidelines. Her hands were on Shray's shoulders as he faced the opposite side and fist-pumped the air. Miraya was looking at Shray proudly and as if she was... in love with him.

She *had been*, actually, but Miraya never realised that it had been so obvious on her face. Not until now.

"I didn't know this picture was taken as well. A few years back I met Pavithra and we had the chance to catch up after a long time. She is working in the airlines," he says.

"Oh. What did you talk about?"

"Just this and that, you know. I always thought she'd become a photographer or something so seeing her without a camera on her neck was weird. While we were talking about school, she asked me about you."

Miraya removed her hands from her feet and sat upright. "What did you say?"

"I told her that I lost contact with you after school and haven't spoken since. She was shocked. She told me that she'd always assumed we'd be close forever."

Miraya scoffs lightly. "But I bet she had hoped otherwise."

"What do you mean?"

"She had a huge ass crush on you, Shray. We even had arguments and fights that lasted for weeks because of you. You always ended up choosing me over her and as if that's my fault, she would blame me."

Shray is surprised. "But you two were so close."

Miraya shrugs. "Well, except for that, she was a good friend. She eased off the blame game when I got together with Siddh."

"Why didn't you tell me?" Shray sits down next to her.

"All the girls you've been in a relationship with in school have treated me like I was their rival. I got used to it. And if I had told you, you would've made things worse by taking my side over theirs," she says. After a long pause, she whispers, "And it wasn't like I didn't enjoy it whenever you picked me over them. I was jealous of the girls you were in a relationship with. Knowing that I mattered to you most and hearing them complain about it was on one side, was something I found a great deal of pleasure in."

"I am sorry," Shray says.

Miraya shakes her head, dry chuckles escaping her lips. "There's nothing to be sorry for." She adjusts her strappy sandals one more time before standing up. "So, what happened then?"

"We were talking about you and she said she recently found a picture that she had taken of us. It was one of her favourite shot, it seems, but it never made the school magazine because we appeared too close in the picture. She sent me this picture later," Shray explains.

"She could've given us the picture immediately in school, right? But she didn't. You know why? Because she didn't want to stir anything between us. I am actually surprised she didn't delete it altogether," Miraya says.

Shray doesn't respond. She finds a small smile playing on his lips.

"What?"

"You've become so cynical," he says.

"I've always been like that."

"Not to this extent."

Miraya turns to him. "So, what, Shray? Is it such a bad thing?"

"No. But sometimes you can stop assuming the worst of every-one and give them a chance," he says, softly.

Miraya exhales sharply, not wanting to argue with him now because they had to meet their parents. "The wallpaper is nice." She doesn't say anything else.

Shray drops the topic cleverly and moves on. "So, what's yours?"

Miraya shows him the picture of him that hadn't made it to the magazine issue of MIRROR. Shray just stares at the picture and then her but doesn't say anything. He simply smiles and nods before leading the way out of her apartment.

"Do you remember our story?"

"Yes. Memorised every single detail."

"And if there's a question asked about us that you don't know the answer to, just stay quiet. I'll step in and do the talking," Miraya says as they get into the elevator. "And—"

She turns to face Shray and her eyes stop at his face. "What happened?" he asks.

Miraya only steps closer to him. Slowly, her hands raise and touch his cheek.

"Miranda—"

"Shhh. It's an eyelash." She tries to peel the little lash off his skin but it's stubborn. She steps a little closer and tries again. There is no gap between them. Their feet are kissing, their chests pressed against each other and their breath mingling. When Miraya stares into his eyes up close, she notices that his eyes aren't black. They are a luscious shade of dark brown, like that of roasted coffee beans.

Miraya hears the elevator doors close and only then she snaps out of her thoughts. "Yup, got it," Miraya says, trying not to make the tremor in her voice obvious. She dusts off the lash.

Shray appears like someone took the remote to his life and pressed pause on it.

"Oh, do you believe in making wishes on the eyelashes? I am sorry I didn't know —"

He visibly trembles and releases a sharp breath. "With you looking perfect in this dress, I am trying my fucking best not to pin you against this wall and kiss you, Miranda. Please don't make it more of a challenge than it already is."

Miraya's eyes go wide and heat rushes to her face. She takes a step back and nods. "I am sorry. I didn't realise," she mutters, looking away.

A part of Miraya wants to scream at what happened and dramatically fan her face but she composes herself.

The ride to the fancy restaurant that Shray had reserved for them was short and devoid of chatter. Miraya took Shray's arm as they entered the restaurant and was shown the way to their family who were already seated.

"Bro, you two really look good together," Vidyuth says, grinning like a drunk fool. Shray rolls his eyes at his brother's behaviour.

"Were you waiting for long?" Miraya asks.

"No, no. We just came," her mother answers. She is in a green and pink sari, her neck adorned with a simple necklace.

Mirays sits next to her mother and Shray next to her. There is an empty chair next to his family so his choice of seat surprises her and her family. Shray's parents only smile.

"He can't stay away from her even for a few minutes," Shray's mother laughs.

It takes a while to order food and Vidyuth keeps making silly jokes to keep the mood light. Miraya's parents engage in good conversation with Shray's and for a second, she feels really happy that they are getting along well. But she catches herself just in time.

This marriage arrangement isn't going to last. There's nothing to be happy about.

Shray's hand finds hers under the table. What's wrong, he seems to ask with his eyes. Miraya shakes her head and goes back to her food.

"So, Shray, Miraya never told us the whole story of how you found each other again. Tell us," Miraya's mother prompts.

"Shray was surprisingly secretive about it as well," Mala Aunty says. "Yes, you have to tell us."

Shray glances at Miraya and then recites the story they had spun. It wasn't entirely fiction but there were slight tweaks here and there.

"Miraya and I lost contact after school. It was such a coincidence when Miraya came to interview me for MIRROR. We began to catch up and it seemed seven years didn't pass at all. It took only one conversation to fall back into our friendship. We kept in touch after the interview and met a couple of times. We didn't see it coming actually — the feelings. It just happened," Shray says, glancing at her.

Miraya smiles and squeezes his fingers in encouragement.

"I became too busy. The only time I could meet with her was after the shoot, which was late in the evening. So, we met in places we wouldn't be exposed to the public. But things got out of hand."

"It's okay, Shray. Only because of that, we got to know you two were in love. Now, we have officiated this alliance in marriage. Everything happens for a reason," Shray's father says.

"I just wish you could have told us," Mala Aunty says, a small pout on her face.

"Ma, we've had this conversation plenty of times." Shray chuckles.

Miraya's parents are silent, forcing smiles on their faces. They knew exactly why their daughter didn't tell them that she was in love with Shray. If she had told them, this alliance wouldn't have happened at all. They would have immediately searched for another potential groom for her.

"So, who confessed first?" Vidyuth asks.

"Shray. We were having a small argument and he yelled it in between," Miraya says, grinning. "It was kinda... romantic." She leans in towards Shray when she whispers the last word.

"That was not how I planned to say it," Shray admits. The others laugh. "But if you are happy, I am happy."

If she didn't know better, Miraya would think they were a couple who were head over heels for each other and very excited about getting married.

Only, she *did* know better.

And it didn't feel good.

Chapter 29

♥

A week passes by.

Shray used to call her everyday, an hour or two after she was done with work. She'd sit on the beach and talk to him about her day and his. What was started as a way to know each other all over again, became a habit and an expectation. And the past week, Miraya was disappointed every day.

Shray never called.

He used to send her these random sweet texts from time to time enquiring if she reached home safely, if she had her meals or if she slept well the previous night. He would also gently remind her not to drink coffee on an empty stomach and to never skip her breakfast. At first, Miraya had thought of it as sweet yet unnecessary. Only now she knows how much those small gestures actually meant to her.

Now all she receives are apology texts stating that he is so tired and has no time. Occasionally, vain promises of calling her the next day were made but never kept.

It's not like they have to let each other know what they do or talk to each other everyday. It is not necessary for a couple in love and it's most definitely not necessary for Shray and Miraya.

But still.

Miraya felt uneasy throughout the week. She felt empty, as if she missed something she didn't even know what. That dull but sure throb in her heart made it difficult to be enthusiastic about anything. She just wanted to snuggle in bed all day and do nothing.

Pressing her feet deeper into the sand, she walks forward, searching for a quiet place to sit down. The beach is abnormally crowded today. As she scans the place, her phone rings. Immediately, as if her reflexes were on fire, she answers and presses the phone to her ear.

"Shray!"

There is silence at the other end but quickly, a booming laughter screeches its way into her ear. "I am not your soon-to-be husband, Miss Miraya. Might I remind you to check the caller ID before assuming it's him? Might I also remind you that you have a best friend named Kishore who lives in Germany?"

Miraya presses her lips into a thin line. "What do you want?" she asks.

"Ouch. Rude. I'll forgive you because I know you are cranky because you miss him."

"I don't miss him. I just had a long day at work."

"You seem to be having long days at work everyday this week," Kishore says, the smirk in his voice bleeding through the phone.

"Shut up."

"Okay, Mira. Can you push Shray off your mind for a few minutes because I have something to tell you. I've been wanting to talk to you about this for quite a while but it just kept postponing for some reason. I don't like keeping this from you for so long."

Miraya spots a place on the beach and drops her sneakers, next to which she seats herself. "Tell me. I am very curious now."

"I have one good news and one...okayish news. Which one first?"

"Okayish one, please."

"So... Radhi dropped out of college."

"What? Why?"

"It became a huge problem. Ma was super angry. My Aunt and Uncle advised against it. In fact, everyone did but Radhi was stubborn. She just went ahead and quit college," Kishore says. "But she has a plan, though. Her friend's mother is a makeup artist. She wants to spend a year working in her studio, learning and earning at the same time. Then she wants to open her own beauty salon."

"Seems like a good plan. She hasn't lost sense of purpose. In fact, she is very strong about what she wants to do. It's a good thing that she got the courage to do it despite what others say."

Kishore sighs. "I know. I am proud of her, really. But I am also scared for her, Mira. What if she doesn't get what she wants? Nothing is certain in life and she is giving up on her education to chase that uncertain dream."

"Kishore, I know that since she is your baby sister, you might have taken the role of a father to her. It's your right to worry about her, yes. But she is an adult. It's her life. Instead of fearing for her, support her and help her get what she wants, no? She will appreciate you that way. Not if you keep telling her to reconsider her decision. She has made up her mind already," Miraya says.

"Ma is not talking to her. Priya is supportive but she feels Radhi should at least earn a degree, just in case. Since I am the only one not against her, Radhi is crying on the phone to me every day. I... want to be by her side, Mira. I just want her to be happy and I can't stand her crying everyday. It's too hard," Kishore says. His voice is painful.

"Do you want me to go check up on her? Talk to her and maybe hang out for a bit?"

"No, no, it's okay. That's the good news, actually. I'm coming next month. I want to stay with Radhi and Ma, sort things out and make sure they are back to normal. Plus, I miss them."

Miraya smiles. "And why is that good news for me?"

"Seriously? Don't you miss your roomie a little? Or are you too busy for anyone but your superstar sweetheart?"

Miraya's face twists at the horrendous nickname. "How do you even come up with these names?"

"It's a talent only best friends specialise in," Kishore says. Miraya rolls her eyes but a smile plays on her lips. "So, did you hear from your father after your talk?"

"No. Not after that."

After the dinner Miraya and Shray had with their families, Appa pulled her to the side to talk to her. "I always thought that whenever you smiled, you were happy. Or that whenever you got what you wanted, you were happy. But today when I saw you with Shray, I realised that the last time I saw you smiling like that was when you were in school. All these years, you've never been truly happy and I had been blind," he said and then turned towards her.

He rested his heavy palm on her shoulder and continued, "I am sorry I lost sight of the difference between your real happiness and the ones you were faking for us, kanna. I am so sorry."

"Pa..."

"Somehow, one thing led to the other and you found the right person for you. It wasn't the way I would have opted for but in the end, seeing you look so happy with him gave me some clarity. Something I had lost sense of since what you did in school. I was so angry and disappointed in you that I refused to forgive you. I stopped talking to you properly and left all your matters to your mother. I thought it was the right thing to do but now I realise how much pain

you would have gone through. I am sorry I didn't forgive you. I am so sorry, kanna."

It was the longest that her father had spoken to her in seven years. Miraya hugged her father tight that day and teared up on his shoulders. Forgiveness from her father was something she had given up on. She had made up her mind that he was never going to give it to her. Not in this life, at least. But unexpectedly receiving it... it was the best feeling.

And it was all because of Shray.

When Shray dropped her in her apartment later, she had hugged him tight. So tight that she could feel his heart drumming alongside hers. "What's this for?" he had asked, his chin on her shoulders.

"You. Just you."

Shray didn't understand what she meant but hugged her back.

"Hello? Miraya?"

"Oh, sorry. I just—"

"Bet you were thinking of him."

Her face turned hot. "No, I wasn't!"

"So, when are you going to stop lying to yourself and just tell him you love him? Hopelessly, might I add," Kishore begins.

Miraya's fingers draw random shapes on the sand. "But what he did—"

"He did what he did seven years ago, Mira. That excuse is getting old. How long are you going to carry that grudge? It is poisoning you. It is keeping you from loving what you love. Do you really want that?"

"Kishore, you don't understand—"

"No, Mira. I understand how much his actions turned your life upside down. I really do. But you are here, aren't you? You are doing well. You have a good job and you have good friends. You think you are happy but you aren't. And what is keeping you from being truly happy? Your ancient grudge against him. Am I wrong?"

Miraya bites her lip and stares at the crashing waves. She doesn't answer.

"After all you've been through, don't you deserve happiness? So what if the one who can make you happy is the one who hurt you seven years ago? Are you refusing to ever let yourself be happy because of that one mistake he made? People make mistakes, Mira. You and me and everyone. You aren't punishing just him for what he did. You are punishing yourself too. Do you realise that?"

Miraya's eyes tear up. She knows that every word that Kishore said is true. But she can't bring herself to take that step forward. How can she just let go of the grudge she had nurtured for seven long years? Shouldn't it have a purpose in the end?

"It's hard, Kishore," she says, wiping the rogue tear that had slipped out.

"Okay, tell me one thing. What do you gain from holding a grudge?"

Miraya draws a blank. "He hurt me, Kishore. Don't you think he should pay for that?"

"Is this a type of revenge? Is that what you want?"

Miraya sighs. "It's not revenge... but it's just... I need to make him regret what he did. He didn't even experience the consequences of what he did."

"He did. He lost you. For seven years. And he was in love with you. Don't you think losing you was punishment enough?"

"This argument is going nowhere," Miraya says.

"Look, let's just say he did what he did out of spite. People in love do crazy things but yes, that doesn't excuse his actions. What he did was wrong, I agree. But why don't you leave it up to karma and just forgive him, Mira? I know forgiving others is hard. But sometimes you've just got to do it. I am so sorry to bring this up but do you realise there's no difference between your father and you? Both of you refused to forgive. Like your father did now, you'll regret it later. And you know how it feels to be at the sword's end of a grudge like that. Think about it, Mira."

Miraya buries her head in her knees. "He doesn't even care to apologise," she says through her cracked voice.

"Then, confront him. Demand his side of the story."

"I don't like to talk about it. You know that."

"Sometimes we've got to do things we don't like, Mira. Take that leap. Break the ice wall you've put between him and you. Allow yourself to love him because I know for a fact that when you love someone you love them with every bit of your soul. Don't compromise on that because of your grudge. It's not worth it, trust me, Mira. I want you to be genuinely happy."

"I love you, Kishore. You know that, right?" Miraya asks as a tear slides down her cheek. She quickly wipes it away.

"I know. I love you too and that's why I want you to stop faking it and lying your way through life. Face the truth," Kishore says.

Miraya sniffles into her sleeve. "I'll try."

"Good. Now let's talk about the movie you recommended. Why the hell would you suggest a movie in which the hero dies? What did I ever do to you, woman?"

Chapter 30

M iraya has been staring at the message for more than ten minutes. What does *Soon* mean? Three more days passed without a call from Shray. And Miraya was slightly worried and greatly pissed at him.

Fiya steps into Miraya's office space. "Hey," she says.

"Is something wrong? Do you have any problems with the story you are working on?" Miraya asks.

"No, no," she says and pulls out an invitation card from behind her back. "I am getting married."

"What?"

"I am getting married to Ashraf. The engagement is on January 30. It would mean a lot to me if you came. And also Shray," she added the last part quietly.

Miraya was surprised. She hadn't even known Fiya was deciding on marriage. That was how distant they had grown. "Congratulations. I mean, I am so happy for you. And of course, I'll come. I am not sure about Shray but I'll try getting him to attend as well," Miraya says. *If he picks up her calls, that is.*

"Thank you so much," Fiya says and she could catch on to the notes of excitement in her voice. "And Miraya, I am sorry I wasn't very understanding of you during the scandal. I feel very guilty for not being there for you."

Miraya waves her off. "That's okay. I could understand that you felt left out so it's partly my fault. I would have honestly told you everything if I knew what was happening in my life. But I was *very* confused. It was too chaotic to explain and that's why I didn't." She adds, "I guess it still is messy."

"You don't owe me an explanation or anything, Mira. I am sorry I behaved like a kid. Only last week, Ashraf sat me down and knocked some sense into me. I've been trying to find the right time to apologise but I bailed on it every time because I was a little scared."

Miraya laughs. "Am I that scary?"

"Sometimes, yeah," she says, wearing a sheepish smile on her face.

"It's nice to talk to you again casually," Miraya says. "Maybe we should catch up—"

Priscilla interrupts her. "Miraya, Mrs Nandhini is calling for you."

Miraya gives Fiya one tight hug before grabbing a pen and a notebook and rushing into Mrs Nandhini's office.

"Come in," she says.

Miraya takes a seat.

"Lakshmi wanted to do a piece on the pearl and gemstone jewellery market in Andaman. She was very excited about it but poor thing, she fell sick last week. She booked tickets to Andaman this week but her father passed away yesterday. She asked me to pass it on to someone else. Are you interested?" Mrs Nandhini says, not looking up from her binders.

"Um, yes. But is Lakshmi okay? Should I check up on her?"

"She is fine, just grieving. Her father was her only parent but he was sick for a while. The doctors had told her to expect it but his death came too soon. I went and checked on her myself yesterday and paid respects. You don't need to worry about it," she says.

Miraya nods. "So, when is the flight?"

"Tomorrow. Lakshmi has sent me the basic research she has done about the markets and the artisans. I will forward you that. Look into it. I'll also pass on the ticket details."

"Okay, sure. Is that all?"

"It will be a two-day trip so you've got to be sincere and smart. Of course, you take your time to be a tourist but also remember you are there for work. You know how this works, right? I trust you will do justice to Lakshmi's idea."

"Yes, Ma'am. Of course." Miraya smiles and leaves the room.

Andaman. She has never been there at all. She has always wanted to go but never found the chance and time to. Plus, it would be a much-needed break from her current worries.

After work, she goes home and begins to pack. Dakshina is on video call, helping her pick out the best clothes. She is insisting Miraya borrow her bathsuit, which was unnecessary for a two-day work trip. "You never know, sweetie," she says.

With a sigh, she dumps the damn suit inside her suitcase. Dakshina grins. "When are you coming back anyway? I kinda miss you, you know," Miraya says.

"Hmm, I think I like it here," Dakshina says, turning back to look at her fiancé. When she returns to the phone, there is a big wide grin on her face.

"Daksh, you promised you would return home after a week. It's so empty here."

"Call Shray. He will gladly keep you company."

"Only if he would pick up his calls in the first place," Miraya mumbles, packing the bag of toiletries. *Not that she would invite him to stay with her or anything.*

The doorbell rings.

"Who is that?" Daksh asks.

"No idea. I wasn't expecting anyone."

"Must be that Shilpa lady, trying to get a peek into our apartment with the excuse of getting milk."

Miraya shrugs. "Maybe. I'll be back in a second."

She pads to the door and unlocks it. Before she can see who the person is, she can *hear* him.

Shray.

"Surprise!" he exclaims. "Missed me?"

Miraya doesn't even spare a glance at him. She turns around and walks back to her room.

"I can't believe I forgot to remind you. Pack the black lingerie, Miraya. Please. You never know. You might regret not taking it with you when you meet a hot guy there," Dakshina says through the call.

"What black lingerie? And which hot guy?" Shray asks, following Miraya into the room.

"You're not supposed to be here! *Get out!*" Miraya screeches. Her face is burning hot and she pushes Shray back into the living room.

Only then does she notice that he is wearing a powder blue hoodie and ripped jeans — truly a sight to behold. He also has a white cap on his head with the lettering IDC in navy blue. Miraya is reminded of sports day practices in school. Shray and Miraya had gotten matching sun caps during one of their school tours to show off later on but they had only worn it twice.

But, what actually brings her jaw to the floor is the beard he was sporting. Shray has never grown one this long.

"Your beard." The words come out of her mouth before she can stop it.

He catches her hands that are on his chest and pins it there. "It's for the movie I am doing. *Nilam.* I have to maintain this look for three more months."

Miraya makes a face.

"What? Don't you like it?" Shray asks.

She pulls her hands away from his clasp. "It doesn't matter if I like it or not," she says and moves to shut the door.

"Why are you so cold today? I thought you'll be happy —"

"No, I am not happy, Shray. I am fucking mad at you. Go sit in the living room. Let me finish packing first!" Miraya says, closing the door.

"Why are you packing?" She hears a muffled question from the other side of the door.

Miraya doesn't answer. She sighs and folds her towel into a square.

"Did I mention black lingerie at the right time? Did Shray hear it?" Dakshina asks, her eyebrows wiggling. Miraya gasps and takes her phone from the bed.

"*God*, Dakshina. You did it on *purpose*?"

She laughs into her sleeve. "Obviously. I knew Shray was coming to meet you. He called me up and asked me what flowers you liked."

"What?" Miraya is confused. "What did you say?"

"Girl, I had no fucking clue. We never talk about shit like our favourite flowers and animals. I just told him to buy whatever looked pretty. Do you have a favourite flower, by the way?"

"No. Never thought about it."

"I know right. Who even sits and thinks about it? All flowers are pretty."

Miraya glares at her friend. "Don't change the topic. I hate you for doing that to me. He heard it, Dakshina. He fucking heard it."

"That was the whole point, sweetie. Now, I am ninety-five per-cent sure Shray is sitting in the living room thinking of you in that lacy black bra and how he's going to peel that off —"

"Shut up. *Shut up.* I am not talking to you. I am hanging up right *now*," Miraya says. She was going to burn that bra tonight.

Dakshina guffaws, slapping the sofa seat. Miraya professes her deep hatred for her best friend one last time before hanging up and throwing the phone on the bed.

She tries to recall the things she was yet to pack but she can't concentrate. Knowing that Shray, the guy who hadn't had the time to even check up on her for the past week and a half, was sitting on her sofa after having heard about her black bra was so messed up. She wants to punch something.

Instead, she maintains her calm and composes herself in front of the mirror. She walks out of the room.

Shray is sitting on the sofa, scrolling through his phone, a huge bouquet of pink roses waiting next to him. Miraya clears her throat and he looks up at her.

"Miranda, I am sorry," he says, standing up and picking up the bouquet. He gives it to her. "I really wanted to text you and call you but I literally had no time. My schedule was so packed that I immediately went to bed every night." There is sincerity in his voice that moves her. She can see that he is hitting himself for not calling her.

"It's okay. We are not dating anyway, right? You are not obligated to call me or anything. I just got mad for no reason. Forget it," she says.

But Shray takes her hand. "No. Don't shut yourself again, Miranda. I like this. I like you being mad at me and I like begging you to give me one more chance. I like bringing you flowers and apologising for screwing up and I like you forgiving me for it with a smile you don't want to share. Don't go back to being closed off. Fight with me, yell at me, be angry at me. Don't shy away claiming that you have no reason to. Don't be a stranger, Miranda. Please."

Miraya's breath hitches at his words. She doesn't know what to say in response. Her mouth opens and closes but nothing manages to escape them.

Thankfully, Shray places the bouquet in her hands. "I am sorry, Miranda. You have no idea how much I missed you," he says.

"Thanks for the flowers," Miraya manages to say, her voice rocky. She turns and walks off to the TV stand to grab the vase.

"Am I forgiven?"

"There's nothing to forgive. You had work and you were busy. I understand," Miraya says. Shray opens his mouth to say something but before that, she adds, "but next time, give me a warning. At least an approximate count of days you'll be going poof on me so that I don't sit and expect your text or call all day."

"Yes, Ma'am," Shray says and there is an apparent grin in his voice. Miraya tucks in a smile and replaces the water in the vase.

He follows her. "So, why are you packing? And what about the black lingerie?"

Miraya spins around to face him and smacks his chest. "For fuck's sake, will you drop it?"

Shray throws his head back and laughs. Open-mouthed, all-teeth, whole-hearted and child-like laughter. It makes her heart beat different.

"I'm sorry. Just wanted to see that beautiful pink colour your cheeks," he says, pinching her cheeks lightly. "So cute."

She swats his hands away.

"So, are you going somewhere?"

"Yes." Miraya clicks a few pictures of the rose bouquet. She unwinds the strings and places the flowers in the vase. "I love the flowers, by the way. They are really pretty."

"Not more than you," Shray quips and Miraya stares at him with a teasing smile.

"Really, Shray?" she asks, crossing her arms across her chest.

He scratches the back of his neck. "Okay, that was a little cliche. I agree. But it's the truth."

"Okay, now stop it." Miraya laughs, even though she can feel warmth creeping up her neck.

"Where are you going?" he asks, following her again as she moves to the TV stand to place the vase.

"Andaman."

"When?"

"Tomorrow."

Miraya leans against the shelf and stares at him as he takes in the information. "What? But I just came," Shray says.

"So?"

With time, Miraya can see that the beard gives off a rugged vibe to Shray which makes him look hot and a little sexy. In a bad boy kind of way. If anyone asked her a few hours ago if Shray could pull off such a look, she would have said No and boy, she would have been terribly wrong.

It is, of course, strange to see him like this but Miraya can definitely get used to it.

"I want to spend time with you, Miranda. I have only two weeks before shooting begins again."

"Not my problem. This is a work trip anyway and I will be back in two days."

"Are you going alone?" he asks.

"Yes. Why?"

Miraya can see the gears in his head spinning, trying to process the information. Suddenly, his eyes light up like a light bulb.

"What if I come with you?"

"And why will you?"

"Because I can, Miranda," he says, rolling his eyes at her lack of enthusiasm. "Think about it. We have always wanted to go on a trip, just the two of us. We even wrote it down in the bucket list we made. Remember?"

"I remember but I don't think—"

"Don't think. Just say yes. It will be fun."

Ten thousand alarms blare in her head, bright red ones, advising her that the idea was nothing but trouble. She cannot agree to this trip, especially if she will have to keep her true feelings confined in her chest all the time during the trip. It would be such a hassle.

"No, Shray," Miraya says, strongly. "It is a work trip so I have to be fully focused on the story I'll be working on. I won't have time to spend it any other way."

"I'll not disturb you. We will just hang out when you are free. We can't hang out here publicly but we can in Andaman. No one will recognise me. We'll just be two friends having fun."

"I don't know..."

Miraya partly feels like it is a good idea. It was her first time in Andaman and it would be nice to have someone with her. One part of her wants to take this chance and have the most fun with him because after they break up, they will never have the chance to. Even if they remain friends.

But trips like these strengthen emotional connections. Miraya wants to tame her feelings down and put out the fire before it spreads, not give it more oxygen and make the fire breathe flames.

She is torn.

"Please, Miranda. It will be worth it, trust me. I am good company."

You are very very good company, Shray. That is the problem.

But Miraya and problems are close-knit besties. Like hot *ba-jjis* on a rainy day. Like Indian auntys and gossip. They always go hand in hand.

So, she ends up agreeing to Shray's plan.

Chapter 31

♥

"Hello," Miraya says with a head nod as she flattens herself to walk past the young man to get to her seat next to the window. It was a shame Lakshmi hadn't chosen the aisle seat.

The man doesn't respond but tucks in his legs to free up space. Miraya nods in gratitude and shimmies past him successfully. She drops her leather baguette bag next to her leg and fiddles with the seat belt.

Her phone rings, rather too loudly. The young man beside her makes a face and a sound of irritance. "Sorry," she mutters, digging into her bag to get her phone.

It was Shray.

"Where the hell are you?" he bellows through the phone.

Anger flares through her. "Where the hell were you? I scoured the entire airport for you and you never picked up my calls. How long was I supposed to wait?"

The young man repeats the sound and only then she realises she was screaming. "Sorry. I am so sorry," she says, cupping her hands next to the mouth to whisper-yell at Shray. "I hate you and I am so mad at you."

"Miraya, the flight takes off at 8:30 am. It's only eight now. I am here."

"Don't you know that you are supposed to be there at the airport before two hours at least?"

Shray sighs. "It is unnecessary."

Miraya had actually missed a flight once. She had accidentally forgotten to switch the PM to AM when she set the alarm and slept through her reporting time. Her parents yelled at her when they found out, the people at work yelled at her and even Kishore had been done with her. After that incident, flight trips made her hyper-punctual. She was always two or three hours ahead of time, sometimes even more, to prevent history repeating.

So it's not her fault that she is cautious. Or if she is early for once in her life.

"Okay, where are you?" he asks, softly this time.

Just like that, her anger simmers down as well. "On the plane."

Shray hangs up.

Asshole.

Sometimes he annoys every single brain cell of hers. Alive or dead.

Slowly, passengers board the flight and she thanks herself for getting on early when she sees the excuse-mes and sorrys thrown around.

Her phone rings again and before the young man beside her can hiss at her again, she presses it to her ear. "What?" she snaps.

"Where are you? I am on the plane. I can't see you."

Miraya stands up, one hand holding the phone to her ear and another clutching the front seat.

"Did you accidentally sit in the wrong seat?" the man beside her pipes, a hint of hope in his voice.

"Unfortunately, no," Miraya says, feeling no longer kind towards him. He was a handsome man with neat clothing and a classy stubble. Even though he looked like a professionally kind-hearted man who'd help old women carry their groceries, he was a genetically annoyed man with a poor sense of patience. She wanted to pluck the expensive airpods out of his ears and crush them under her feet.

Miraya waves her hand when she spots Shray's face in the crowd. He locks eyes with her and then with the man beside her. He makes a face.

"Come over," Shray says.

"Where?"

"To my seat. I'll sit next to that man. You sit here comfortably," he says.

"But you don't fly economy. It wouldn't be right for me to take your business class seat. And people might recognise you if you come here," she says, adding the last part quietly.

"Shut up and switch seats with me, Miranda. Don't talk morals now."

"No. I am sitting here. You are sitting there. End of topic. Bye," Miraya says and hangs up. She shifts back to her seat and puts the phone on airplane mode.

The mandatory announcements come in and the safety measures are demonstrated. The plane takes off and the seat belt sign goes off.

Miraya nestles a romance book in her lap. The man beside her mutters something under his breath.

"Sorry, did you say something?" she asks.

"I just said romance books are a fool's way to waste money and time," he says.

Miraya's jaw drops. "Are you calling me a fool?"

"You did waste your money and time on a romance book. That does make you one, does it not?"

Oh, he better take that sentence back.

"Excuse me, Mr whoever you are, no one asked for your rotten opinion," she fires.

His eyebrows raise. "If I remember correctly, you were the one curious to know what I was thinking."

"That was because I thought you said something to me!"

"It's not my problem," he says, shrugging his shoulders.

"Nor should me 'wasting time and money on romance books' be," Miraya says, air quoting his words. "I suggest you keep your baseless thoughts to yourself, Mister."

The man makes a sound, accompanied by a smile that slights her. It pisses her off so much. She just can't sit beside a man who is so rude and offensive. She stands up and pushes past the man. "What the hell are you doing?"

"Why do you care?" Miraya shoots back and walks straight, passing the toilets. The air hostess stops her.

"I need to talk to someone. He is seated in the business class section."

"Ma'am, you should be seated in your seat. You can't move around unnecessarily."

"You don't understand. This is necessary," Miraya says. "It will take only a moment."

The flight attendant lets her go. She scans every one of the rich suits and branded shoes in the seats and narrows down on the messy mop of hair. Shray has his legs propped up on the sofa-like thing and scrolls through his phone.

"Shray."

"What are you doing here?" he says, sitting up straight.

"Can we switch?" Miraya asks, biting her lips.

Shray smirks and crosses his arms over his chest. "I thought you did not want to. *End of topic.*"

"That man beside me—"

Shray loses his grin. He immediately shoots question after question. "Did he misbehave? Did he try to make a pass at you? What did he do?"

"No. He is an asshole."

"Why? What did he say?"

"He called me a fool."

Shray leans back against his seat. "He was being honest. How does that make him an asshole?" Shray asks in all seriousness. But in the end, a smirk tugs at his lips.

"I forgot that you were an asshole too," Miraya says, turning back on her heels. What was she even thinking when she asked him to switch seats? Where had her self-respect gone when she decided to do that?

"Miranda!" She thought she heard Shray call but she never turned. She was so pissed, spewing invisible fumes when she rudely barged into her seat.

Miraya glared at the man next to her as she took her book and harshly flipped the page. He rolled her eyes at her. The audacity this man has for unabashedly bashing her and her choice of genre! She wanted to smack him with her book.

"Women these days," the man mutters.

Okay, that's it.

"Excuse me? Just how high do you think of yourself? I understand that you may have different opinions, however dumb they are, but do you think you are entitled to speak them out loud even though you know it may be offensive to others? Do you not care about the feelings of others? And what did you say? Women these days? What does that even mean, you— you— *man*!"

"Man? That's the best you can come up with?" He laughs. "Look, women, in the name of being true to themselves, are being silly and immature. Romance books. At the age of —what," he scans her up and down, "— 25? Don't you have something real you can focus on?"

"Why does it even bother you? It's not your problem."

He looks around and sees the others tuning into their argument. "Look, don't raise your voice against me. I won't be ridiculed by a woman like you."

Miraya is so close to punching him. So close.

"Woman like me?"

"Yes. Dumb, arrogant, inde—"

"I wouldn't finish that sentence if I were you," a voice comes.

Shray.

The man turns to him. "And who are you?"

A round of whispers echo through the plane. Shray is hard to recognise with the beard but it isn't impossible.

"None of your damn business." Those five words make Shray look so damn hot and sexy, more than any other heroic dialogue in any of his movies. The way the words cut through his hardened jaws and present themselves like a sharp knife makes her heart sigh. Even though it feels great to defend oneself, it feels even better to be defended by someone else. Preferably by Shray in his rugged beard and messy hair.

All her reasons to be mad at him evaporate into thin air.

The man raises his eyebrows. It goes up so high that it hits his hairline. Shray glares at him.

The flight attendant steps in. "Is there a problem here?"

"No," Miraya quickly says.

"Actually yes," Shray says. *Don't make this into a big deal*, she screams with her eyes. He ignores her. "I would like to exchange seats with this man."

"Why should I—" the man starts.

"It is a business class seat," Shray interjects. The man shuts his mouth.

"He feels very stuffy here which makes his brain slow and murky. Maybe a little space would help him think better," Shray artfully suggests.

"Would that be okay for you, sir?" The attendant asks the man. He doesn't look at Miraya or Shray while packing his things and moving out of the seat.

Shray smugly takes his seat. "Shouldn't you be thanking me, Miranda?"

"I could have handled it myself," she says, looking the other side, hiding a smile.

"Yes, you could have. But I couldn't help myself. I wanted to slap him when I heard him call you names."

"And yet you offered him the expensive seat."

"Yes but a seat next to you is all I care about. I would give away thousands of those seats if I could sit with you in this crampy space," Shray admits. Miraya can't help but blush at his words.

"Do you think people recognized you?"

"I don't care about it, Miranda. This trip is about you and me. No one else," he says and then yawns like a cow. "I am so damn tired. Can I lay my head on your shoulders?"

Sure, she almost says. "Is this why you wanted to sit next to me?" she asks.

He shrugs.

"Use this." She throws him the neck pillow she brought.

He grumbles but uses the pillow to lay his head back and close his eyes. Miraya watches him toss and turn in his seat for a while but a few minutes later he settles into a position. When Miraya looks up from her book, she finds him lying so awkwardly, curled up on himself in a way that will surely bring him aches everywhere.

She puts down the book and slowly lifts the arm rest between them.

"Shray," she whispers.

"Hm?"

"Come here," she says, guiding his shoulders to her side so that he can lean on her. He doesn't even open his eyes when he nestles his head on the crook of her shoulders. His warm breath hits her skin, pricking her with goosebumps everywhere. She bites her teeth.

Miraya wraps an arm around him so that his head doesn't slide off.

He whispers something that sounds a lot like I missed you. Miraya could've misheard it but still it warms her heart.

Miraya presses her lips to his hair and lays her head on his.

Chapter 32

"**Y**ou should have booked a room, Shray," Miraya says, hitting his shoulders. "There is no use whining about it now."

"I thought I'll just pay for one in whichever hotel you were staying in," he mumbles, sitting on the chair in the reception area. Miraya paces in front of him.

"It's holiday season. Everything is full. The bookings open two months early here. Why didn't you think about it?"

Shray takes her hand. "Miranda, I barely had time to book a plane. It was all last minute. You know that," he says.

She sighs and takes a seat next to him. "You should have at least asked me about it."

"I know. I am sorry."

"Now what should we do? Should we check for availability in any other hotel? Just for you?"

"I am not leaving anywhere without you," Shray says.

Miraya glares at him. "What else do you expect me to do?"

"I'll just crash in your room, Miranda. On the sofa. I'll not bother you at all when you work. I'll keep to myself," Shray pleads. Miraya considers him with a suspicious glance. Is he planning something by any chance?

"I am not planning anything," Shray says.

Miraya's palms fly to her mouth. "Did I say it out loud?"

"No, but I can tell by the look in your eyes. I promise, Miranda. I'll be good."

Shray and Miraya had been friends for so long but they had never slept together in the same room. Sometimes, during their study sessions, Miraya would fall asleep in his bed. In the morning, she would find him sleeping in Vidyut's room. It was too weird, sharing a room. So, Miraya was nervous.

"Miranda?"

She glances at him.

"You've been staring at that flower vase for far too long. What is going on in that pretty head of yours?"

"Nothing," she says. "You can stay with me. But no one knows about this, understand?"

Shray grins. "Got it," he says, picking up both of their bags. Sometimes she wonders how Shray became such a popular actor. He was way too idiotic and child-like.

Miraya kicks off her slippers and crashes on her bed as soon as she is inside her room. Shray drops off the luggage and opens the blinds. From the bed, Miraya can see the view. It's beautiful. The sea. The calming blue. The colorful tourists, dotting the white sand. It is not too sunny or cold. The weather is just perfect. Perfect to take a walk along the beach.

But Miraya needs rest. At least a nap. Otherwise she can't do her work.

Curling her legs under the sheets, she closes her eyes. Miraya can feel Shray's footsteps move here and there. She thinks she can leave him to unpack his bag and settle in but his footsteps keep her awake. It's too distracting.

"Shray."

"Hmm?"

"Come here."

He pads over to the bed.

"Sit."

He does.

Miraya closes her eyes again.

"What? Why did you call me?" he asks.

"Just shut up and sit here. I can't sleep when you keep moving around the room," Miraya says.

She could tell without seeing that Shray was rolling his eyes. "I'll just check if the kettle is working. I need something hot to drink," he says, getting up.

Miraya closes her palms around his calf. "Stay here. Please."

Shray sighs. "Fine, *madam*," he says and leans back against the headboard. Miraya doesn't realise she still has her hand coiled around Shray's leg. Shray doesn't mind. He picks up his phone and texts his mother to let her know about his whereabouts.

Without the WiFi password, Shray doesn't know what to do with his phone. So he tosses it on the bed and stretches without waking up Miraya. Shray pauses mid-stretch and stares at her, suddenly taken aback by how beautiful she looked even while sleeping. Her cheek is pressed to the pillow and her body is curled to one side. The black strands of her hair are all over her forehead, splayed out on the pillow like a dark mess.

Shray reaches out and pushes her hair back so that it doesn't fall over her eyes. Miraya snuggles into his touch more and inches closer to where he was sitting. Shray freezes when she does it, fisting his fingers in the air to resist the urge to pull her close and tuck her under his chin.

Shray remembers that Miraya's response to someone carding her hair was to close her eyes and let her head fall back. She would often claim she fell asleep in the salon but Shray and her friends never believed it. They thought she was cracking a joke.

But Shray believed when he saw it happen. He realised that the quickest way to put her to sleep was to play with her hair. She would be out like a light.

It was during the time when Miraya's parents left her for two days in Shray's home to attend a funeral elsewhere. Shray's mother's happiness knew no bounds at the possibility of caring for Miraya like she would a daughter. Shray and Vidyuth hated that Miraya grabbed all of their mother's attention for those two days.

One evening, when his mother oiled Miraya's hair, Miraya fell asleep. Shray and his brother had thought she was pretending but she actually fell asleep with her head on his mother's lap.

And now Shray's fingers automatically move through her raven hair. He watches her chest rise and fall evenly, her face so at peace without the constant worry or tension that lined her face.

Shray realises at that moment that this feeling of watching her sleeping safe and sound with him beside her is all that he ever needs in his life. It's all he ever wants.

□□□□□□□□□□□□□

When Miraya wakes up, Shray is in the shower. Her hand clutches her grumbling stomach, reminding her that she hasn't eaten all day.

Just as she picks up the menu card lying on the bedside table to order something, the doorbell rings. She bundles her hair into a ponytail and pads over to answer it.

"Your lunch, Ma'am," the woman says, bringing in a tray of hot food. Miraya stares at her quizzically, wondering if Shray had ordered the food. And as if to answer the question, Shray walks out of the bathroom in a towel, dripping an army of water droplets from his hair and his chest. Smooth, hard-planed, tempting-to-run-her-hands-over chest.

"…. wake you up?" Shray asks, which registers in her mind only belatedly.

"Huh?"

"I asked if the doorbell woke you? I thought I'd take a quick shower before the food came but before that — Miranda?"

"Huh?"

He tilts his head. "Why are you walking backwards?"

"I am?"

The back of her legs hit the sofa. But she can't take her eyes off him. Shray slaps his hair to push the water off the strands. Watching him do that while he had nothing on except a towel which sat low around his waist, sucked the air out of her lungs. He was beautiful. So fucking beautiful that she can't bear to take his eyes off him. She wasn't even embarrassed because he was art and art deserved to be stared at and appreciated.

"It's nothing you haven't seen before, Miranda," he says, an obvious tease climbing up his voice. Heat creeps up her neck, warming her face.

"I've s-seen this before?" she asks dumbly.

"You haven't? I thought you watched all my movies."

"Oh. Right. The movies," Miraya says, blinking. With a pang of disappointment, she realises that probably every woman in the state had seen him like this.

Not without a screen between him and them. Not with him standing so close to you that you can smell his green apple-flavored shampoo, her mind reminds her in consolation.

Only then, she realises the woman who came to deliver the food was still waiting at the door. Also staring at Shray.

"Would you put on some damn clothes?" Miraya says to him, stepping in front of him to block his view of the woman.

"Women are so hard to read," he mumbles, his shoulders falling as he walks over to the closet. On the way, he leans close, so *close*, that his lips almost brush the shell of her ear, "It really seemed like you didn't want me to," Shray whispers. She shivers, white-hot desire shooting through her veins all over her body.

Miraya doesn't dare respond to him and instead focuses on the attendant. "You asked for extra blankets but we only have thin sheets available. Is it okay?" the woman asks.

"Why not blankets?"

"We don't really provide extra blankets or extra beds, Ma'am," she says.

Great.

"Please bring the sheets anyway," Miraya says. "Thank you for your help."

She is about to shut the door when the woman starts again.

"And Sir said the TV remote wasn't working. Can I check it?"

"I don't think both of us would need the TV. Thank you," Miraya says, slightly annoyed. The woman smiles, which looks very much forced, and leaves.

"What did you mean by 'we won't need the TV'?" Shray asks, putting on a white t-shirt. "Why would we not need the TV? What else would we be so busy doing that we won't need the TV?"

Miraya catches on to what he was implying only seconds later. "You dirty-minded idiot," she says, smacking his shoulders.

"What? I just asked an innocent question. What naughty things did you think of?" His smirk is so big that it looms over the entire vibe of the room. "Come on, Miranda. Don't be shy to share those dirty thoughts of yours."

Her face heats up. "Don't you dare turn this on me. You started the whole thing!" Miraya lungs forward and Shray climbs up the bed.

"No, I didn't. It was you who implied to the woman that we were going to be so busy having sex that we wouldn't need the TV!"

"*Shray Nivas!*" If her face wasn't flaming red before, it was now. Miraya climbs the bed but he gets down and sprints across the room. Miraya chases him.

"Shit, there's not enough space to run here!" Shray shouts, jumping over the table.

Miraya climbs over the sofa and tackles him to the ground. They fall with a thud but Shray takes most of the weight. He winces.

"You asked for it," she says, blowing her stray hair away from her face and smacking his chest once more for good measure. He grabs her hands and places it on his heaving chest.

"Do you think after hearing all the noise from our room, people would think we were having mindblowing, earth-shaking sex?" Shray says.

"Shray! Stop it!" Miraya punches his shoulders, her face turning hot.

"Ouch. Okay, okay," he says, securing his hold on her hands. "I'm sorry. I love teasing you. Especially if it makes you blush. Your face is red." There is a fondness in his voice that melts away the annoyance in her.

"I hate you." The words are weak with a hint of a smile on her face.

"You look beautiful," he says, bringing her palms to his lips and placing a lingering kiss.

Miraya's breath catches. Only then she realises they are in a very compromising position. Both her knees are on either side of his hips and her palms were pressed to his chest. She was basically straddling him.

"Shray, don't," she breaks, especially when she sees the look in his eyes. They look at her as if she is the only thing that matters in the world, as if she is his everything. It makes her stomach drop and feel anxious and nervous at the same time.

"You know I love you, Miranda. What's there to lose?"

"You can't do this to me. You can't make it difficult for me," she says, snatching her hand back and standing up.

"Then I'll make it easy, Miraya. Tell me what to do and I'll do it."

She doesn't look at him. "I just... I am confused, okay? I really want to love—" She hears the sharp intake of air from Shray and pauses. "You know what, I don't want to talk about this. I have work to do and I have to focus on that. I can't have this conversation right now."

"Miranda..."

"Please, Shray. Understand," she says, before grabbing her clothes and rushing off to shower.

Chapter 33

♥

By the time Miraya returns back to the hotel, it's seven in the evening. She should have worn something full-sleeved or carried a jacket just in case because it was turning colder as the darkness rolled in. Her cotton indo-western top was doing less to save her from the chilly air.

She wraps her arms around herself, clutching the jingling pouch of jewellery that she couldn't resist buying when she went to work on the story. Since Miraya had sat down with them, given them a chance to explain their hard work and their difficulties, the artisans had saved her the time of bargaining and sold her some beautiful pieces of jewellery for optimal price.

Miraya steps into the elevator, feeling a little warm inside. She pulls out her phone and notices that there is a message from Shray that he is waiting in their room if she wants to have dinner with him. She had barely eaten anything after the hurried lunch she had with Shray. Speaking of which, it was the most awkward lunch she has ever had. They hadn't spoken while they ate and Miraya told him goodbye without meeting his eye when she left.

In truth, she had expected or hoped that Shray would tag along with her since he was very persistent with the idea of them spending time together. When he did no such thing, she wondered if she had been too harsh or stirred up tension between them again. He had been on her mind all day, to no one's surprise, but she felt bad about leaving things the way she did.

When she rings the bell, Shray opens the door. "How was it? You look so tired."

Miraya runs her hands over her face. "It was good. Interesting. I might have to go again tomorrow if the pictures I clicked aren't good enough," she says, dropping her bag on the sofa and her jewellery pouch on the bedside table.

"What about dinner?" Shray follows up after her, picking up her bag and hanging it on the hook on the wall. He grabs the pouch and places it on her side of the closet.

"Are you hungry? I was thinking we can have a late dinner."

"But aren't you hungry?" Shray asks. Miraya shakes her head and pulls out her laptop. "Why don't you have these?" He gives her a packet of chips.

"Where did you get it?"

"I went out, took a walk. I bought a bunch of these from a local store."

Miraya takes it and stuffs a few chips in her mouth. She is just glad there is no awkwardness between them again. They were back to being casual and that was a good sign.

Miraya types out her notes and a few things she wanted to elaborate on. She had a rough creative idea about how to present this story and it aligned with what Lakshmi had in mind. Putting the story and the information into words and shaping it artfully was going to take much more time.

"Do you need help?" Shray asks, sprawling himself next to her on the bed. He lays so close to her, without a moment of hesitation. If it would have been anyone else, she would have judged them for not knowing what personal space is but because it's Shray, she likes the proximity. She likes that he feels familiar enough to cross that line with her and feel normal about it.

"Would you transfer the pictures from the camera to my laptop?" she asks. "I'll freshen up and we can go have dinner."

"Sure, okay," he says and shifts to a sitting position to work. She hands over the laptop to him and stalks into the bathroom.

The first thing she notices is two toothbrushes in the cup, standing side by side. Shray's toiletries are stacked on one side of the counter beneath the mirror. Miraya's toiletries are on the other side, neatly arranged unlike how she had left it. A laugh escapes her lips. It was almost as if Shray and Miraya were married. Miraya would be the messy wife and Shray would be the orderly husband, tidying up after her.

Miraya's mind wanders to dream of what it would be to be actually married to him. Maybe they would be curled up together in bed every morning until one of them has to get ready for work. Maybe they would brush their teeth together, standing beside each other across the mirror. Maybe Shray would make her breakfast when he has a day off and kiss her goodbye when she leaves to work. Maybe when she returns from work, she would be greeted with a tight hug from him and they'd spend the rest of the evening watching movies or cuddling.

The pictures in her head were so beautiful that she yearned for them all. Getting married to Shray would be a dream. She knows it like the back of her hand. But she can't just keep pretending nothing ever happened between them in school.

Miraya splashes water on her face and stares at herself in the mirror. She has only one more day with him. They can be anything they want. Miraya wants to take whatever she can get now if she can't afford a future with him.

Dabbing a towel on her face, she steps out of the bathroom and finds Shray watching something on her laptop. "What are you watching? I don't think there were any videos in the camera," she says, looking over his shoulder.

Her eyes widen and she snatches the laptop from him. "I gave you one job, Shray! Why are you snooping around on my laptop?"

Shray quickly gets to his feet. "Look, I wasn't snooping around. It was a mistake, Miranda. I was actually double-checking if the files were transferred and I saw a folder named Ferdinand. I clicked it out of curiosity because we had that joke going on between us in school."

"You weren't supposed to see that," Miraya cries, almost defeated. She crashes down on the bed, clutching her laptop to her chest.

He comes to her side and wraps an arm around her shoulders. "Hey, it's okay. I'll tell you something, Miraya. No one, not another soul, has kept track of my milestones like you did. Not even me. I don't even remember what my first commercial was. It felt so good to see everything, so neatly organized."

"Your first commercial was for that headache balm," Miraya says, hiding her face in her hands. "But that's not the point. I am so sorry."

"Miranda, look at me."

She doesn't.

Shray pries her hands off her face and turns her towards him. "There's no reason you should be sorry. I should thank you. Because Miranda, this is the most touching thing anyone has ever done for me. The first thing I felt when I saw all the pictures and the video clips of me, labeled with the date and my milestone, my eyes teared up. I seriously wanted to cry. It meant so much to me that even if we weren't in touch, you still supported me in your own way. And you were proud of me. That makes me very happy."

"So, it's not creepy?"

He laughs. "Miranda, you idiot woman, of course it's not creepy. I fucking love you for it. I want to take you in my arms and kiss the hell out of you."

Miraya looks up at him. His eyes move from her lips to her eyes. "I—I just... even though we weren't talking, I couldn't help but be proud of you. I mean, I know how much you wanted it. Even though I hated you, I felt like a proud friend. Like I had been there with you all along. Sometimes— sometimes when I miss you, I go through these pictures to remind myself that you are in a different world than mine and that you are happy. It's so ironic considering I was also mad at you but I guess I couldn't help it. "

Shray's hands cup her cheek. "I wasn't entirely happy, you know. I missed you. I missed you every single day and wished you were by my side."

Miraya's eyes tear up. Her lip trembles and she bites it to keep it in place. "Don't say that. Don't —"

"Can I kiss you?"

Her eyes stare into his dark brown eyes and she sees herself in them. That look. Shray is giving her that look again — the one which screams that she is the only thing he can see. Like she is his everything.

When she doesn't answer, Shray's eyes turn sad but yet understanding. He tries to cover it up. Before that, something just snaps free inside her.

Miraya places her palm on the nape of his neck and brings his head closer. Shray's breath catches but before he could process what was happening, she presses her lips against his.

Shray takes a moment to recover from the shock but wastes no more time before cupping her chin and bridging them closer. He kisses her like he had been starving for years and years. Carnal. Animalistic. Like he wants to taste all of her at once.

Miraya's eyes fall shut. At this moment, everything is Shray.

Shray, Shray, Shray.

Her hands wander into his soft hair, gripping the strands gently but firm as the kiss turns wet and needy. She releases a gasp when he bites her bottom lip, making her want to press into him more. Fueled by hunger and greed, Miraya climbs on his lap. Shray squeezes her hips and brings her closer to him.

His lips leave hers and move to feather kisses over her jaw. He nips and bites at the skin as his lips move to her throat, burying his face in her neck as he sucks the skin there. Miraya sighs and bites her lip as he pushes the strap of her top aside to cup her shoulder with his mouth. "I love you," Shray whispers, his beard scratching against her skin, making heat pool downwards in her body.

"Can I—um, take this off—" Miraya breathes, tugging at his shirt.

"All yours," he whispers, never stopping the kisses. Before she can tug off her shirt, Shray sucks at the skin near her collarbone and a strange sound of pleasure, which she never knew she could elicit, ripped out of her. "Ah, so this is your weak spot."

She can hear the fondness in his voice and she closes her eyes shut again as he gives special attention to it. Her fingers clutch his shirt and before she can change her mind, she tugs it off him. Oh, how many times had she wondered what it would be like to be held by him and pressed flush against his chest.

Miraya's hands wander, drawing patterns and shapes, feeling the ridges of his toned body and making him gasp a little when she slightly presses her nails to his skin. Shray captures her lips again and his hands roam from her hips to the insides of her shirt. "Is this okay?" he asks.

Miraya doesn't think. She immediately nods. She wants his hands on her.

His hands move farther, upwards, running over the strap of her peach-coloured cotton bra. "Can I take your shirt off?" he asks.

"I should have worn that lacy black bra," she mutters in a moment of regret but pulls it off herself.

Shray breathes heavily. He stares at her."I swear to fucking god, you will be the death of me. You look-you look... perfect. So utterly fucking beautiful," he breathes, peppering a kiss on her shoulders for every word. Shray rolls her over the bed so he is on top of her and presses his lips to her neck softly.

"You are perfect," he whispers again, kissing the outline of her bra. "Black lingerie or not."

Miraya smiles and tugs him up to press her lips to him. Shray's fingers trail downwards, across her chest, grazing her skin in a tease. Miraya reflexively arches against him, pressing her chest into his fingers for more. Just when Shray's fingers go around to the hook in her bra, Miraya's phone rings.

Both of them turn to the direction of her phone and then glance at each other. When Miraya purses her lips in apology, Shray rolls off her and walks to her bag to fish out her phone.

"Who is it?"

"Dakshina," he grumbles, tossing it to her. "I don't like her so much now."

Miraya laughs and answers the phone.

Chapter 34

Miraya can't stop smiling. She had left the hotel early in the morning to dig up more on the life of the jewellery artisans. When she was talking to a young girl who helped make bracelets, there came a slight tap on her shoulders. She simply could not believe that Shray had traced back to her because she never once mentioned where she was going to be.

Shray chose to hijack the camera and do his own thing when Miraya refused to give him attention. When she was satisfied with the content she gathered and the work she had done, Miraya joined Shray and they walked together.

That's when Shray decided to hold her hand.

Miraya glanced at him and then went back to staring forward, a small smile playing on her lips.

And she hasn't stopped since then.

None of them chose to speak about what happened between them the previous night. Miraya was anxious when she woke up with her cheek pressed to his chest and his arm curled around her waist. They had slept in the same bed together. They had kissed and made out and almost had sex.

But none of those scary details made Miraya regret it. She was anxious about discussing what happened because she doesn't have an explanation for losing control and acting on her desire. Whatever she says will make no rational sense. That scared her.

But since both of them had silently come to an agreement to not bring it up but continue on that path, it was okay. For one day, she would forget all her inhibitions against giving Shray every bit of herself and act on what she wants.

Him.

When they go back to India, this glossy dream will shatter and she will have to face reality. She will have to think of a way to fake-break up with Shray to stop the marriage.

But today, she was just going to live in the moment. With Shray, in his arms, next to the iridescent waves and beachy sand.

"What are you thinking?" Shray asks. He is wearing a pale pink translucent shirt and denim shorts. Coincidentally, his outfit matches with her pink floral sundress.

"Nothing," she says, leaning into his side.

Shray lifts her hand and presses a sweet lingering kiss over her knuckles. As if he wasn't the least bit aware of Miraya's heart exploding into pink glittery goo inside, he removes his hands from her hands and circles it around her waist, pressing their sides.

"I love this. You, me, here and the fact that I can show you off to these people," Shray says.

Miraya smiles and sighs, feeling like someone tipped a bucket of warm sunshine on her, brightening her life. She gripped his shirt tighter and leaned closer to Shray. A delicious mixture of mandarin and musk and something so entirely him fills her nose and like every woman in a romance book, she wants to bottle it up and wear it around her neck.

"You smell so good," she mumbles, placing a hand on his chest.

"I know."

Her eyes narrow and she smacks his chest. "You've been given so many compliments that it's gotten to your head."

"I don't care about what the others say, Miranda. I only care about what you do," he says. Miraya pulls away from his hold and crosses her arms across her chest, a smirk playing on her lips.

"Oh really? I think I remember someone whining over an article just two weeks back saying they got called cute instead of sexy. It looked a lot like you but I guess I was wrong. My bad," Miraya comments.

"Fine. Maybe I care about what others say. But the words that come out of your mouth are —" he raises his arm over his head, "here. Nothing can top it."

"Oh, really?" Miraya says, pressing herself back to his side. He wraps an arm around her and quickly presses a kiss just next to her ear.

"Really," he whispers hoarsely in her ear. Miraya trembles in his arms, a shaky breath leaving her lips, too dazed to take another step forward. Satisfied with her reaction, Shray smirks and pulls her along to keep up with his arrogant steps.

□□□□□□□□□□□□□□□□

Shray and Miraya have lunch in a small cafe fashioned like a hut. She spears the sweet garlic shrimp on her plate with her fork and stuffs it into her mouth. Shray wasn't a big fan of seafood. He could tolerate shrimp and liked squid but he hated fish and crab. His preferences made no sense — not that it had to — but back in school, it had always bothered her that he didn't like what she loved.

She had been pushing him to try eating fish since school but now Miraya was more mature about it. She knew that all his preferences and dislikes were a part of him.

"Can I ask you something?" she starts.

"Sure," he says as he pours himself a glass of water.

"Did you ever date anyone after school? Any exes or flings?" This question has always been on her mind.

It takes Shray by surprise. But he quickly wipes the look away and says, "Yes. I was in a relationship. It was very private and no one knew about it."

"Oh." The disappointment is quick to boldly colour her face. "Um, how long did you date?"

"Four years."

"Oh." Surprise, shock, and disapproval greets Miraya. Four years is a lengthy commitment. "Were you close? I mean, how close were—"

Shray leans forward with a teasing glint in his eyes. "Miranda, if you want to know if I had sex with her, then yes. I did. We dated for four years. What do you expect?"

"Oh. Right," she says, covering a wince. Both of them knew that Miraya was expecting a negative answer to all of her questions, secretly hoping she had been the one in his mind all along. It was a cruel thing to expect, especially when she had no plans to save this complex relationship between them.

Only when she glances up from glaring at the plate for too long, she realises that Shray is smirking at her. "Oh, Miranda. My sweet sweet jealous Miranda," he says in adoration. "Did you really believe it?"

Miraya frowns. "What—"

"I lied, you beautiful idiot. Do you really think I would've dated someone else and had sex with her when you were the only person fucking with my mind for eleven years and counting? Can't you see that I am blind to anyone else but you?"

"But it never stopped you from getting into relationships in school," she argues.

He laughs. "Miranda, those weren't relationships. Those were just my failed attempts at shaking you off my mind. It never worked. Not even once. You're like... the she-hulk inside my heart. No one is a match for you. You are invincible," he says, raising his hand above his head.

Miraya's lips curl at his terrible attempt at a Marvel reference.

"No need to get jealous. I am all yours, Miranda. Yours to do with what you will," he says.

Miraya's heart sinks at his words. Because what she was going to do with him is leave him and break his heart.

□□□□□□□□□□□□□□□

After lunch, Shray suggests sightseeing. Miraya knew that if they got into it, it would take more than a day to see all of this place. And as the amber light dims and the crystal skies darken, Miraya grows anxious. Their day was ending. The hours were slipping past them like invisible waves, leaving a ripple of ache in her chest with each one gone. She wants to tie herself to Shray for the rest of the day and she doesn't care about where they go or what they do.

Miraya wants to just exist beside him. Close to him. Be held by him.

"Have you tried sea walking?" Shray asks.

"No. I always wanted to try it but I never had the chance to go," she says.

"Maybe we can go now. I heard it's really good —"

Without a warning, the sky cracks open and pours rain. It starts with a drizzle but just when Miraya shrugs it off as nothing, rain pounds. "Shit. We have to find shelter!" she says, moving to the side.

But Shray doesn't move. Instead, he tugs her back. "What are you doing? Come on!" Miraya pulls at his hand but he simply shakes his head with a grin on his face.

"Dance with me."

"What?"

"I said dance with me," he repeats, staring into her eyes. With the coldness drenching her and her view of him blurring with a curtain of rain, she shivers.

"You're crazy to joke like that. Come on." She pulls him again but he doesn't budge.

"You know, the Miraya I used to know in school would have done it without a second thought."

She snatches her hand from him. "Well, that Miraya is dead now, Shray. If you are looking for her, you are on a hopeless search."

"No, she is not dead, Miranda. I've seen her when you laugh at cat videos at two in the morning, when you sleep with your hands tangled in your hair, when you look at seafood like it's your lifeline and when you look at me. She is not dead. You have just conveniently trapped her inside with something you are stubborn to let go and do you know what I see? I can see her struggling to get out. She wants to be free."

Shray's words feel like a brutal punch to her gut. Something inside her shatters. The noise of rain falls deaf to her ears.

"Come on, Miranda. One dance. Today was supposed to be our cheat day." He stretches out his hand once more, his hair and face dripping wet, rivulets of rain soaking his shirt and making it transparent. Miraya bites her teeth, holding back the tears and the urge to run away. She takes his hand.

Shray immediately tugs her close to him, pressing his chest against hers. His arm wraps around her waist and the other holds her hand. He stares into her eyes. "Dance with me."

So, she does. She moves with him as if she is in a trance, guided by the heat of his hands on her body and his bold gaze. Shray spins her around and pulls her back to him, whispering in her ears, "Do you know how hot you look right now? Drenched from head to toe, dress clinging to your skin, your neck dotted with raindrops that I want to wipe away with my lips. *God.* What an oxymoron you are. You make me feel alive and kill me at the same time."

"What an oxymoron you are. You make me love you and hate you at the same time," she whispers, her lips brushing his in a dangerous game but not enough to kiss. Shray's eyes darken, almost turning black with desire and temptation. He pushes his hips against hers and Miraya gasps. *Two can play this game,* his eyes seem to say.

Unable to resist, she leans in and presses her lips against his lips. Miraya has seen movies and read books in which people kiss in the rain. Only now does she know what they were talking about. It's a rare kind of bliss, a mix of something completely wild and something completely delicate. Shray's lips slide over hers, coaxing the little control she has and the access to her tongue wordlessly. Miraya's hands grip his shirt, leaning into him more and surrendering under his touch. Despite the icy shower of rain, all she can feel is hot. Burning hot, every inch of her skin.

Her fingers crawl upwards, tangling into his wet hair, gripping the slippery black locks for balance as she feels her knees go weak. It's amazing how another person, a mere human like her, can make her feel so vulnerable yet bold at the same time.

Shray groans when she bites his lips and that throaty sound from him sets her body on fire.

Suddenly, Shray pulls away from her.

Miraya blinks at him, hot and flushed, looking at him with confusion.

Then he sneezes. Once, then twice.

Her lips curl into a teasing grin. "So much for dancing in the rain," she says, throwing an arm over his shoulders and leading him towards shelter.

"Shut up."

Chapter 35

Shray steps out of the shower, leaving the bathroom filled with steam and the mirrors fogged up. Miraya is not in the room. He dresses himself and picks up his phone to call her but before that the door opens and she walks in. A brown paper bag is nestled in the crook of her arm.

"What's that? And where did you go?" Shray asks, followed by a loud sneeze.

Miraya doesn't answer his question. "Dry your hair," she says, grabbing a towel from the closet and throwing it at him. It hits his face.

She pulls out a tiny bottle of honey, ginger, turmeric powder and a few lemons. Shray stares at her. "What are you doing?"

"I called your mother," she says, pouring water into the kettle.

"What for?"

"I remember you saying your mother had a special tea that she would give you when you caught a cold. So I called her to ask for the recipe," Miraya says, casually as if there's nothing special about it. She breaks a piece of ginger, peels the skin off and smacks it a few times with the back of her bottle before dropping it inside the kettle. "You have to work, Shray. You can't afford falling sick. Your job is not like mine. No one will notice I'm gone if I take an off but your absence affects so many other people and their time."

When the water boils, she pours it into a cup and adds a pinch of turmeric, honey and a few drops of lemon juice. Shray simply shuts his mouth and watches her as she stirs the drink. She sips it a little and squints, going back to add a drop more of honey. She sips it again and nods with approval, walking towards him.

"Here. Drink up."

"Thank you," Shray says, taking the cup from her.

Miraya sits down next to him and watches him as he drinks it. "Funny how you didn't utter a word against drinking the tea. Your mother told me it would be hell of a challenge making you drink it."

"I like to do that with my mother. It's fun because she bribes me with the good stuff. Once, she bought me new shoes when I drank and ate whatever she gave me for a month with no complaints."

"So, you don't want anything from me?" Miraya asks.

Shray's eyes immediately turn to her. "I didn't think you would give me if I asked. I've been wanting an answer out of you for a long time."

Miraya recoils back. "Forget I asked anything."

"Thought so." Shray throws his arm around her shoulders and pulls her close to him. "This tea is not so bad."

"I'll make it for you again in the morning before we leave for the airport," she says, placing a hand on his chest. "Do you want to take a nap? I'll wake you up for dinner."

Shray places the empty cup on the table and pulls her onto the bed. "Only if you join me."

"You always liked to be pampered, didn't you?" she asks, her eyes carrying a teasing glint. When Shray replies with a heart-stopping smile and a shrug, she crawls towards him and wraps an arm around him. Shray pulls the covers over them and then snuggles into her chest, his arms wrapped around her waist, fingers tracing the strip of skin under the hem of her t-shirt.

"Where is that famous black lingerie, anyway?" he asks, lips against her skin.

"Shut up and go to sleep."

□□□□□□□□□□□□□□□□

The bright lights in their room falsely leads Miraya to believe that the day isn't ending just yet. Only when she checks the time on her phone, she realises it is eight in the evening. Shray and Miraya are supposed to have dinner and that's it. That's the end of their day. Panic settles inside her.

"Miraya? You ready?" Shray asks, buttoning down his maroon shirt.

She dabs her lipstick on and grabs her phone. "Yeah. I'm ready."

Miraya and Shray decided that the open restrobar that the hotel had was fancy enough for a casual dinner. It looked pretty in the day and the hotel staff promised that it looked prettier at night. When they step into the restaurant, they realise that the staff weren't wrong. The place really looked aesthetic with emerald green tiles and copper-coloured decor. Fairy lights and creatively designed lanterns lit the room, mellow and cosy with a hint of romance. The slow music playing in the restaurant added to the vibe.

Shray and Miraya occupy the table in the open, facing the beach. It's cold but Shray is quick to offer her his jacket. "Thanks," she says, quickly pressing a kiss to his cheek, surprising him.

"What's this for?"

"Because I can."

Shray's eyes resemble two golf balls. "Did something happen to you that I didn't know of? Did you hit your head or am I with Miraya's overly affectionate secret twin sister?"

"Very funny," she says, seating herself. "If you don't like it, just say so." Miraya is at the edge of a cliff, vulnerable and anxious. It's making her be extra, to do something, *anything*, to hold on to the rope that will save her.

"Kiss me in this crowded room and I will never blink an eye. No complaints," Shray swears with his palm on his chest.

Miraya shakes her head and looks through the menu. Her eyes pin onto the alcohol menu. Maybe this will help her stop thinking about the deadline that she has given herself and focus on the present. Because right now all her thoughts are about the sky, fearing the hues becoming darker and darker with time. She wants to drag back the sun that's gone to sleep and hammer it back in its place so it's day again. Forever. She wants to hold time by the throat and keep it strangled in her pocket. She'd be happy stuck with Shray for the rest of her life in this beautiful coastal town.

Miraya was regretting so many things. She thought she'd satisfy the craving of loving Shray that gnawed underneath her skin and her heart by indulging in it for a day. Put an end to the misery. Make her heart full with that one sip.

How horribly wrong and stupid she had been. Loving Shray was like drinking ambrosia. One sip was never enough. She wanted more and more and more. Her heart would never be full without him.

"I want a bottle of wine," she says.

"What?" Shray looks up from the menu.

"I don't care what you order to eat but I need alcohol," Miraya says firmly, tossing the menu card back onto the table.

"Miranda, is something wrong?"

"Absolutely not. Why do you think so? We can drink alcohol to celebrate as well, right?" she says, adding as much enthusiasm as she can muster.

Shray isn't convinced. His eyes pause on her for a moment, scanning her face, trying to decipher if she isn't well.

"Please, Shray."

"Fine. You always get what you want anyway," he mutters the last sentence under his breath and calls the waiter.

Everytime the grim thought of the day ending flashes across her mind, she takes a long gulp of the drink, relishing the delicious burn in her throat. Initially, Shray doesn't notice her drinking too much. He is focused on his food and the conversation he thinks Miraya is enjoying. But she isn't even listening.

She chews on the juicy meat, studying Shray as he cracks a joke. She laughs in response but her eyes capture every detail of him, wanting to staple it as the wallpaper in her mind. His dark brown eyes looking glassy under the fairy lights, his beard trimmed to perfection, black locks pushed into place with expertise. Child-like laughter with eyes crinkling so beautifully that she wants to kiss them. The very out-of-place friendship bracelet on his wrist that he wears like a trophy. His thin silver chain around his neck glints under the lights, easily outpowered by the twinkle in his eyes and the shimmer in his smile.

Miraya is a fool to let him slip away, knowing that he would be the best thing that would ever happen to her. Her heart wants to forgive him, burn her resentment up and cling on to him like he was her lifeline. But the best years of her life that he had stolen from her was a loss that she'd always mourn. She had been a prisoner in her own home because of him. There was no way he could give back her girlhood if she demanded it. It was irreparable. So were the scars on her heart, the wounds that refused to heal.

Miraya pours herself another glass of wine and presses it to her lips. Taking a long sip, she places the glass back on the table but instead ends up placing it on the plate with peppered mushrooms.

"Miranda!" Shray says, prying the glass out of her hold. She blinks and realises her mistake.

"I'm sorry. I didn't see," she mumbles.

"Your cheeks are red and I know it isn't because you are head over heels for me. You've drunk too much," he says, handing her a glass of water.

"No, I'm perfectly fine, Shray," Miraya says, gulping some water just to wipe that worry in Shray's face.

"Are you sure? I feel like your mind is somewhere else."

"No, I'm with you."

He leans back and crosses his arm across his chest. "Okay, tell me the question I asked you right before you almost spilled your drink on the table."

"I don't know...?"

Shray chuckles. "So cute. I asked you if you dated anyone in the past few years."

Miraya's hand reaches for the glass and she gulps the drink. She can feel it getting to her head. "No, no, I didn't," she whispers, tightening the grip on the glass.

"What about Siddh? Did you get back in touch with him?"

A piercing crack comes in response as the glass in her hand shatters into shards. Shray's chair screeches back when he rushes to her side, hissing, "Miraya! What's wrong with you?"

Miraya doesn't feel the gaze of the people in the room which would've, otherwise for the alcohol, set her aflame with embarrassment. Shray peels the shards that have embedded into her skin carefully as the restaurant staff crowd them. Tears roll down her cheeks and her body begins to tremble. "Shit, shit." Miraya can hear Shray's curses like a faraway echo as he wraps his arms around her tightly, pressing his lips to her head desperately, barely containing his panic. He holds her bloody hands in his gently, then slowly pulls her to his feet. "...first-aid kit... room... tab...thank you." She can only catch a few words because her head is swirling with the past. Her breath quickens and her body shakes within Shray's arms.

He walks her to the quiet part of the beach, where no one is around. He sits her down and rubs her back. "Miraya, listen to me, okay?"

Her heart thuds against her chest and even though the wind is strong against her face she struggles to breathe. "I-I can't breathe," she stutters, clutching her chest.

"Miraya, can you hear my voice?"

She nods.

He takes her hand and sandwiches it between his. "Okay, focus on my voice, okay? Just do what I tell you."

Her chest heaves higher and Shray wraps his arms around her tight, his chest pressed against her back. "Now take a deep breath for me, will you?"

A whimper rips out of Miraya. Her grip on Shray's hands is deathly. Her blood is all over his hands. "It-it hurts."

"Deep breath, Miraya. Just one," he whispers into her ear.

Miraya closes her mouth and inhales sharply. She lets it through her mouth.

"Good girl. Now one more," he says, squeezing her better hand and kissing her head.

She does as he says and then twice again. Slowly, her body calms down. Breath goes back to normal and her heart slows to a steady pace. But her tears doesn't stop. She stares at Shray through her blurry eyes and cries again, not holding back her tears. "It's all because of you. How long are you going to pretend, Shray? How long should I wait for you to realise what you did to me? You ruined my life!"

Shray sucks a sharp breath.

Miraya untangles from him and pushes away his hand. "I am tired of it, Shray. I am sick. Don't you even want to apologise for what you did? How could you be so heartless? Who gave you the right to come back into my life after what you did and make me fall in love with you again like a stupid girl? You betrayed me. And you have the nerve to ask me about Siddh. If you never liked him and I being together, you could have just fucking told me, Shray! Why did you have to go behind my back and get us caught? You just threw away our friendship like it never meant anything to you. It might have seemed like a simple situation when you did it but do you even know that one incident uprooted my whole life?"

"Miranda—"

"Don't call me that. I never should have talked to you again and I never should have fallen hopelessly in love with you again. It's just so easy to love you and fucking hard to hate you. But you know what? I really do hate you, Shray! I hate you for never hiding the chits I trusted you with, I hate you for choosing your cowardly crush against our friendship. If you really loved me, you wouldn't have done it, Shray! You betrayed me like it was so easy for you. Are you happy? Now that you know that my parents never looked at me the same way after the incident? Now that you know what happened then scarred my life forever?"

"Miranda, your hand," Shray says.

"Don't change the subject! I never should have agreed to this trip. I never should have talked to you again."

"It's bleeding too much, you idiot," he says, taking her hand. She shakes his grip off her and stands up to walk away from him. But Miraya's vision sways. She feels nauseous and dizzy.

She makes it a few steps forward and then her vision blacks out.

Chapter 36

When Miraya wakes up, she wakes up with a terrible headache. She raises her hands to clutch her head and only then she notices the white bandage around her hand. Feeling disoriented, she slowly pushes herself up and finds Shray sitting on the chair next to the bed, watching her silently.

"Good morning," he says.

She runs her better hand through her hair and tames it down. She feels salt tracks on her skin, dried-up and tightening her face. "Good morning. Didn't you sleep?"

"I couldn't."

She raises her eyebrow. "Why?"

Shray raises his eyebrow at her in return. "You don't remember what happened yesterday?"

Miraya squints her eyes as the curtains flutter open and beams of sunlight pierce the room.

Take a deep breath, okay?

Focus on my voice.

"Yeah. I remember. I had a panic attack."

"That's it?"

"It isn't very clear," she says, realising she is in different clothes. "Why? Did I do something?"

"You're honest when you are drunk, do you know that?"

"Huh?"

Shray leans forward and slowly takes her hands. He presses a kiss on both of her knuckles and keeps it under his lips. "Our plane is in five hours. Since you like to be there two hours early, and you need at least an hour to get ready, will you give me an hour? I want to talk to you. It's important."

"Is it about the panic attack? I get them occasionally but it's nothing to worry about."

"It's not about that."

Miraya doesn't see the harm in it so she agrees. "Okay then. I'll take a shower and then we'll talk. Alright?"

"Yes."

"Is everything okay? You seem... sad."

Shray forces a smile on his face. "How could I not be, Miranda? Today's the last day."

"Oh. Right," she says, contracting his sadness. She picks up her towel and her clothes and walks into the shower. She throws the bandage in the bin and inspects the wound. It's just two thin cuts, dry out of blood. When the water hits her skin, the cuts sting like a bitch. She hisses and pulls it back from the water and at that moment, everything that happened last night rushes to her mind.

The screaming, the accusing, the crying...

You are honest when you're drunk.

Now she knows the meaning of his words. Now she knows what Shray wants to talk about.

He finally knows the truth. He knows the reason why she has been at war with him.

And if he is going to talk about it, he is going to give excuses. Miraya doesn't need to hear them. It won't change the fact that he was the reason her life was ruined. There was simply no other plausible explanation for the chits getting confiscated and not his cigarette. He had never hid them in the first place and that was the only explanation.

Why he did it and what made him take that decision was something she did not need to hear.

Miraya takes a long time showering. When she steps out, she finds Shray nowhere in the room. She dresses herself and sits in front of the mirror, hoping he doesn't return soon. She needs to kill time before he can seize a window of opportunity to start the discussion.

When he returns with breakfast for two, she forces a smile and nods gratefully. But she doesn't speak a word. Nor does he before disappearing into the bathroom.

Miraya packs her clothes, being careful not to disturb the wound in her hand. She finds Shray's stuff already packed. Miraya is making Shray's tea when he steps out of the shower and starts to get ready. Neither of them speak a word.

There is an hour more to kill.

Miraya becomes anxious.

She goes to eat her breakfast but the cuts on her hand make her opt for the spoon instead. Even with the spoon, she isn't doing a great job at it. "Let me," Shray says, taking the spoon from her and feeding her. Miraya doesn't want to argue so she lets him feed her.

"Thanks for the tea," he says.

"No problem."

She doesn't even ask if he is doing better.

After he finishes his breakfast, Miraya helps him clear everything out. There are thirty minutes more and she can feel Shray searching for an opportunity to begin. When he opens his mouth, she blurts out, "Can you dress my wound?"

"Yeah. Yeah, of course. I forgot about it," he says, quickly moving to get the medical kit.

He covers her wound with speed but he does a neat job at it. He finishes it in ten minutes.

"I'll go check if I left anything behind in the bathroom." Miraya stands to leave but Shray grips her wrist.

"I already checked."

"Okay, what about the bedside drawer—"

"I know what you're doing, Miranda. You remembered everything, didn't you?" Miraya purses her lips and looks away. "We are having this conversation now no matter how much you try to evade it. It's important you know what really happened that day. I always thought you knew."

Miraya brings her hands to ear like a child. "I don't want to hear it. I don't want to talk about it. It's going to do nothing other than make me relive it and you don't know how hard it is for me. It nearly killed me, Shray."

"Miranda, it's not what you think—"

"No, Shray! Please. Don't. I don't want to have this conversation. I don't want to know why you did it."

"But I didn't —"

Miraya moves away from him and takes her bags. "I am leaving if you speak another word about it."

She can sense Shray getting frustrated. His eyes are growing tired and angry and desperate by the moment. But like a flip of the switch, his eyes begin searching for something. He goes to the bedside table and tears a paper out of the notepad.

He scribbles something on the paper and marches towards her. "People have their own versions about what happened. In your version, I can see the reasons why you assumed it was me who did it. If I were you, I would have done the same. But your version is wrong. You don't have the entire story. Since you are so stubborn not to hear it from me, I'll give you a choice."

He takes her hand and presses the paper into her palm. "Everything you want to know is here. If you are curious, check it out. Do it at your own pace. It's your call whether you want to keep believing something that didn't happen or know the truth of that day."

Miraya is stunned at his words. She doesn't know what to say.

Shray grabs his bags and walks out of the door, waiting for her outside, his eyes teary. He looks away when she follows him with her bags.

When they leave the elevator, Shray whispers, "I really hope you check it out."

Only on the plane, when she is sitting next to some stranger, does she read what is on the paper.

Pw: MIRAYA_not_Miranda

□□□□□□□□□□□□□□□□□□□□□

The next three days are agony.

Miraya can't sleep, can't work in peace and can't eat well without thinking of the note that Shray had pressed into her hand, claiming it had the key to her past. She should be curious to dig deep into it but all she is is frightened. Another fear is conjured and nurtured in her mind now. What if she had wasted the best years of her life believing a lie? What if Shray was right? What if I had been completely blindsided by what I saw that I didn't bother to second-guess Shray's betrayal? At least given him the benefit of the doubt that came with a decade-long friendship they shared?

As her mind piles up with these thoughts, she wonders if the Miraya back in high school would have given this so much thought before recklessly diving into it. She probably wouldn't have. Miraya was brave back then. She thought she was invincible, that no one could touch her and that nothing affected her. But, her blind optimism and recklessness crumpled into shards of cynicism and paranoia when her best friend struck her where it hurt. As much as Shray was stubborn to believe that high school Miraya was still alive, she knew that it was not a possibility.

Miraya's experiences had hardened her. She was no longer like a sponge, absorbing all that life threw at her with a bright attitude and slowly becoming heavier with her emotions and feelings. Now, Miraya is like a rock, already too heavy to soak up any more hurt. She's keen on dodging anything that makes her harder at the same time more brittle, because she is scared someday she might actually break.

Miraya grabs the paper from her wallet and flattens it out. The email ID and the password on the note were familiar. During eighth grade, Shray and Miraya had created that email for fun just so they could talk to each other during computer classes. They had fought over deciding on an email and a password so they had played rock paper scissors to choose who would pick what. Shray got the email and Miraya got the password.

It's so stupid and silly now that she thinks about but at that moment, when they laughed at the screen during class and glanced at each other from across the room, they thought they were the coolest of all. The other students thought they were crazy, or secretly in love, or that they were unnecessarily theatrical. But it had been their secret.

Miraya had completely forgotten about the existence of it after they had stopped having computer classes. She had assumed Shray had completely forgotten about it like she did but she was wrong. So she was really curious as to what was in the inbox and how the truth of her past can be revealed after she opens it.

Miraya traces the letters on the paper, contemplating whether to give in to her curiosity or not.

She remembers the last time her grandmother had come to visit. During their walk to the temple, she had advised her.

"Closure is tricky, Mira. Sometimes it's a healing balm, sometimes it's salt on your wounds. You should know when to seek it."

Miraya had asked, "How do I know when to seek it?"

"When the pieces you are missing mess with your peace of mind, that's when."

Her past has been messing with her peace of mind forever but she had never known there were pieces missing until now. Now it disturbed her more.

Should she take the leap? Should she dive deep into whatever this is?

Rubbing her forehead with her index fingers and her thumbs, she stands up and goes to the kitchen to pour her some coffee. She had made a huge batch and stored it in a flask when she returned from her office with a pile of work to do. It was almost 3AM. She was done with her work but she can't go back to sleep.

Might as well take a look at the haunting riddle of her past.

Pouring a generous amount of coffee without a sound as to not wake Dakshina, she goes back to her room and settles in her chair before her laptop.

Miraya takes a sip of the coffee and then rests it on the table. She picks up the paper and then takes a deep breath.

Here goes nothing.

Chapter 37

T he email has 2190 unread messages. Every single one of them is self-sent. Miraya's fingers tremble as they scroll down and navigate to the earliest mail. There are a few read mails stacking the bottom row, which are messages Shray and Miraya had sent to each other during their computer classes. She clicks on the first unread mail.

Dear Miranda,

I forgot this mail ID exists. I was going through my old phone one last time before I lent it to Vidyut and found that I was signed in through this mail. It's been two years since we used it and I thought, if it is coming back to me after two long years, it is for a reason. It means something. You know me. I can't let such a thing go easily.

I wanted to tell you but I decided against it when a better idea came to me.

So... I have decided to use it as my secret journal.

Okay, go on, laugh all you want. I know you are as you are reading it. But this is something I desperately need. I am going fucking crazy keeping these feelings in. Sometimes, I just want to get it all out because I am afraid I will struggle to breathe and end up dying. But sometimes, I look at you and smile because I am so in love with you but you don't even realise it when you smile back, so radiant, like the damn sun. That moment is worth all the pain.

Look, I am a coward. You might think I am not (I've heard you vouching for my bravery to the boys) but let me tell you, I can't take a damn risk when it comes to you. Losing you will kill me. I know you are raising your killer eyebrows at me as if I am insane but don't ask me how, I just know it, okay? I will disintegrate if I lose you. I love you so much, Miranda. I LOVE YOU.

That felt nice, getting it all out in capital letters.

Anyway, I honestly don't know when you will get to read all this shit or if you will ever. But I really hope you end up doing it. Because this is a piece of my heart that no one has ever seen. It's been sealed shut until now.

If somehow you get your hands on this, feel more than welcome to take a peek. It's all yours, anyway.

Love,

Your Shray

Anticipation and nervousness knots tight in her stomach. She braces herself and clicks the next one. Then the next one, and the next one. With every email she reads, she grows more curious and hungry for more because Miranda through his eyes is the most beautiful and precious girl in the world. It's so easy to fall in love with her.

Hey Miranda,

I'll let you in on a secret. Do you know what's my favorite part of getting hurt? You fussing over me.

You should have seen yourself in the hospital. Face so red and eyes so puffy, standing in your uniform like a little girl heartbroken over her broken toy, your hands not staying still. You know what I realised then? That you are the most beautiful girl on the entire planet. Because even though you ugly cry, the concern, the anger, the love and the affection streaked on your face makes you glow so bright that I want to drop on my knees and beg you to love me and never let me go.

And when you scold me as if I had hurt myself on purpose, as if I had gone and damaged what belonged to you — it makes me love you more, if that's possible. When I grin and smile as you scold, you think I deserve a beating. You punch me on my shoulders or smack my chest for making you worry.

I wonder. What have I done to deserve you? But then I don't care about it because even if I don't deserve you, I am never letting you go. I know that much.

Love,

Your Shray.

Miraya reaches for a tissue and sniffles into it, unsure whether to smile or cry at his words.

My Miranda,

So, something happened today. You didn't know about this because I didn't tell you.

I got into a fight with Raghu. It was after PE period. Both of us went back to the sports room to keep the basketballs. He talked about you. Asked me if I was in love with you. Of course I denied it. He laughed. 'Man, you are insane if you don't want her for yourself. I mean, did you notice during the game?' he asked. I was so confused. He told me to stop playing dumb and then whispered into my ears... something so filthy and insensitive about your body. I just lost it there, Miranda. Hit him square in the jaw.

I think he knew he was talking shit so he didn't bother to complain or make a scene about it. I warned him to keep his eyes the fuck away from you and stormed off. You asked me why there was a cut under my knuckles. I lied and said I got scratched by the shelves. You scolded me to be careful. It killed me that I lied to you.

I am sorry, Miranda. I know you won't want me to hide things like these from you but even though you pretend not to be hurt by what people say, I know you are fragile in the core. You have a glass heart but it's guarded with steel doors. And I promise you, if someday I get past those doors, I'll never ever cause the slightest crack on your heart. NEVER.

Love,

Your Shray

So many unsaid promises. So many words. As she reads each of them, she begins rooting for him. She wants him to keep his word. She wants him to be the man who honors his promises.

Hey,

During English class today when you sang our song, I was so happy at first. But that happiness turned into bitterness when I realised you were looking at Siddh and singing it. For him. Do you know how that made me feel? I felt like a loser. It was as if you took a knife and put it through my chest.

And I don't blame you.

It's not your fault. You have no clue about my feelings and that's okay. I wish you'd give me a warning when you brutally assault my pathetic lovesick heart like that.

Love,

Shray

Her memories flash before her, but each of them burns differently in her mind now after reading his perspective.

She scrolls through the messages and finds it never-ending. It is going to keep her up for hours more if she reads every single one of them. The questions in her mind are thirsty for answers. She needs them now. She can't afford to get lost in a love spiral with Shray and his delicate rosy words.

She recalls the dates the incident happened, numbers she always wanted to forget but never did. She clicks on that mail, taking a deep breath before beginning to read.

Dear Miraya,

I am so sorry about what happened today. I swear when you told me to hide the chits, I really did. Even though I was pissed that I have to cover up for you and Siddh, I ignored my aching heart and did it. I have no clue how the teachers found your chits. I didn't know how they missed my cigarettes. When the teachers asked me whose chits they were, I told them it wasn't mine. But I never told your name. I swear. I would never do that. When the class teacher came, she recognized your handwriting and Siddh's. I couldn't save you anymore. I knew denying it would only make things worse so I kept shut.

I am so sorry. God, I can't imagine how you must be feeling right now. Were your parents harsh with you? Did you cry? I know a hug can't heal everything but I wish I could hug you and tell you that I am always with you.

I called you so many times but your phone was switched off. I came by your house but your father told me not to come anymore. I asked my mom to call your mom just in case I can hear something about you, but your mom never picked up. I am going crazy here.

I hope you know that I'll always be here for you. I know you will get through this. I love you.

Love,

Your Shray

That's it? Where were the so-called pieces she was missing? Where was the full story?

She frowned. Shray had been so confident when he had pressed the note in her hands. It should be here somewhere.

Miraya opened the next mail, written the very next day.

Miranda,

YOU WON'T BELIEVE WHAT HAPPENED TODAY! *Today was a complete mess. I am so angry and betrayed and completely livid after hearing what really happened yesterday.*

I found out who was behind you getting caught. I was thinking about it and it was really odd. A lot of it didn't make sense. Then, I was in one of the bathroom stalls and the boys were talking about what happened to you and Siddh yesterday.

"They pulled the chits out of Shray's bag, man. I think they hid it there but somehow the teachers found it."

"Sad. Miraya is the only girl in the class who's not annoying, man. I felt so bad watching her get scolded."

"Wait, did you say Shray's bag? I saw Sona digging through Shray's bag when I was coming out of the classroom. I asked her what she was doing and she said Shray told her to keep something inside. So I didn't think much of it. Do you think she has something to do with it...?"

I stormed out of the bathroom and immediately found Sona. She was laughing with the girls as if nothing ever happened. I saw red, Miranda. I didn't even think about talking to her alone. I just confronted her in front of the whole class.

"Did you do it?"

"What? Shray, I don't know what you are—"

"Why did you touch my bag yesterday? I never told you to keep anything inside."

The look on her face said everything, Miranda. I could practically see her trying to come up with a way to escape. "Don't bother denying it. A lot of people saw you going through my bag. Tell me the truth. Did you take out the chits from that secret zip?"

Her walls were breaking down but before that anger replaced the vulnerability. Her eyes held fury. "Yeah, so what, Shray? It's not like

I falsely accused her of anything. What she was doing was wrong. I just made it easy for the teachers to catch her red-handed."

I swear to God, I would have slapped her if she wasn't a girl.

"Why? I thought you were our friend. Miraya shared everything with you. She was so close to you. She trusted you."

Sona scoffed. "She never trusted me and she most definitely did not share everything with me. The only person she considers a friend is you, Shray. No one else. We are just people she talks to."

"What did she ever do to you?"

"Everything. I work so hard to be where I am but her? She just skates through life like she is the goddamn ruler. On sports day, she is the star. Everyone is after her, treating her like a queen. I am much prettier than her but Siddh, the one guy I like, falls for Miraya. The teachers love her. She is so popular among the juniors. Even though I am always right next to her, no one pays me attention. No one recognizes me. I heard someone call me 'the short girl who tags along with Miraya' and do you know how infuriating and self-demeaning it is to be defined in terms of her?

"I am good at sports too, I study better than her, I sing too. I am good at everything but why don't I get the credit? And you. You make her feel like she is a goddamn queen. She didn't do her homework one day and I was so glad that at least one teacher sent her out as punishment. Then, you decide to join her as well. I heard you laugh when you came inside the class later. How come she gets to enjoy even punishments? She is happy all the fucking time. She gets what she wants. Nothing hurts her at all. How? I was furious. I was tired of being the side character, Shray. I was always overshadowed by her even though I worked harder than her. I want to be the main character for once. So I took her out of the story."

I was baffled. I couldn't even process what I was hearing, Miranda. She pretended to like you all the time.

"You know what, Sona? Joke is on you. The school is still buzzing about Miraya even after you pulled this shit. Nothing's going to change. You will still be invisible, Sona, and worse, you are going to lose the little respect you had."

The whole class was shocked, Miranda. No one expected for Sona to be such a cunning bitch. I always thought she was the sweetest person but turns out she is so fake. I can't believe she has hated us for so long and had pretended she was a good friend all this time. I can't believe we didn't see through her shit.

I want to talk to you. I miss hearing your voice. I called you again today. So many times. I am worried, Miranda.

I miss you, you know. I miss you so so so much. I wish you'd call.

Love,

Your Shray

Miraya can't swallow. Her mouth has gone dry. And nausea treks through her throat. The bitter realization is deep-hitting, shattering her to the core. Out of all people, *Sona?* She had lost her best years because of her. She had spent all these years thinking she was such a saint. Miraya felt shame and anger and disgust at her dumb self. She had been such a self-obsessed, foolish girl that she had overlooked Sona's pretense. Miraya had wasted her precious time because she had been so victimised that she'd refused to give Shray the benefit of doubt.

Sona's petty actions had cost her time and tears and memories but most importantly she had robbed Shray from her. Shray was her villain for seven years when he could have been something else.

Nausea. She can feel the bile rise up her throat. She rushes into the bathroom and throws up, gripping the icy marble of the sink so tightly that her knuckles pale. Her head is down, her body hunched in pain as she screams and cries, letting the hot tears flow down her face. Tears of grief, pain, anger and regret.

And all she can think of as she slides down onto the bathroom floor, stuffing her fist into her mouth to muffle her cries, is Shray. The look on his face when she told him to stay away from her, when she had heartlessly dismissed his advances to reconnect again, when she had stuck a knife in him as she spat out that she hated him so much.

That look haunts her, carves out her peccancy under her skin to make sure she remembers her cruelty towards the man who did nothing but love her with everything in him. That look of hurt in his eyes, him being destroyed by her words but still loving her nevertheless. It flashes in her mind, consuming her with guilt and regret.

The air she breathes feels like acid. Her tongue scratches against the dry walls of her mouth. Everything hurts. Her body, her mind and her heart.

It's death by a thousand cuts.

Chapter 38

Miraya climbs out of the car and shuts the door, wrapping her arms around herself. The streetlights shimmer, casting a melancholic glow on her puffy, tear-stained face. It feels eerie to be the only one wide awake on a dead street alongside all the houses sitting under a roof of darkness, accompanied by absolutely no sound except for the wind. Her shoes scratch against the road as she walks to Shray's house. The watchman is asleep and it gets a few loud thumps on the glass windows to wake him up from his nap. "Who are you?" he asks, groggily.

"Miraya. I've come here before, remember? I want to meet Shray."

"Are you insane, woman? At this hour?"

"It is an urgent matter. Can you please let me in?"

The old man grabs his spectacles and wears them. He steps out of his booth and leans over the gate. "Oh, you. I know you. You came that day with Sir."

"Yes, yes. Can you let me in? I want to see him," Miraya says, holding onto the cold metal of the gate.

The old man considers. "Sir told me to let you in if you ever come again. So I think it should be alright for you to go inside. But Sir is not here."

Miraya's voice wavers. "Why? Where is he?"

She had not heard from him after he had dropped her at her apartment that evening. He said he didn't have any work for a week. Where could he have gone?

"I don't know the details of his whereabouts. But he is not in the house. He left this afternoon," the old man says, scratching his beard and pulling the beanie on his head tighter.

"Did he say when he might be back?"

Miraya was desperate. She wanted to talk to him immediately. There was too much in her heart. It was pulling her down, curling her mind into madness like quicksand.

"I don't know. But I think he will be back by tomorrow. Otherwise, he would have told me," he says. "Do you want to wait inside?"

"I-I can?"

"You look quite shaken up and whatever it is that you want to talk about appears to be important. Sir has also been like that for a few days so I think that has to do with you. He will want you to wait inside," the man says.

Sir has also been like that.

God, she has put him through so much unnecessary pain. She feels the sobs rattle in her chest.

"Have you called him?" he asks, before letting her in.

She hasn't. Whatever she needs to say should be said in person. The moment Miraya hears his voice, she will break. She can't afford to do it through a phone call.

But she lies.

"Yes, but he never picked up."

The watchman nods and then lets her in. He leads her to the house. He is a lean tall man, skin thin and loose enough to show his veiny arms. His grey thin moustache gives him a stern appearance.

He pulls open a window and pushes his arm inside to grab a key from the flower pot inside. "Here."

"Thank you," she says, taking the key from him and unlocking the door. As soon as she switches on the lights, the watchman goes back to his booth. She closes the door and stares at the empty living room, so devoid of colour. At a time like this, when her life is so grey and bland, it would do her better to surround herself with some colours instead of the minimalistic black and white shit.

Everything feels cold. She sits in the living room, the same place she had sat the other day and pulls her knees to her chest. The time is 4:35 am. Her eyes are tired and heavy and hot from crying but she refuses to give it rest. She has to talk to him. It was her first priority.

Miraya feels like a lonely ghost in the house, staring at the walls, waiting for someone to come and warm the place with their presence. Her gaze moves around, trying to find something to focus on before the silence consumes her. She stops at the back of the door. Her breath catches as she recalls the kiss they had shared, pressed against that door. Their first kiss.

So much has happened since then that the kiss feels like ages ago. She had been so angry at that time and the kiss had felt so wrong but right at the same time. Now that she knew that her anger was baseless and false, she feels like a punctured doll, betrayed by life. If only she had cared enough to know more about what happened to her instead of jumping to conclusions. If only she had given him a chance. If only she had shoved her demons aside and had the guts to face the situation instead of running from it like a fucking coward.

If only.

She would've saved a lot of pain and hurt for the both of them.

Miraya wipes her tears and blinks away the ones ready to spill.

What a fool she had been. She would never forgive herself.

Miraya stands up and decides to distract herself before she crumbles under the weight of her thoughts. She climbs the stairs, heading for Shray's room. The lamps shed light on a simple room with a big closet. The bed is well-made, as if the sheets were changed and ironed to perfection. On a makeshift shelf hammered to the right wall are his awards. There are three of the big prestigious ones on the top, followed by the smaller ones. Miraya traces her fingers over it, a smile breaking its way through her sad face. She was so proud of him. Wholeheartedly. No inhibitions this time.

On the other wall there are frames. Pictures of his mother and him, one with Vidhyut, one with the three of them including his Dad. The next one is a picture of him with his inspiration, the great veteran actor he grew up dreaming to be. Among them, is a picture of him and Miraya. Miraya is on his back, her head just above his, one hand holding a trophy up in the air. Shray is wearing red stripes on his face, his mouth open in laughter and his eyes glittering. The most attractive thing about the picture is not the trophy in her hand but the happiness on their face. There is no mask of any sort, no lies, no pretence. Both of them are glowing with happiness, pure simple joy.

She traces a finger over Shray's face.

Could they go back to being this happy? Is it possible? Or is it too late?

Miraya bites her trembling lips and sits down on the bed. She stares at emptily at the picture.

After a while, she gets under his sheets to hide from the cold, in hopes of finding some lingering warmth of Shray. She finds it when she closes her eyes in comfort, wrapped in the familiar scent of him. Like home.

She doesn't realise it when sleep swallows her.

□□□□□□□□□□□□□□□□

She is back at the beach. The sun is bright but not blinding. The air is soothing and fresh, lacking the usual sultry tinge it carries. Miraya is on the sand, laying on a thin towel as she watches the white clouds move against the bright blue sky. Like swirls of white paint on a blue canvas. Like a hypnotic illusion.

She could keep watching it forever. The way one soft cloud teases another and moves away before the other could catch it. The way the other clouds huddle together and whisper about the two, giggling at how flirtatious they are. Watching the clouds is so calming and so relaxing, especially with the push and pull of the waves posing as the melody of beauty in the background.

The white smears thin out and spread, mingling to sculpt their own art. *So beautiful*, she thinks.

You are beautiful, the cloud whispers back. She can feel a cool feathery touch, pushing away her hair from her face. Miraya closes her eyes.

After a long time, she feels peaceful. As if there's no pain in this world. Miraya rolls on her side and her eyes widen when she finds Shray laying next to her. He smiles at her and then pulls something over her. A blanket. She can't see it but she can feel the thick fabric cover her.

Before she can ask Shray why he brought a blanket to the beach, she feels him pull away from her. Away, far away.

No. Stay. Stay.

"Stay," she says, blinking her eyes open.

She is not in a beach.

She is on a bed in Shray's room. Her hand around Shray's wrist.

She had been dreaming.

"I'm not going anywhere," he says. Miraya blinks twice. He is wearing a blue and white checkered shirt, his hair out of place, exhaution lining his eyes and his face. Shray is really next to her, sitting on the empty space on the edge of the bed.

Miraya sits up. "Where were you?" she asks, swallowing the briny taste in her mouth.

"Last minute shoot," he says. "I heard from Raman *Anna* that you came at 4, wanting to talk to me. You could've waited for a few more hours and gotten some sleep before driving here."

"But I wanted to talk to you as soon as I can."

"I guess you read the emails?" Shray asks.

Shame swallows her all over again. "Shray–" she begins.

"We can talk tomorrow, Miranda. I'm not going anywhere," he says, his fingers caressing hers in assurance.

"No. I can't keep to this myself any longer. Can we talk now, please?"

Shray sighs and settles himself next to her. "Okay, go on."

"I'm so sorry," she says. "I'm sorry I hurt you. Because of my self-ishness, I refused to give you a chance to explain. I misunderstood you and lost so many years together with you. I am so sorry, Shray."

At this point, Miraya doesn't even bother to hide her tears. She is sobbing, sniffling into the back of her hands and wiping tears away as it flows. "I was a coward. I thought ignorance is bliss. I thought not knowing your excuses would do me good because I was so scared of opening up that chapter of my life when all I wanted to do was close it shut. I feared that talking to you would make me relive it all. I suffered a lot, Shray. My parents — they took away my freedom. They hated me at one point. I hated *myself*. It was so bad that time, Shray. It was hell. I was so scared that I'll break again. That's why I never—"

"Shhh, it's okay, Miraya. Come here." Shray pulls her to him and cradles her against the chest. "I understand, okay? You don't have to explain. I'll admit that you really hurt me in the past few months but it was nothing compared to the pain when I lost you. So when you just appeared before me after so many years, even though you were antagonistic, I was so fucking happy that you were back in my life in some way. It hurt when you pushed me away the more I tried to come closer but I couldn't stay mad at you. I couldn't give up on you."

"Why?"

He smiles at her. "I am an optimist, Miranda."

Miraya stares at him.

"And because I love you too much."

She cries more.

"Should we talk about something else?" Shray whispers. "Something distracting?

"No. I want to talk about this. Us."

He sighs. "Okay, what do you want to know?"

"Tell me more about what happened that day."

Shray narrates it all over again. She picks up on the anger in his voice when he comes to the part where Sona talks shit about her and she couldn't help but crack a smile at that. "I thought you knew. You refused to speak to me when you came to write your exams. But I thought the news would've reached you somehow through Pavithra or someone. I never imagined you would be led to lead a life believeing a lie. I am so sorry."

"It's my fault. I shouldn't have doubted you."

"Miranda, if I was in your shoes, I would've been convinced of the same about me."

She purses her lips. "But you would've forgiven me."

"Yes. I would've forgiven you. Not immediately but sooner. I wouldn't carry that with me for all these years."

She lowers her gaze. "It's just that— when my life crumbled into pieces, I wanted to blame someone. It was so convenient to put everything on you. That anger which later turned to bitterness and then hatred– I poured it all to grow my resentment towards you. I am so sorry. I am so so sorry, Shray. Can you please forgive me?"

"Miranda, Miranda," he sings lowly, smiling. He frames her cheeks. "Of course, I forgive you, you idiot. I'm not going to lose you over the past. Not again."

"You promise?"

Shray looks at her fondly and caresses her skin, swiping away the tears. He presses his lips to hers and whispers, "I promise."

"I'm really sorry, Shray," Miraya says.

Shray groans and leans back into the bed. "Apologies don't really suit you, you know? I told you that I forgave you. Why are you apologizing again?"

"Because it shouldn't be this easy, Shray! Let me beg for it. Let me work for your forgiveness."

"Stop being so boring, Miranda. There's no fun in watching you repeat the same thing over and over again. Besides, forgiving others isn't always supposed to take time, you know. As long as you know the person would never do that again, forgiveness can be quick, simple and easy. And I know you won't hurt me again."

"I won't." Miraya looks up at him through wet lashes. She bites her lips and then climbs on his lap. Her thumbs draws arches over his cheek and her hands frame his face. "I'm sorry," she whispers, staring into his eyes.

Shray groans in frustration. Like he is so done with her. If she wasn't sitting on his lap, he would've left the room. "What's this for now? I told you–" he begins.

"For taking way too long to say this."

"Say what?" he asks, his voice becoming softer. The anticipation in his voice hints that he has already guessed her words.

"I love you," Miraya whispers, brushing her lips across hers like a feather, barely there. "Like you mentioned in one of the mails, I have a fragile heart but they're inside steel doors. Maybe those doors can't be broken. Maybe it can't be moved. But you found another way in. You *melted* your way inside my heart a long time ago, Shray. I was too much of a coward to accept it. I am so sorry I messed up. But I don't want to waste any more time. I want you all to myself. I want to be yours."

Shray places his lips on hers and slowly, gently kisses her. "You have no idea how long I've waited to hear these words," he whispers between kisses.

When they pull away, resting their foreheads against each other, Shray asks, a hint of curiosityin his voice. "So... are you thinking what I am thinking?"

Miraya grins. "Yes. Let's get married."

"For real?"

"For real."

Epilogue

The alarm blares through the silence in the room and Miraya rolls away from Shray, trying to find the damn phone. Shray groans at the sound and nudges her with his elbow. "Switch off the damn thing!"

"I'm trying," Miraya says, propping herself on her elbows to locate the device.

"Well, make it fast," Shray mumbles, pulling the sheets over him.

"You do it then!" Miraya kicks his leg but he doesn't even move. She realises the sound is coming from Shray's phone, which is in the pockets of his discarded jeans. "It's yours, you idiot."

"Just switch it off, Miranda."

Miraya sighs and fishes out the phone. Once she dismisses the alarm, Shray calls, "Come back."

"Not you bossing me around the first thing in the morning. I can still choose not to marry you, you know," she says, climbing back into bed.

Shray's eyes open and a lazy grin appears on his face. "You love me too much to leave me."

Miraya scowls at him but Shray brings her close to his chest and tucks her under his chin. "Don't go to work today," he whispers against her hair.

"I should."

"Please, Miraya. Let's stay in bed all day."

She runs her hands through his dark locks and smoothes the lines on his forehead. "I wish I could. But I have to go. I'll stay the night today, okay?"

"I still don't like it that you are leaving but fine."

Miraya chuckles. When she looks at him, sleeping next to her, his eyes closed as if there is no more worry in the world, it feels quite surreal. She always imagined loving Shray but she had thought it would be just that. A figment of her imagination. Only in her head. A dream. Now that she is tucked in his arms, breathing the same air as him and wrapped in his warmth and smell, she feels like she has accomplished the greatest feat of her life. She had fought all the demons and won the war in her head. Shray was hers as she was his.

It was beautiful.

Pressing a kiss on his forehead, she untangles from him and heads to the closet. It is enormous. Everything is so neatly arranged. She realises with dismay that if Shray took a glimpse at her closet, he would probably call off their marriage.

Miraya finds a white button-up shirt that she can style it appropriately to wear to work. After a quick shower, she walks out of the bathroom smelling like Shray's green apple flavoured shampoo. She keeps an eye on Shray's sleeping figure as she puts on her clothes. Just as she pulls on her jeans, he stirs. "Don't you dare open your eyes," she says, hastily tugging the material upwards.

"Are you naked?" he asks, a smirk lacing his voice. "Why would I *not* open my eyes, Miranda?"

"Because I said so, you idiot. Just for a few seconds. If I catch you peeking, you're dead."

"Fine, fine. And you said *I* was bossing over you."

Miraya rolls her eyes and zips her pants.

"Are you done?"

"Yes, you can open your eyes," Miraya says, untangling the towel from her hair.

Shray raises an eyebrow. "Is that my shirt?"

"Yes. So?"

He shakes his head quietly, leaning on the headboard and watching her with a fond smile. Miraya's heart wavers when she catches how he is looking at her.

"Stop that," she mumbles, drying her hair.

"Stop what?"

He knows what she is talking about.

"Staring," she says.

"You are beautiful. Especially in my clothes. So damn beautiful," Shray says, walking over to her. His hair is a mess but he doesn't care. "It's only a problem if I don't stare at you."

Miraya's breath hitches when he wraps an arm around her and traces the slope of her neck with his nose. His beard scratches against her skin but all it gives her is shivers. She leans back against his chest.

Shray peppers kisses all over throat, her neck and her jaw, spinning her around to capture her lips at last. "I love this. Waking up with you. Watching you get ready. Kisses in the morning," he whispers against her lips. "I can get used to this."

"Not yet, Mister. We aren't even engaged yet."

"And who's fault is that?"

"Shut up."

"When are we going to talk about that to our parents?" Shray asks, balancing his chin on her shoulders.

"Tell me when you will be free so I can discuss the dates with Ma. Now remove yourself from me because I already think I'm running late and you're not helping."

"*You* could remove yourself from me," he teases, running his hands over her waistline, starting to inch lower. Miraya feels desire burn beneath her skin and all she wants to do is press herself to him so she could feel all of him. But then she won't ever be leaving the house.

She snaps out of it and pushes him away from her. "Get out of here."

"Do you mean it, Miranda?" he whispers hoarsely. His morning voice isn't any help to her case. Her body reacts without her permission and he chuckles.

"Fuck off, Shray," she says, pushing him away. Her face feels hot. "You're banned from coming anywhere near me until I say so!"

"We'll see how long you last." Shray lightly slaps her butt before cackling his way into the bathroom.

□□□□□□□□□□□□□□□□

Miraya opens the door and grins at Dakshina and Ranav. "Thank you for coming!" she says, hugging both of them.

"Well, I'm never missing an opportunity to get a tour of Shray's house," her best friend says. Miraya takes the bag from her which has her dress and whatever she needs to get ready for Fiya's engagement party. "Make yourself at home."

"Oh, I will. Where is your man?"

A faint pink blush crosses Miraya's face when she refers to Shray as her man. "He is upstairs. In the shower."

"Aren't you joining him?" Dakshina asks casually, making Ranav shake his head at his fiancee.

"I would have if you two had arrived a little later," Miraya says. She knows that Dakshina was going to put her through a lot of teasing since Miraya did the same when Ranav and her friend got together. It was only fair that she took the teasing like a pro.

Dakshina doesn't expect that so she whips her head at her in surprise. Slowly, she smiles.

"What?"

"You're glowing, do you know that?" Dakshina asks then looks at her calculatively. "You're not pregnant, are you?"

"Of course, not!"

"Ranav, back me up. She is glowing, isn't she?"

Like the loyal fiancee he is, he agrees.

"Did you have sex last night?"

"*Dakshina Gopinath!*" Miraya's face heats up. "That's a very personal question."

"No, it's a very simple question. There are only two answers to it. Yes or No," Dakshina says, plopping down on the sofa.

Miraya shakes her head. "I'm going to get ready." She is halfway up the stairs when she asks, "Are you sure you guys don't want to join us? Fiya will be more than happy to have you there."

"I would love to but Dakshina and I have an appointment with a marriage counselor. It's the only slot we could get so we can't afford to miss it," Ranav explains.

"Okay, then. It would have been nice if you came along with us."

"I know, Miraya. But have fun with Shray, alright? You know that a lot of attention is going to be on you today. One thing is that you have to get used to it since you've decided to marry him. But if anything goes wrong or makes you want to get out of there, or if you need us to come pick you, just call us. It doesn't matter if we are in mid session. We'll come right away," Dakshina says, walking up to where she stood.

"I will. Thanks, Daksh. Will you be here when I finish getting ready?"

She checks the time on her watch. "No, we'll say Hi to Shray and we'll leave. Only then we can make it there on time."

Miraya hugs her. "Okay, I'll see you later."

"When are you planning to come home? Wait, are you *ever* planning on coming home?" Dakshina asks, crossing her arms across her chest.

Miraya rolls her eyes. "It's only been two days. You stayed at Ranav's for a week and more."

"I am planning a wedding, Miraya. What excuse do you have?"

She sighs. "Fine, I will. But not today. Shray is off to Assam for a shoot tomorrow. I want to stay with him tonight."

"I never thought I'd see the day when you become lovesick. But here we are," Dakshina says, smiling. "It's a good look on you. You seem really happy."

"I am happy. It's a nice change from always worrying over something. Now I feel confident that I can face anything, you know. With Shray by my side, I feel stronger. Braver," Miraya admits.

"I can see that."

Daksh pulls her back into a hug and then whispers, "I packed the black lingerie just in case. I think Shray would like that."

Miraya slaps her friend's shoulders in disbelief, trying not to blush. "Would you ever let go of it?"

"I made you buy it. I want to make sure you find good use for it. Don't blame me for being the best friend you can find on this entire planet."

Miraya shakes her head and sighs. "Fine, whatever. I'll go get ready now."

Miraya hugs Ranav and heads inside Shray's room. He is standing in front of the tall mirror, turned towards the side as he rolls his sleeve up.

"Let me," she says, dropping the bags on the floor and reaching out to help him. She folds the lilac shirt into neat rolls upwards and buttons it just below his elbows.

"Did you do your eyebrows?" he asks, a mild inquisitive frown on his face.

"Wow, you are fast. It took you a day to realise it. I expected you to take two more days," Miraya says dryly.

Shray gives her a sheepish smile and offers her his other hand. "You look beautiful either way. It's hard to spot a difference."

Miraya shoots him a look and buttons the material. "Your flattery won't always work on me."

Shray wraps an arm around her waist and tugs her to him so that she crashes against his chest. "But this will."

He frames her face and tilts it just so that he can kiss her. Miraya's fingers curl around the collar of his shirt as her other hand tangles with his hair. Their lips slide against each other, slow and wet but slowly turning greedy for more. Kissing Shray is like being injected with a dose of all the good things in the world. It makes her curl her toes in pleasure, heart expand in her chest with love and mind blackout, shutting out everything else except what matters. Shray.

Miraya's hand comes to rest on his chest as he maneuvers her to press her against the wall. Shray's lips move from her lips to her jaw. He nips the skin and leaves delicious tingles of pleasure all the way down to her throat. A filthy sound rips from her throat when Shray licks the spot at her collarbone, making him respond with a low groan from his side. He sucks the skin into his mouth and she closes her eyes as she holds him tight.

Marks. He is leaving marks. No.

Miraya pulls away from him and smacks his chest. "No hickeys, you idiot. I told you this morning!"

He licks his lips and shrugs. "I don't care."

"I can't go to the party like this, you fool."

Shray dips his head and kisses the spot again, staring at it fondly like a painting he had created. "Haven't you heard of makeup? Just cover it, Miranda. If you need help with it, just ask me."

Miraya eyes him with disapproval. Always nonchalant. Always playful. It wasn't fair that she had to be the serious one in the relationship.

"Dakshina and Ranav are waiting downstairs. They'll leave soon so don't keep them for too long. I'll go get ready."

"Okay," Shray says, kissing her one more time on her lips, brief but hard enough to make her head spin.

She watches him as he runs a hand through his hair and corrects it. The lilac shirt hugs his body, especially his chest and his arms. The first button is undone, somehow elevating his look. The black formal pants he is wearing are tailored to fit him, so *perfect*, making it hard to believe that he was hers. All hers.

"Stop that," he says.

"Stop what?"

"Staring."

"It is only a problem if I don't stare at you, Shray." She grins, pleased that she got a chance to use his line on him.

"Fair enough. I won't argue with that," he says, biting his lips to hide a smile, before leaving the room.

□□□□□□□□□□□□□□□□

Miraya fastens the oxidized silver *jhumka* on her ear when Shray walks back into the room. "Are you done? It's getting late, Miraya," he says, striding up to her. She sits on the chair in front of the mirror and Shray roots himself just behind her. He grabs his comb and rolls it over his hair to push the strands back.

"I'm almost done. Clip this bracelet on for me, will you?" She hands him the bracelet with emerald stones and stretches out her hand. Obediently, Shray crouches down and straps the thing on.

"There you go, wife," he says, kissing her knuckles lightly.

Miraya peels her hand away from him and turns to face him. "Aren't you getting ahead of yourself?"

"I am an optimist," he shrugs.

Miraya traces his eyebrows with her fingers, smiling at the way he closes his eyes at her touch. Shray leans in, expecting her to kiss him but she turns away and applies her lipstick.

"Tease," he grumbles as he stands up and irons out his shirt. Miraya checks herself in the mirror one last time before using the perfume and grabbing her *duppata*.

"Yup, I am ready now. How do I look?"

Miraya is in a bottle-green sleeveless monochromatic *sharara* suit. The leaf neckline shimmers with its gold-coloured stonework and the *duppata* shines with matching *zari* borders. She humors him by twirling in her outfit, making the pleats of the pants glide elegantly when she moves.

"So?" she asks again.

"Alexa play Speechless by Dan + Shay," Shray says, stepping close to her.

Miraya chuckles, pleased with his answer but she doubles over in shock when a foreign voice pierces the silence. "*Playing Speechless by Dan + Shay from Spotify.*"

"I thought you were just joking!" Miraya says, cupping her palms over her mouth and laughing.

"I don't joke when it comes to you, Miranda."

She hides a smile. "What now? Will you ask me to dance with you?"

He grabs her hand and twirls her around. "I might. But we are getting late," he whispers, pressing a quick kiss behind her ear.

Miraya shakes her head and grabs her purse. They leave the house and get into the backseat of the car, shortly after which the driver starts the car.

A few silent minutes later, Shray reaches for her hand and places it on his thigh. "You know that you might be getting a lot of attention today, right? Are you really sure you want me to come with you? It's not too late to change your mind, Miranda. I don't want to spoil your day with Fiya."

"I want you by my side, Shray. You are coming with me as my boyfriend." Her forehead creased. "Wait, boyfriend is too weird —"

"Just call me your husband."

Miraya rolls her eyes. "Anyway, as I was saying, you are coming with me as my *future* husband. Not as an actor. I want you with me and Fiya wants the same. She won't be offended if you borrow the spotlight from her for a little while."

"You will also be under that spotlight, Miranda. The last time —"

"The last time was hard because we weren't together. I was scared and anxious of playing the part of your girlfriend. I was terrified of the stares because I was scared all of them were dismissive and judgemental. I feel the same now as well but this time I know that what they think doesn't matter. All that matters is that I am with you, where I belong. I am confident I can handle the attention if you are by my side," Miraya says, squeezing his hand. "And I have to get used to it anyway so might as well take slow steps forward."

"I will always stay by your side if that's what you want. You know I will."

Miraya faces him. "I know you are worried. Not only about me dealing with the attention now but also about the future. Whether I will be able to handle all of it and still want to be with you." She lifts her hand to his cheek. "I love you, Shray. That means I love everything about you — the good, the bad and the in between. Just like I know you do about me. Aren't you tolerating my messiness and my absolute lack of punctuality? Aren't you okay with me knowing to cook just five dishes? Don't you get annoyed with me hogging the mirror everyday but then brush it off because you love me?"

"I get it. But the media — it's not easy, Miranda. I've heard about so many broken relationships because of it.

"Look, I know the media is not pretty but it comes along with you and I am ready to tackle it, okay? I can. I will. I thought you were the optimist. I thought you were extremely hyped about our relationship. I thought you wanted us, Shray. Where is all this doubt coming from?"

Shray captures her hands between his. "I want us more than anyone, okay? But more than the reality of us, what I want is for you to be happy. I am just scared in the long run, you will find my life to be too much. That the media will eat away your peace and happiness."

"You make me happy, Shray. You. As long as you are there with me, you don't have to worry about my happiness. Please shut up about it already."

Shray sighs. "Okay, then. I gave you a disclaimer, Miranda. Keep that in mind."

Miraya leans back and snorts. "All disclaimers are considered null when it comes to us. We are a fucking team, Shray. We get through shit together no matter what."

"Like old times?" he asks, watching her with a lazy smile.

"Like old times," she whispers, smiling in return.

"God. I love you."

"Yes, you've mentioned it a couple times." Miraya chuckles.

"Well, watch me be a broken tape recorder and say the words to you forever."

She leans close to him, intertwining their hands together and whispers, "And watch me never get tired of hearing it."